OOK OF
RDOS

BY
CARL POSEY
**AND 67 OF
THE WORLD'S TOP
COMIC ARTISTS**

PARADOX PRESS
NEW YORK

THE BIG BOOK OF WEIRDOS
published by Paradox Press. Compilation
Copyright ©1995 Paradox Press. All Rights
Reserved. Factoid Books is a trademark of
Paradox Press. Paradox Press is an imprint of
DC Comics, 1325 Avenue of the Americas,
New York, NY 10019. A division of Warner
Bros. — A Time Warner Entertainment
Company. Printed in CANADA. First Printing.

See page 222 for individual story copyright
holders.

Cover by Tom Taggart
Title page illustration by Roger Langridge
Interior publication design by Brian Pearce
Lettering by Rod Ollerenshaw

TABLE OF CONTENT

INTRODUCTION

BY GAHAN WILSON

Face it — you just did a weird thing.

I don't know where you did it — you could have been in a bookstore, or maybe in a friend's house — but you saw this book and that funny little voice in the back of your head, that voice that sounds like you talking out loud but which only you can hear, that voice that tells you to *do* things, said: *"Pick it up! That book about **Weirdos**!! You know you want to read it!"* And you did pick it up, and here it is in your hands.

Now, you shouldn't be concerned or wonder if this means you're going crazy, because picking up this book and reading it is a perfectly sane and logical action; being interested in Weirdos makes sense. *Not* being interested in Weirdos is unwise, and can even be dangerous. For example, should you see a tall, heavyset Weirdo clumping toward you on the sidewalk and pulling something glinty and sharp out of a greasy paper bag as he looks at you sidewise and asks God, *"Should I?"*, if you see all that and you don't become interested enough in him to at least quickly and quietly cross the street, getting out of his path and clear of his field of vision, then you are very likely to end up as a brief item on that evening's TV news (featuring a badly-lit shot of your pooled blood congealing on the sidewalk).

This is not to imply by any means that interest in Weirdos is only negative — if you can spot the right Weirdo you can make a fortune (Henry Ford, page 151), find salvation (Georges Gurdjieff, page 60), or experience the absolute tops in literature (Fyodor Dostoyevsky, page 91), art (Vincent van Gogh, page 131) or theater (Sarah Bernhardt, page 96). Without Weirdos to lead the way, in fact, we all would still be wrapped in the rotting hides of animals, crouching around fires in caves, and dying miserably of old age at around sixteen years old. Actually, we wouldn't be anywhere near that well off, because the fire wouldn't be there if some Weirdo hadn't been nutty enough to think of lighting one indoors, and we'd still be shivering in our bare flesh if another Weirdo hadn't been perverted enough to try to wear an animal instead of just gulping it down!

The truth is, you have to be pretty weird to invent a light bulb or create surrealism or put together the FBI, and if you think your totally unweird Uncle Fred could come up with "The Tell-tale Heart" or "Swan Lake" or "Plan Nine from Outer Space," think again. He's probably never even heard of them. (Come to think of it, do you *have* any unweird relatives? I don't think *I* do.)

Of course, the great problem with Weirdos is that they can, and often do, mislead the rest of us in a highly spectacular wrong direction. Adolf Hitler (page 25), for example, was absolutely certain World War II was for our own good (not to mention the Holocaust); Walter Freeman (page 156) was altogether convinced that turning the emotionally troublesome among us into passive vegetables via prefrontal lobotomies was the greatest idea since sliced bread; and it's an absolute certainty that Ivan the Terrible (page 16) would have been astounded to learn he'd go down in history as Ivan the Terrible.

Let a really talented Weirdo make a serious mistake and the rest of us can end up having truly spectacular problems. But what would happen if, because of this potential danger, the Non-Weirdos of the world somehow managed to perfect a society where no Weirdo ever got the chance to do his or her own thing (which is self-contradictory, when you think about it, as the whole scheme is 100% pure Weirdo). Where would that put us?

I think it would put us to sleep, and far, far too many of us are already born asleep, live out our whole lives asleep, and, finally, die asleep. Could we possibly stay awake if we knew how the plots of all the movies or television shows would end? What if no book ever surprised us? Suppose every painting you ever saw reminded you of every other painting you'd ever seen? Would you even bother to bite into any more pies or sandwiches if the contents of every one were totally predictable?

Imagine how it would be if everybody always agreed on everything, and you knew exactly how everybody had spent last night because they'd spent it just the same way you'd spent it yourself, and you could tell what would be happening in your life two years from now because your life would be just exactly the same as your two-years-older neighbor.

Are you still awake?

The fact is that it would be a dreadful mistake to eliminate Weirdos, no matter what the dangers, no matter what the costs. If we did not have Weirdos in our population, we would have to make them up.

But not to worry, there is not even the slightest danger of Weirdo scarcity in ourselves or others. Look back over any day you spend and I guarantee you will discover a generous abundance of the Weirdo factor both in others and in yourself. Watch the news, see who runs the country, see who owns it, see who's trying to build it up and who's trying to destroy it, and you will be at ease: There is absolutely no chance of a Weirdo shortage.

Be aware, though, that this invaluable Weirdo factor requires intelligent maintenance. And that is another proof that you weren't crazy at all when you picked up this book, because if you study carefully the little stories contained in *The Big Book of Weirdos* you will discover that they offer endless

helpful suggestions and examples that will assist you enormously in succesful Weirdo management, both interior and exterior.

You'll learn that some kinds of Weirdo quirks are extremely handy. Being able to make millions by outguessing everybody else on the stock market, or succeeding in showbiz as an escape artist, for instance, are only two examples of Weirdo talents that can be counted as a definite plus. (If *you* possess such talents, you may feel free to make use of them as often and as unreservedly as you like.)

There are also generous examples of the little pitfalls that now and then present themselves and which you should be on your guard against. Absorb the contents of this book and you will learn that it's a danger sign if you find yourself indulging in odd peculiarities such as sleeping in a coffin instead of a bed, or if you seem to be losing control over that nagging obsession you have about germ contamination. You will even be made aware of the riskiness lurking behind what may seem benign or even laudable practices, such as mass feeding of city pigeons, or the possibly overenthusiastic collecting and stacking of moldy old newspapers.

Keep this book with you always, consult it carefully (without moving your lips and speaking aloud in public, if possible) every time you have that funny feeling that things are slipping out of control, and there is an excellent chance that you will avoid a sufficient accumulation of negative Weirdo factor to push you over into outright insanity.

It's worked for me.

So far, at least.

At least, I *think* it has.

GAHAN WILSON was officially declared "born dead" by the attending physician in Evanston, Illinois, but survived anyway to become a cartoonist published in periodicals as diverse as *The New Yorker, Playboy, Gourmet, Punch,* and *Paris Match.* He has written two mystery novels (*Eddy Deco's Last Caper* and *Everybody's Favorite Duck*) and is currently writing *The Big Book of Freaks* for Paradox Press.

CHAPTER ONE

AUTOCRATS AND DICTATORS

It's been said that power corrupts — and that absolute power corrupts absolutely. What isn't usually mentioned is how darn *weird* absolute power makes people... or how weirdness often seems to be a prerequisite for obtaining power in the first place. Blame it on inbreeding, doubtless a contributing factor among dynastic rulers like Elagabalus (*page 8*) and Caligula (*page 11*), or poor upbringing (Hitler, *page 25*), or just a sadistic nature (Ivan the Terrible, *page 16*), but the reasons why are almost beside the point: These rulers, despots all, were really strange. And with absolute power at their disposal, they treated their countrymen and kingdoms as their own personal playthings... as often as not, with disastrous consequences.

FOR FOUR YEARS, A FLASHY TEEN RULED THIRD-CENTURY ROME WITH WILD EXTRAVAGANCE, BIZARRE HUMOR, AND SCANDALOUS SEXUAL BEHAVIOR. HIS NAME?

ELAGABALUS

EVEN BEFORE HE BECAME ROMAN EMPEROR, THE BOY WAS AN EXOTIC.

DESCENDED FROM SYRIAN ROYALTY, HE WAS HIGH PRIEST OF THE SUN GOD, ELAB-GEBAL -- HENCE HIS NICKNAME, ELAGABALUS.

HE LOVED TO DRESS UP IN SILK ROBES AND DANCE HIS CULT'S ELABORATE RITUALS.

BUT JULIA MAESA, HIS GRANDMOTHER, THOUGHT HE SHOULD RULE ROME.

MY LITTLE KING!

SHE ARRANGED A CONVENIENT MUTINY THAT LED TO THE SITTING EMPEROR'S DEATH.

I SWEAR MY ALLEGIANCE, EXCELLENCE.

AND I SWEAR...

...TO HAVE THE BLOODY TIME OF MY LIFE.

ROME HAD SEEN PLENTY, BUT NOTHING LIKE THIS.

HE FAVORED ORIENTAL COSTUMES AND HEAVY MAKEUP, WITH TONS OF GOLD AND PRECIOUS GEMS.

HE IS WHAT HE WEARS.

HE GLIDED WHEN HE WALKED, TO SUGGEST A NEVER ENDING DANCE, AND GOLD AND SILVER DUST WAS SPRINKLED AHEAD OF HIM.

A VORACIOUS PARTY ANIMAL, HE SPENT HIS DAYS FLIRTING WITH MEN AND WOMEN.

WHO'S NEXT? WHO CARES?!

A RECKLESS CHARIOTEER, HE STAGED RACES THAT SAVED ON HORSEPOWER...

BY USING OTHER ANIMAL SUBSTITUTES!

GO ROMULUS, GO!

HIS NAVY TRAINED ON CANALS FILLED WITH WINE.

WHAT A WAY TO GO!

HE ORDERED A MOUNTAIN OF SNOW RAISED IN HIS SUMMER GARDEN.

I JUST ADORE THE APRÉ, DON'T YOU?

HE SERVED FOOD MADE OF WOOD, IVORY, AND MARBLE, AND SUCH DELICACIES AS SPIDER JELLY AND LION-DUNG TARTS.

PLEASE! HAVE ANOTHER!

AFTER FOUR INDULGENT YEARS, HE KNEW THE END WAS NEAR,

AN IDEA WHOSE TIME HAS GONE,

SOMEBODY GET A ROPE,

DETERMINED THAT HIS FATE WOULD BE SHAPED ONLY BY HIMSELF, HE ASSEMBLED A SUMPTUOUS SUICIDE KIT.

HE HAD A SUICIDE TOWER BUILT ON GOLD PAVEMENT, IN CASE HE DECIDED TO JUMP.

OBSESSED WITH THOUGHTS OF SUICIDE, HE FAILED TO SEE THAT EVEN HIS GRANDMOTHER HAD TURNED AGAINST HIM.

SOON, MY WILD BOY, YOUR TIME WILL BE UPON YOU.

SHORTLY, A VIOLENT OUTBREAK AMONG HIS PALACE GUARDS...

...CAUSED HIM TO FLEE WITH HIS MOTHER.

THE TWO FINALLY FOUND A PLACE WITHIN THE PALACE WALLS TO HIDE FROM THE REBELLIOUS GUARDS... A SLIT-TRENCH URINAL.

WE'LL BE SAFE HERE, MOTHER.

BUT WHEN THE GUARDS SOUGHT MOMENTARY RELEASE AFTER A HARD DAY'S BATTLE...

TAKE THEM!

I DON'T DESERVE THIS!

HIS 13-YEAR-OLD SUCCESSOR FARED BETTER --HE LIVED TO THE RIPE OLD AGE OF 26.

GAIUS CAESAR-CALIGULA

...BETTER KNOWN SIMPLY AS CALIGULA, RULED ANCIENT ROME FOR FOUR SHORT, HORRIBLE YEARS--AND ENTERED THE WORLD'S LANGUAGES AS THE EMBODIMENT OF CAPRICIOUS CRUELTY.

HE WAS NOT ALWAYS BAD. BORN IN AD 12, HE WAS THE SON OF GERMANICUS, A POPULAR WARRIOR --AND THE NEPHEW AND ADOPTED SON OF THE REIGNING EMPEROR, OLD TIBERIUS.

SEEING HIM IN BATTLEDRESS, HIS FATHER'S SOLDIERS GAVE HIM A NICKNAME.

AH, CALIGULA!

"IT MEANT "LITTLE BOOTS."

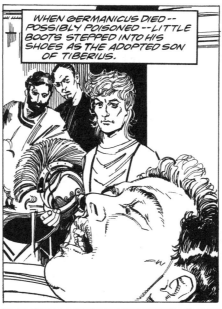

WHEN GERMANICUS DIED -- POSSIBLY POISONED -- LITTLE BOOTS STEPPED INTO HIS SHOES AS THE ADOPTED SON OF TIBERIUS.

TIBERIUS TAUGHT THE BOY ALL HE NEEDED TO KNOW ABOUT DEGENERACY OF EVERY KIND.

CALIGULA, JOIN IN, JOIN IN.

NOT NOT. NOT YET.

IN AD 37, CALIGULA'S PATIENCE PAID OFF. THE 78-YEAR-OLD TIBERIUS SICKENED.

ACCORDING TO SOME HISTORIANS, CALIGULA HELPED HIM DIE.

GOODBYE, DISGUSTING GEEZER.

THE ROMAN SENATE GAVE HIM THE THRONE.

IT SEEMED AN INSPIRED IDEA...

...AT FIRST.

CALIGULA CUT TAXES, RESTORED THE ARISTOCRACY THAT TIBERIUS HAD GUTTED, DECLARED A GENERAL AMNESTY--ROMANS LOVED HIM.

BUT EVEN THEN, A CERTAIN "SPITEFUL" NATURE BEGAN TO EMERGE.

HE DELIGHTED IN TOSSING GOLD COINS TO THE GROUND IN FRONT OF HIS SUPPORTERS SO THAT THEY WOULD HAVE TO SCRAMBLE TO RETRIEVE THEM.

CATCH THEM OR THEY'LL ROLL AWAY!

THEN, JUST SIX MONTHS INTO HIS REIGN, CALIGULA CAUGHT AN ILLNESS THAT BROUGHT WITH IT RAGING FEVER AND DELIRIUM.

FOR WEEKS HE LAY STRAPPED DOWN TO HIS IMPERIAL BED, WRITHING AND SCREAMING IN AGONY.

THE CALIGULA THAT ROSE FROM THE SICK BED WAS A DIFFERENT MAN.

THE FEVER HAD AFFECTED HIS BRAIN AND LEFT THE EMPEROR MAD.

HE DECIDED TO BE AN ABSOLUTE MONARCH, MODELED AFTER THE PHARAOHS OF EGYPT.

DOWN, ALL OF YOU, DOWN! HOW CAN YOU STAND MY GLARING LIGHT?

HE DRESSED HIMSELF UP AS THE HEROIC MORTALS OF MYTHOLOGY...

NOW I'M HERCULES, AND I'M OFF TO DESTROY CERBERUS. RIGHT?

RIGHT?

BUT IT WASN'T LONG BEFORE HE MADE THE JUMP INTO GODHOOD...

DO WE NOT KNEEL BEFORE APOLLO? DO WE NOT QUAKE? DO WE NOT SHIVER IN OUR....LITTLE BOOTS?

HE ORDERED HIS SUBJECTS TO WORSHIP HIM.

REMEMBER, MY CHILDREN, THOSE WHO PRAY... MAY STAY.

RUMOR HELD THAT HE'D REPLACED A JUPITER STATUE'S HEAD WITH A LIKENESS OF HIS OWN...

SACRILEGE? CAN A GOD LIKE ME BE SACRILEGIOUS?

...AND THAT, LIKE THE PHARAOHS, HE MARRIED HIS SISTER, DRUSILLA.

BROTHER... IS THAT YOU?

OH, YES, AND APOLLO AND MARS AND KING TUT AND YOUR HUSBAND TOO.

SOME HISTORIANS SAY THAT HE DIDN'T SEAT INCITATUS, HIS HORSE, AS A ROMAN CONSUL...

OF COURSE, OF COURSE.

...BUT NO ONE THOUGHT OF HIM AS JUST ANOTHER HARMLESS ROMAN ECCENTRIC.

BE AFRAID. BE VERY AFRAID.

CALIGULA'S EXTRAVAGANCE WAS LEGEND AND HE BUILT A BRIDGE OF SHIPS ACROSS THE BAY OF NAPLES FOR A MOCK BATTLE...

...AND SPENT A FORTUNE ON THE SPRUCE GOOSE OF THE DAY: A GALLEY WITH TEN BANKS OF OARS.

TO KEEP THE PEOPLE HAPPY, HE GAVE THEM BREAD...

...AND CIRCUSES.

WHEN HE HAD SPENT THE LAST OF TIBERIUS'S HOARDED MILLIONS...

GODS JUST NEED AN ENDLESS SUPPLY OF GOLD.

...HE BEGAN STRIPPING THE ARISTOCRACY THAT HE HAD ONCE REVIVED.

BUT, MAJESTY... YOU RUIN ME.

WOULD YOU PREFER BEING CRUCIFIED FOR TREASON?

CALIGULA BROUGHT HIS TRADE-MARK SPECIAL TOUCH TO HIS COST-CUTTING MEASURES.

A... SUICIDE CAKE, HIGHNESS... HOW THOUGHTFUL.

AND SWEET. I INSIST THAT YOU TRY IT.

HE RAISED TAXES ON EVERY-THING, EVEN STREETWALKERS.

SHALL OUR EMPEROR TAKE YOUR SHARE OUT IN TRADE?

NO! HERE... TAKE IT ALL!

A CASINO AND BORDELLO WERE SET UP IN THE PALACE TO RAISE STILL MORE GOLD.

PLACE YOUR BETS, CITIZENS!

BUT SADISTIC CAPRICE WAS HIS STRONG SUIT.

I CAN DO ANYTHING, AND TO ANYONE.

WHEN THE EMPEROR TORTURED SONS...

...HE LIKED THEIR FATHERS TO WATCH.

AAAAAAAAAAIIIIIIEEEE

AFTER HE TOOK A WOMAN, HE LIKED TO TALK ABOUT IT TO HER HUSBAND.

A LITTLE PLUMP IN THE THIGH, BUT VERY PNEUMATIC, MARCELLUS. VERY.

NO ONE EVER JUST SAID NO.

INCREDIBLY, WITH THE POPULACE TURNING AGAINST HIM, HE STILL RELISHED RIDICULING AND HUMILIATING THE ROMAN ARMY.

MARCH TO THE ENGLISH CHANNEL AND THERE ENGAGE NEPTUNE!

BRING ME SEASHELLS TO PROVE YOUR VICTORY!

BE A GOOD LITTLE GIRL, CASSIUS CHAREA, AND SEE THAT THEY DO IT!

GRRR... YOUR WILL BE DONE, SIRE.

IT WAS NO WAY TO TREAT A CENTURION IN THE PRAETORIAN GUARD.

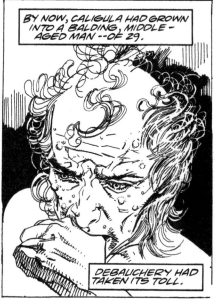

BY NOW, CALIGULA HAD GROWN INTO A BALDING, MIDDLE-AGED MAN -- OF 29.

DEBAUCHERY HAD TAKEN ITS TOLL.

HE SUFFERED EPILEPTIC-LIKE FITS...

...AND TERRIBLE TWITCHING, SLOBBERING CONVULSIONS.

SURROUNDED BY PEOPLE WHO WISHED HIM DEAD, CALIGULA MAINTAINED HIS FOOLHARDY COURAGE.

I AM TAKING A WALK THROUGH THE STABLES... ALONE.

WITHOUT GUARDS, WITHOUT WEAPONS, HE MADE HIS USUAL ROUNDS.

IT WAS AS THOUGH HE WAS DARING THE DISSATISFIED POPULACE TO TRY TO ELIMINATE HIM.

FINALLY HIS ENEMIES TOOK HIS DARE. A GROUP LED BY CENTURION CASSIUS CHAREA CAUGHT HIM IN THE IMPERIAL THEATER, AND STABBED HIM 30 TIMES.

TO THE VERY END, HE URGED THEM ON.

I'M... STILL ALIVE... I'M STILL... ALIVE...

AND SO HE WAS. BUT NOT FOR LONG.

15

THE 17-YEAR-OLD BOY CROWNED CZAR OF RUSSIA IN 1547 WAS CALLED IVAN GROZNY - IVAN THE AWESOME. BUT HE HAS COME TO US THROUGH HISTORY AS...

IVAN the TERRIBLE

TERRIBLE? MOI?

ORPHANED AS A BOY, IVAN WAS ABUSED AND BEATEN BY THE RELATIVES WHO HOARDED THE POWER OF RUSSIA'S EMPTY THRONE.

CRUELTY BRED CRUELTY.

HE DROPPED DOGS FROM CASTLE TOWERS...

...AND GALLOPED HIS CHARGER INTO CROWDS.

HE LIKED TO INTRODUCE POLITICAL PRISONERS TO HIS HOUNDS.

AND THIS IS BORIS.

HE WAS REALLY TERRIBLE. BUT ALSO SMART.

IN 1547 IVAN PUT DOWN A MUTINY...

... AND FINALLY WON THE CROWN OF RUSSIA.

FOR A TIME, HE STOPPED BEING TERRIBLE. HE MARRIED ANASTASIA, FATHERED SIX CHILDREN ...

...AND WAS A WISE, REFORMING RULER.

BUT IN 1553, AN ILLNESS AS TERRIBLE AS IVAN NEARLY KILLED HIM.

I AM A DEAD MAN, SWEAR ALLEGIANCE TO MY SON, DMITRI.

ALAS, EXCELLENCY, PRINCE DMITRI...

"...PRINCE DMITRI IS DEAD."

THE RECUPERATING CZAR BROODED IN SECLUSION, AS IF WAITING FOR FURTHER CALAMITY.

EXCELLENCE... THE CZARINA... ANASTASIA... SHE...

MY ANASTASIA IS DEAD!

IVAN BECAME TERRIBLE AGAIN.

HE HAD SCREAMING FITS...

...AND AWFUL DREAMS OF POISONING AND IMPALEMENT.

≡SOB!≡

ENRAGED, HE STABBED HIS FAVORITE SON TO DEATH.

FAILURE TO TIP YOUR HAT TO THE CZAR...

...COULD HAVE SERIOUS CONSEQUENCES.

SOMETHING WRONG, SIR AMBASSADOR?

NO.... OH, NO.

HIS POWER WAS ABSOLUTE.

THOSE HE DIDN'T LIKE, HE KILLED.

A CERTAIN DISPLEASING JE NE SAIS QUOI.

SOME SAID HIS FITS AND RAGES WERE MADNESS. OTHERS THOUGHT SYPHILIS MIGHT BE AT WORK HERE.

ARRHHH

I HAVE A DREAM.

IN 1565 IVAN DIVIDED HIS KINGDOM. ONE PART, CALLED THE OPRICHNINA, CAME UNDER HIS ABSOLUTE CONTROL.

MY ABSOLUTE CONTROL.

HE SENT HUNDREDS OF SECRET POLICE --OPRICHNIKI-- TO CRUSH DISSENT.

A NEW WORLD ORDER.

INFORMERS WERE EVERY-WHERE.

OF COURSE I'D LIKE TO GET OUT OF THE OPRICHNINA... I MEAN...

PEOPLE BEGAN TO DISAPPEAR.

ANYA! ANYA! GOD HELP US!

HIS SIEGE OF NOVGOROD KILLED 30,000 PEOPLE -- BRUTALLY.

MANY OF THOSE WHO SURVIVED IVAN DIED OF STARVATION.

WHEN HE TIRED OF KILLING HIS SUBJECTS, HE TURNED ON HIS FOLLOWERS...

...AND HAD THEM FLAYED AND BOILED FOR IMAGINED SINS.

OPRICHNINA EXPERIMENT IS OVER.

HE WAS AWE-INSPIRING --TERRIBLE, THAT IS --TO THE DEATH, WHICH CLAIMED HIM IN 1584.

BUT, TO HIS CREDIT, HE PAID FOR PRAYERS FOR A FEW THOUSAND OF HIS MANY VICTIMS.

NOBODY'S ALL TERRIBLE.

KING LUDWIG II of BAVARIA

...HAD IT ALL -- LOOKS, MONEY, BRAINS, AND THE AFFECTION OF HIS SUBJECTS.

BUT HIS REAL DOMAIN, IT TURNED OUT, WAS A KINGDOM OF THE IMAGINATION, FILLED WITH OPERA AND GREAT CASTLES.

THAT'S WHY HIS PEOPLE AFFEC- TIONATELY CALLED HIM THE DREAM KING...

...AND WHY, AT THE END, HE WAS KNOWN AS MAD KING LUDWIG.

MADNESS RAN IN THE FAMILY. AUNT ALEXANDRA BELIEVED SHE'D SWALLOWED A PIANO...

...AND DANGEROUSLY MELANCHOLY BROTHER OTTO WAS EVENTUALLY DECLARED INSANE.

AUF WIEDERSEHEN, OTTO.

LUDWIG HIMSELF HAD BEEN HEARING AND SEEING THINGS FOR YEARS.

LUUD... VIG... OH, LUUUUD VIG...

SHUSH!

WHILE STILL A BOY, LUDWIG HAD SEEN SOMETHING THAT CHANGED HIS LIFE FOREVER.

IT WAS THE OPERA LOHENGRIN...

...BY RICHARD WAGNER, ONE OF THE GREAT TALENTS--AND EGOS--OF THE DAY.

ZO...YOU LIKE MY OPERA, YOUNG MAJESTY?

IN THE OPERA, LOHENGRIN, A GERMAN KNIGHT, IS GUIDED TO A DAMSEL IN DISTRESS BY A BEAUTIFUL SWAN.

I HAVE NEVER SEEN SUCH BEAUTY.

HERR WAGNER, WHEN I AM KING, YOU WILL NEVER WANT FOR ANYTHING AGAIN.

IN THE MEANTIME, LUDWIG ORDERED THAT IMAGES OF SWANS COVER THE ROYAL WALLS...

...AND PRACTICALLY EVERYTHING ELSE.

WELL, SO I ADORE SWANS? THE KING CAN ADORE ANYTHING HE WISHES.

HIS SUBJECTS ADORED HIM JUST AS ZEALOUSLY. THEY REJOICED WHEN LUDWIG TOOK THE THRONE IN 1864. THEY LIKED THE LOOKS OF THIS TALL, YOUNG, BRILLIANT MAN.

LONG LIVE LUDWIG, LONG LIVE THE KING!

LUDWIG SOON SENT FOR HIS FAVORITE COMPOSER.

HERR WAGNER ...KING LUDWIG WAITS FOR YOU IN MUNICH!

IT'S ABOUT TIME!

HERE YOU CAN COMPLETE YOUR GREATEST WORKS, RICHARD.

YOU ARE TOO GENEROUS, YOUR MAJESTY.

HE OFFERS ME EVERYTHING I NEED TO LIVE, TO CREATE, TO PERFORM MY WORKS. I AM ONLY EXPECTED TO BE HIS FRIEND.

WAGNER IMMEDIATELY EMBARKED ON HIS MONUMENT TO HIMSELF -- A MUSIC PERFORMANCE HOUSE AT BAYREUTH, 100 MILES NORTH OF MUNICH.

THEY AIN'T SEEN NOTHING YET.

HIS OPERA SETS DEFIED THE IMAGINATION --WHOLE FORESTS...

...AND CAVERNS DRAPED WITH STALACTITES.

BUT THE CITIZENS BALKED AT SUCH EXTRAVAGANCE, AND SENT WAGNER PACKING BACK HOME.

THE KING WAS SORRY TO SEE HIS HERO GO, BUT NOT FOR LONG. LUDWIG WAS BECOMING VERY BUSY.

UNDER HIS GUIDANCE, THE REMARKABLE CASTLE NEUSCHWANSTEIN -- NEW SWAN'S CRAG --WAS BUILT IN THE ALPS.

IT JUMBLED TOGETHER EVERY STYLE, FROM EVERY CULTURE. BUT LUDWIG WAS ALREADY WORKING ON ANOTHER MASTERPIECE...

...WHICH WAS LINDERHOF, A SMALL COPY OF FRENCH KING LOUIS XIV'S PALACE AT VERSAILLES.

LUDWIG HAD ALSO BEGUN BUILDING HERRENCHIEMSEE --A VIRTUAL DUPLICATE OF VERSAILLES, STILL INCOMPLETE WHEN THE ROYAL BUILDER DIED.

BUT THESE IMPOSSIBLY EXPENSIVE CASTLES WERE JUST THE TIP OF LUDWIG'S ICEBERG OF STRANGENESS.

LUUUUD... VIIGGG. OH, LUUUUUD-VIGGGG.

AH! IT'S YOU! WHERE HAVE YOU BEEN?

AT STATE DINNERS, HE SEPARATED HIMSELF FROM HIS COMPANY WITH A WALL OF FLOWERS AND LOUD MUSIC.

HE HAD SPECIAL CHAPELS BUILT SO HE COULD HEAR MASS ALONE.

THE WINTER GARDEN HE ADDED TO THE MUNICH ROYAL PALACE ROOF WAS A VIRTUAL JUNGLE.

LUUUUD... VIIIIG, OH, LUUUUD VIIIGG.

IS THAT YOU?

WHOLE ACTING TROUPES PERFORMED FOR WHAT SEEMED EMPTY HOUSES...

...WHILE THE KING, SEATED ALONE, WATCHED FROM BEHIND DRAWN CURTAINS.

TO MAKE SURE HE SAW AS FEW PEOPLE AS POSSIBLE, LUDWIG ROSE AT DUSK AND WENT TO BED AT DAWN,

LUUUD... VIIIGG,

I'M COMING!

HE LIKED TO TRAVEL —

PROVIDED NO ONE SAW HIM.

HE ALSO PRETENDED TO TRAVEL, HAVING HIS COACH TAKE HIM A CERTAIN DISTANCE IN LAPS AROUND THE ROYAL RIDING STABLE.

HE INVENTED PEOPLE -- AND LAUGHED AT THEIR JOKES.

SO HE SAID, "NOT WITH MY WIFE!"

OH, LOOIE, HO, HA, OH, LOOIE...

OH, LUUD... VIG... OH, LUDDY.

THE ROYAL DREAMINESS BEGAN TO LOOK LIKE SOMETHING ELSE.

BAVARIANS BEGAN TO WONDER WHERE THEIR KING HAD GONE.

IT'S SIMPLE; HE'S GONE NUTS.

THE DREAM KING BECAME MORE AND MORE TYRANNICAL. HE FORBADE SPEAKING BAVARIAN DIALECT, AND SNEEZING, AND COUGHING...

SNIFF! SORRY, HIGHNESS.

FOR THAT YOU WILL BE EXECUTED!

LUUDDVIGG... NOT VERY NICE, LUUUDVIGG.

OHH... NEVER MIND.

THE PUNISHMENTS WERE NEVER CARRIED OUT. LUDWIG MIGHT BE CRAZY, BUT HE WAS NEVER CRUEL.

UNTIL NOW, IT'S BEEN LUDWIG'S MONEY. BUT HE'S BROKE. NOW HE'S SPENDING OUR MONEY.

SOMEBODY GET A SHRINK.

SOMEBODY GET A ROPE.

WHEN BAVARIA CUT HIM OFF, HE SENT MINIONS TO THE ENDS OF THE EARTH TO BORROW, AND WORSE.

IF YOU CAN'T BORROW, THEN BEG. IF YOU CAN'T BEG, THEN STEAL!

THE BURGHERS HAD HAD ENOUGH.

GENTLEMEN, DR. BERNARD VON GUDDEN IS A FAMOUS PSYCHIATRIST. HE HAS SOMETHING TO SAY.

GOD HELP US, THE KING IS MAD.

THIS IS NEWS?

LUDWIG WAS SENT TO BERG PALACE ON THE SHORES OF LAKE STANLEY, WITH GUDDEN, THE PSYCHIATRIST WHO'D LABELED HIM INSANE.

I CAN BEAR THAT THEY TAKE THE GOVERNMENT FROM ME, BUT NOT THAT THEY DECLARE ME INSANE.

LUUUUDVIGG...

ONE JUNE AFTERNOON, THE DEPOSED KING AND GUDDEN WENT OUT FOR A LAKESIDE STROLL.

I'M COMING.

WHAT, YOUR HIGHNESS?

OH... NOTHING, SORRY.

HOURS LATER, THEY WERE FOUND DROWNED IN A FEW FEET OF WATER. THE KING HAD EVIDENTLY KILLED HIS DOCTOR, THEN HIMSELF.

OH, MY GOD, YOUR HIGHNESS!

NO ONE KNOWS WHAT REALLY HAPPENED -- EXCEPT THAT POOR LUDWIG HAD FINALLY AWAKENED FROM HIS DREAMS.

Adolf Hitler

THE NAZI DICTATOR WHO TOOK GERMANY TO EUROPEAN DOMINANCE -- AND TOTAL DESTRUCTION -- IN JUST A DOZEN YEARS BETWEEN HIS RISE TO POWER IN 1933 AND HIS DEATH IN A BERLIN BUNKER ON APRIL 30, 1945.

"TOTAL DESTRUCTION"? EXCUSE ME, BUT I BEG TO DIFFER...

OF COURSE, YOU CAN CALL IT WHAT YOU LIKE, BUT I PREFER TO LOOK AT IT ANOTHER WAY.

I MEAN -- DIDN'T GERMANY BOUNCE BACK AFTERWARD? HAVE YOU LOOKED AT THE DEUTSCHMARK LATELY? HAVE YOU?

YOU CALL THAT DESTRUCTION? I DON'T. I CALL IT TOTAL VICTORY.

I WAS THE CREATOR OF ALL THAT. THE FUEHRER. IT'S ALL MY WORK.

AND THIS -- -- THIS IS MY GREATEST ARTISTIC TRIUMPH.

25

PEOPLE ARE ALWAYS BLAMING DAD FOR WHAT I BECAME. "HE DID IT BECAUSE HIS FATHER WAS A BRUTE," THEY SAY.

"MY FATHER GREW UP IN THE AUSTRIAN VILLAGE OF SPITAL, RAISED BY A FARMER THERE.'"

CLARA, WHERE IS THAT ADOLF NOW?

I'M RIGHT HERE, FATHER.

THIS IS JUST A TASTE OF WHAT YOU DESERVE, YOU SNIVELING WRETCH.

"AND YES, YOU MIGHT CALL HIM A BRUTE."

DON'T WORRY, MAMA.

"LISTEN TO THIS: STRUGGLE IS THE FATHER OF ALL THINGS..."

"IT IS NOT BY THE PRINCIPLE OF HUMANITY THAT MAN LIVES OR IS ABLE TO PRESERVE HIMSELF ABOVE THE ANIMAL WORLD..."

"...BUT SOLELY BY MEANS OF THE MOST BRUTAL STRUGGLE." GUESS WHO TAUGHT ME THAT? YOU GOT IT. I LEARNED IT FROM MY DAD.

FATHER WAS FULL OF SURPRISES. FOR INSTANCE, WE NEVER KNEW WHO HIS FATHER WAS... BUT SOME SAY IT WAS A GRAZ MERCHANT NAMED FRANKENBERGER. CAN YOU IMAGINE? A JEW?

"PEOPLE HAVE MADE MUCH OF THAT LITTLE TIDBIT ABOUT MY FATHER. I TELL YOU, MY SUSPICIONS IN NO WAY INFLUENCED MY POLICIES..."

"...BUT I MUST ADMIT I FLEW INTO A RAGE WHENEVER HEARING THE NAME OF HIS HOMETOWN OF SPITAL."

"BUT THEN, I WAS ALWAYS FLYING INTO RAGES... POUNDING MY FISTS AND KICKING WALLS. IT WAS JUST MY NATURE.

"I WAS JUST A VERY INTENSE GUY. IN FACT, MY INTENSITY... MY HATRED, MY ANGER, WHAT SOME CALL MY..... MADNESS,..."

"...WERE MY GREATEST ASSETS. HEY, I WASN'T JUST SOME EVIL GENIUS. THE PEOPLE LOVED ME --THEY THOUGHT ME REFRESH-INGLY HONEST AND CHARMING."

I HAVE NEVER SEEN A HUMAN CAPABLE OF GENERATING SUCH A CONDENSATION OF ENVY, VITUPERATION, AND MALICE.

EVEN THE SWISS WERE FULL OF COMPLIMENTS.

AS FOR THOSE LIES ABOUT MY NEVER GROWING UP:

I WANT SNOW WHITE AND THE SEVEN DWARFS AGAIN TONIGHT, BY THE WAY, AND KING KONG.

IT'S FROM THE FUEHRER, HE SUGGESTS WE LEARN ABOUT FIGHTING RUSSIANS FROM READING KARL MAY NOVELS.

WHAT, THOSE COWBOYS-AND-INDIANS SAGAS FOR BOYS?

WHAT'S WRONG WITH BEING A LITTLE YOUNG AT HEART?

JESUS.

SUCH CRUEL LIES. THEY SAY I WAS A LOUSY ARTIST IN VIENNA ....

...AND THAT I DODGED THE AUSTRIAN DRAFT BEFORE WORLD WAR I BY MOVING TO GERMANY. SUCH CRUEL LIES.

THERE'S THAT HITLER FELLOW. AWFUL PAINTER.

HE'LL NEVER GET INTO THE ACADEMY.

"SO I WASN'T ADMITTED. SO WHAT? I ALREADY KNEW WHAT MY FUTURE WOULD BE.

"I'D KNOWN SINCE SEEING WAGNER'S OPERA RIENZI IN 1906. I WOULD CREATE A THIRD REICH, A NEW ROMAN EMPIRE."

I WAS GOING TO BE BIG.

"REALLY BIG."

BUT PEOPLE REFUSE TO RESPECT MY ACCOMPLISHMENTS. INSTEAD THEY MAKE FUN OF THE WAY I USED TO ENDLESSLY REPEAT THE SAME TASKS, DAY AFTER DAY.

FETCH, BOY.

EVERY DAY WE WALK DOWN THE SAME PATH, AND I CHASE AFTER THE SAME STICK. I NEED SOME VARIETY IN MY LIFE!

"I CERTAINLY HAD NO TROUBLE SEEING MY OWN GREATNESS. LOOK: I HAD NO RANK, I WORE NO MEDALS. MY UNIFORM WAS SIMPLICITY ITSELF.

"AFTER ALL...WHO NEEDS MEDALS...I HAD ABSOLUTE POWER.

"OKAY, SO MAYBE I WAS NOT EXACTLY ADAPTABLE. MAYBE I GOT LOCKED INTO THINGS. NO BIG DEAL."

WHEN SNOW WHITE IS OVER, I WANT TO SEE...SNOW WHITE!

28

UPON THE DEATH OF EGYPT'S KING FAUD I IN 1936, A 16-YEAR-OLD BOY BECAME THE NEXT TO OCCUPY THE WORLD'S OLDEST EXISTING THRONE. THEY CALLED HIM...

KING FAROUK

AT FIRST, HIS PEOPLE REJOICED.

I START MY NEW LIFE WITH A GOOD HEART AND A STRONG WILL.

I PROMISE TO DEVOTE MY LIFE AND MY BEING TO *YOUR* GOOD, TO BEND ALL MY EFFORTS TO CREATE *YOUR* HAPPINESS.

NO KING HAD EVER SPOKEN DIRECTLY TO THE PEOPLE OF EGYPT BEFORE--OR PROMISED THEM ANYTHING.

LONG LIVE FAROUK! ALLAH BE PRAISED!

FAROUK MEANT WELL. BUT HIS UPBRINGING HADN'T PREPARED HIM TO BE DEVOTED TO ANYONE BUT HIMSELF.

WHAT'S GOOD FOR *ME* IS GOOD FOR THE PEOPLE!

WEALTHY BEYOND IMAGINING -- WITH PALACES, YACHTS, PLANES, A HUNDRED CARS, AND THOUSANDS OF ACRES OF LAND -- FAROUK WANTED *MORE*.

MORE!

FORGET IT, AHMED. IT'S THE KING.

OH, ALLAH, NOT FAROUK AGAIN!

blam blam blam

MORE!

THE SEARCH FOR **MORE** TOOK HIM ON MAD SHOPPING SPREES IN EUROPE.

HE SPENT FORTUNES COLLECTING WATCHES, JEWELS, COINS, PAPER-WEIGHTS...

...AND WOMEN.

I THOUGHT *"OBJECT OF DESIRE"* WAS JUST A PHRASE!

BUT EVEN FAROUK'S EXCESSES COULD NOT EASE HIS TERRIBLE ITCH TO ACQUIRE.

I NEED MORE THINGS! I NEED *MORE* MONEY! *MORE!*

SO FAROUK BECAME A THIEF.

THE ITALIANS ARE LOSING, SIRE. WE CAN SIMPLY DIVERT THEIR GOLD INTO YOUR ACCOUNTS.

NAZIS BUTT KICKED

DURING WORLD WAR II, FAROUK'S THUGS PLUNDERED THE CONFISCATED VILLAS OF GERMAN DIPLOMATS.

WHEN THE COFFIN OF THE SHAH OF IRAN'S FATHER PASSED THROUGH CAIRO, FAROUK'S MINIONS RELIEVED IT OF A CEREMONIAL SWORD AND MEDALS.

BUT HE ENJOYED IT MOST WHEN HE DID HIS OWN STEALING.

MORE!

FAROUK CLAIMED HE'D LEARNED TO PICK POCKETS FROM A CONVICT HE'D FREED.

NOT BAD, YOUR HIGHNESS.

ACTUALLY... VERY *GOOD,* YOUR HIGHNESS!

SO GOOD, IN FACT, THAT HE DIDN'T CARE WHO HE ROBBED.

THIS HEIRLOOM WATCH WAS GIVEN TO MY ANCESTOR, THE DUKE OF MARLBOROUGH, BY QUEEN ANNE.

GOOD GAWD! SOMEONE'S PINCHED MY WATCH!

NOT TO WORRY, MR. CHURCHILL! I'LL FIND IT FOR YOU!

I RAN THE MISCREANT DOWN AND... UH... I PICKED *HIS* POCKET!

YEAH, RIGHT... THE BLOODY THIEF OF CAIRO!

IT WAS JUST TOO MUCH FOR A GROUP OF EGYPTIAN ARMY OFFICERS -- INCLUDING COLONEL GAMAL ABDEL NASSER.

THIEVING PIG!

MORE!

IN 1952, AN ARMY COUP SENT FAROUK INTO EXILE... ALONG WITH A SECRET HOARD OF GOLD.

UP WITH NASSER! DOWN WITH FAROUK!

THE NEW REGIME AUCTIONED OFF THE ROYAL PACK RAT'S VAST COLLECTIONS OF PRICELESS JUNK.

LESS!

FAROUK LIVED ON IN EXILE UNTIL MARCH 1965, WHEN THE 280-POUND "BOY PHARAOH" COLLAPSED AND DIED -- OVER A HEAVY MEAL, OF COURSE.

NO MORE...

CHAPTER TWO

ONWARD, CRACKPOT SOLDIERS

MILITARY MEN

What is it about a man in a uniform? So determined, so forceful, so brave, so... bizarre. Perhaps it's the pressure of warfare that fragmented these soldiers' minds and drove them into the kingdom of the weird... or maybe they were born strange and kept their tendencies secret until military service allowed them to blossom. How else to explain Hiroo Onoda (*page 34*), the Japanese soldier who refused to surrender until thirty years after the conclusion of World War II? Or the legendary Lawrence of Arabia (T.E. Lawrence, *page 36*), known as a hero to millions of movie fans but remembered as a delusional, battle-crazed warrior by those who knew him. Or Idi Amin (*page 44*), undoubtedly the weirdest military mind of our time, who waged a paranoid war on his own people while the world watched in disbelief. For these and other military weirdos, war is not just a job... it's an adventure.

LT. HIROO ONODA

...CAME TO THE TINY PHILIPPINE ISLAND OF LUBANG IN DECEMBER 1944, WHEN HE WAS 23. HIS ORDERS: TO WAGE GUERRILLA WAR AGAINST AMERICAN AND FILIPINO FORCES. NEVER HAS ANY OFFICER, IN ANY ARMY, FOLLOWED ORDERS MORE CLOSELY.

LT. ONODA, YOU WILL CONDUCT GUERRILLA WARFARE UNTIL FURTHER NOTICE.

YES, SIR.

YOU WILL NEITHER SURRENDER NOR DIE BY YOUR OWN HAND. AS LONG AS YOU HAVE EVEN ONE SOLDIER, YOU WILL CARRY ON.

YES, SIR.

IT MAY TAKE THREE YEARS, LIEUTENANT, IT MAY TAKE FIVE.

YES, SIR.

AND, ONODA,... DON'T WORRY. WHATEVER HAPPENS, WE WILL COME BACK FOR YOU.

YES, SIR.

AS ORDERED, ONODA SWUNG INTO ACTION.

RA-TA-TA-TA-TA!

BOOOM!

RA-TA-TA!

AI-EEE!

TA-TA-TA-TA!

EIGHT MONTHS LATER, JAPAN SURRENDERED.

BUT NOT LIEUTENANT ONODA.

IN 1949, ONE OF HIS FEW MEN DISAPPEARED.

SOON AFTERWARD HE FOUND A NOTE FROM THE MISSING MAN.

"WHEN I SURRENDERED, THE PHILIPPINE TROOPS GREETED ME AS A FRIEND."

A CLEVER TRICK...

...LIKE THEIR RUMORS THAT THE WAR HAS ENDED, AND JAPAN HAS LOST. IF THE WAR WERE REALLY OVER, MY COMMANDER WOULD HAVE TOLD ME.

ONODA WENT BACK TO WAR.

AH, ANOTHER CLEVER RUSE.

IN THE 1950s, THE JAPANESE GOVERNMENT SENT ENVOYS AND A BANNER BEARING THE SIGNATURES OF ONODA'S FAMILY, URGING HIM TO COME HOME.

IN 1959, THE GOVERNMENT SENT ONODA'S BROTHER TOSHIO.

HIROO, PLEASE, THE WAR IS OVER. NO ONE WILL HARM YOU. PLEASE COME HOME...

EXTREMELY CLEVER. THIS IMPOSTOR LOOKS AND SOUNDS JUST LIKE MY BROTHER.

ALL JAPANESE WOULD HAVE CHOSEN SUICIDE RATHER THAN SURRENDER. BUT I SEE JAPANESE. THEREFORE, WE HAVE NOT SURRENDERED. THE WAR CANNOT BE OVER, I MUST GO ON.

BY 1972, ONODA WAS THE ONLY WARRIOR LEFT.

THAT SAME YEAR, HE CAME UPON A MAN NAMED NORIO SUZUKI, WHO'D COME LOOKING FOR HIM.

DON'T KILL ME, OLD BUDDY. I'VE COME TO TAKE YOU HOME. LISTEN...

SUZUKI WAS CONVINCING.

I WOULD CONSIDER... SURRENDER... IF I WERE ORDERED TO BY MY COMMANDER.

LEAVE IT TO ME, PAL.

SUZUKI FOUND A FORMER SUPERIOR OFFICER, YOSHIRU TANIGUCHI. FINALLY ORDERED TO SURRENDER, LIEUTENANT ONODA HANDED HIS SWORD TO A FILIPINO OFFICER ON MARCH 9, 1974.

THE 52-YEAR-OLD OFFICER HAD BEEN AT WAR FOR ALMOST 30 YEARS.

FIGHTING ON THE DESERT FRINGES OF WORLD WAR I, THOMAS EDWARD LAWRENCE HELPED CREATE THE MODERN ARAB NATION AND A LEGENDARY FIGURE:

T.E. LAWRENCE (OF ARABIA)

BUT UNDERNEATH THOSE FLOWING ROBES LIVED A COMPLEX, OFTEN NEUROTIC, LITTLE MAN, WHO SEEMED TO HAVE NO REAL IDENTITY OF HIS OWN.

HIS FAMILY HAD STARTED HIM OFF THAT WAY.

THE "LAWRENCES" WERE NOT REALLY THE LAWRENCES, SINCE THEY NEVER REALLY MARRIED.

OTHER THAN THAT, THEY WERE PROPER VICTORIANS.

I SAY, THOMAS--

CALL ME T.E.

DRAWN TO MILITARY ARCHAEOLOGY--THE STUDY OF ANCIENT FORTIFICATIONS AND WEAPONRY--AT OXFORD...

...T.E. SOON ESCAPED TO THE ANCIENT DESERT AROUND THE EUPHRATES RIVER.

THE WASTELANDS OF ARABIA FELT STRANGELY LIKE HOME TO HIM.

ALLAH BE PRAISED!

WHEN HE WASN'T EXCAVATING, HE WAS AMONG THE DESERT PEOPLE, LEARNING THEIR WAYS AND MANY LANGUAGES.

HE WAS PARTICULARLY ENAMORED WITH THE BEDOUIN WANDERERS, WHOM HE SAW AS OPPRESSED BY THE TURKS.

THE ENGLISH IS RIGHT, AHMED...WE ARE OPPRESSED EVEN AS WE WANDER...

ONE DAY, MY FRIENDS, ALLAH WILL FREE YOU.

ALLAH IS GREAT.

WHEN WORLD WAR I BROKE OUT, BRITAIN FOUND ITSELF FIGHTING TURKEY IN THE MIDDLE EAST--AND LAWRENCE FOUND HIMSELF AN INTELLIGENCE OFFICER IN CAIRO.

HOW MANY TROOPS ARE YOU TURKS AMASSING, OSCAR? TELL THE TRUTH THIS TIME.

LESS THAN ONE HUNDRED, I SWEAR BY THE OLIVE GROVES OF MY GRANDMOTHER!

LAWRENCE WAS SOON BORED WITH INTERROGATING PRISONERS.

HE'D HEARD OF ARAB GUERRILLAS FIGHTING THE TURKS ALONG THE RED SEA, AND LONGED TO JOIN THEM.

BUT LOCKED AWAY IN HIS INTELLIGENCE OFFICE, HE COULD DO LITTLE MORE THAN CONTINUE HIS INTERROGATIONS...

ALL RIGHT, SIR-- TWO HUNDRED TROOPS, NOW, REMOVE YOUR HAND FROM THE FLAME!

SOON, THOUGH, HE HIT UPON AN IDEA...

WE MUST HELP THE ARAB REBELS, SIR.

WE MUST SHOW THEM WE'RE ON THEIR SIDE.

WELL, LIEUTENANT, AND HOW SHALL WE DO THAT?

SEND ME, SIR.

YOU, LAWRENCE?

AS AN IDEA, IT WAS BETTER THAN NOTHING. LAWRENCE WOULD JOIN THE ARAB REBELS.

AND BY THE WAY, LAWRENCE... WHAT HAPPENED TO YOUR HAND?

I PLAY WITH FIRE, SIR.

AT FIRST, THE ARABS WERE SKEPTICAL...

BY ALLAH, TAKING ONE OF THE BRITISH INTO OUR FOLD IS A STIFF PRICE TO PAY FOR ARMS!

...AND T.E. DID LITTLE TO REASSURE THEM.

I SAY-- WHERE CAN I GET SOME DECENT DESERT APPAREL?

BUT ONCE IN ACTION, HE WON THE REBELS' TRUST.

THEY LIKED HIS COURAGE...

...AND ADMIRED HIS COLD-BLOODEDNESS.

LAWRENCE SOON BECAME KNOWN AS A MAN WHO WOULD TAKE GREAT RISKS...

...WHICH, COMBINED WITH HIS INTELLIGENCE SKILLS, ...

...PLEASED HIS ARAB COMPATRIOTS GREATLY.

THE ARAB RAIDS, HOWEVER, ANNOYED THE TURKS.

THIS ENGLISH MAN, I WANT HIM!

BIT BY BIT, LAWRENCE'S GUERRILLAS FOUGHT THEIR WAY TO THE NORTHERN TIP OF THE RED SEA.

IN JULY 1917 THEY TOOK THE KEY CITY OF AQABA.

I SAY—CAN YOU TELL ME WHERE TO FIND MR. LAWRENCE?

SORRY, MASTER, NO SPEAK ENGLISH.

MY NAME'S LOWELL THOMAS, MR. LAWRENCE. YOU MAKE WAR, I MAKE PEOPLE FAMOUS.

I'M HERE TO PUT YOUR WAR ON FILM.

MR. THOMAS, YOU MAY PUT IT WHEREVER YOU WISH.

THUS LAWRENCE BACKED INTO FAME.

FOR BOYS WHO WATCHED HIS EXPLOITS ON NEWSREELS, LAWRENCE'S WAR WAS A DREAMLIKE ADVENTURE...

...FOR LAWRENCE, IT WAS A HARD REALITY.

IN FACT, HE SEEMED TO BE EXPLORING HOW HARD REALITY COULD BE.

THE TURKS WOULD SHOW HIM.

THEY CAPTURED LAWRENCE IN NOVEMBER 1917.

BRING THE ENGLISH MAN TO MY QUARTERS.

MR. LAWRENCE... I PRESUME?

DON'T...

THE BOY'S DREAM OF ADVENTURE HAD CURDLED INTO A NIGHTMARE...

...A NIGHTMARE FROM WHICH NEITHER HIS SPIRIT NOR HIS BODY WOULD EVER AWAKEN.

WHEN HE WAS RELEASED AND RETURNED TO BATTLE, LAWRENCE FOUGHT LIKE A ROBOT, SEEKING PHYSICAL AND MENTAL EXHAUSTION ...AND, PERHAPS, DEATH.

WHEN THE WAR ENDED IN 1918, LAWRENCE WAS A LIEUTENANT COLONEL--BUT HIS IDENTITY HAD BEGUN TO FLICKER OMINOUSLY.

COLONEL LAWRENCE? ARE YOU WELL?

COLONEL LAWRENCE IS DEAD, YOUR HIGHNESS.

HE ABANDONED THE DISTINGUISHED SERVICE ORDER, THE ORDER OF THE BATH--AND HIMSELF.

IN 1923, HE ENLISTED IN THE ROYAL AIR FORCE AS JOHN HUME ROSS.

WHEN THE RAF DROPPED HIM, HE JOINED THE ROYAL TANK CORPS AS T.E. SHAW. LATER HE TRANSFERRED BACK TO THE R.A.F. HE WAS NEVER T.E. LAWRENCE AGAIN.

HE WROTE HIS MONUMENTAL AUTOBIOGRAPHY, SEVEN PILLARS OF WISDOM, AND REMAINED THE DARLING OF HIS ARISTOCRATIC ENGLISH FRIENDS. BUT HE LIVED AS THE LOWEST-RANKING AIRMAN, TENDING SEAPLANES...

...AND, PERHAPS, REMEMBERING HIS WAR IN THE DESERT.

IN 1935, AGED 46, LAWRENCE WAS RETIRED FROM THE R.A.F.

THERE IS SOMETHING BROKEN IN THE WORKS. MY WILL, I THINK.

THAT SAME YEAR HE HAD A FATAL MOTOR-CYCLE ACCIDENT...

...FACING, AT LONG LAST, A PAIN HE COULD NOT ENDURE.

THE GREAT IMPOSTOR

ABOARD THE ROYAL CANADIAN NAVY DESTROYER *CAYUGA*, OFF THE COAST OF WAR-TORN KOREA IN 1951, A TENSE MEDICAL DRAMA BUILDS TOWARD A CLIMAX.

SURGEON-LIEUTENANT JOSEPH CYR WORKS FEVERISHLY TO SAVE THE LIVES OF WOUNDED SOLDIERS.

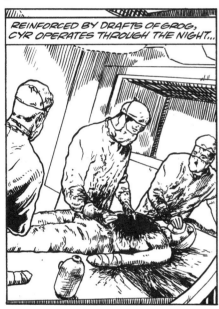

REINFORCED BY DRAFTS OF GROG, CYR OPERATES THROUGH THE NIGHT...

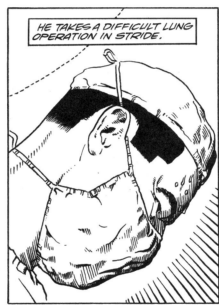

HE TAKES A DIFFICULT LUNG OPERATION IN STRIDE.

THOSE WHO WERE THERE THAT NIGHT TALKED OF A "MIRACLE DOCTOR".

IT'S A MIRACLE, ALL RIGHT.

A MIRACLE THAT THE PATIENT SURVIVED.

BUT ONE DOCTOR, READING ABOUT THE *CAYUGA* SURGERY, DIDN'T THINK MUCH OF THE MIRACLE.

THIS CAN'T BE!!

HIS NAME WAS DR. JOSEPH CYR, AND HE WAS STILL IN CANADA.

HE BLEW THE WHISTLE.

THE "DOCTOR" WAS REALLY 30-YEAR-OLD FERDINAND WALDO DEMARA OF LAWRENCE, MASS...

...WHO'D ALWAYS HAD AN IDENTITY PROBLEM.

LIKE A CLIMBING PLANT, HE NEEDED SOME STRUCTURE TO CLING TO. HE TRIED THE CHURCH...

...BUT DIDN'T FIND WHAT HE SOUGHT. SO HE BEGAN BECOMING OTHER PEOPLE, WITH OTHER CAREERS.

WITH NOTHING BUT SMARTS AND DETERMINATION, HE BECAME A CIVIL ENGINEER...

LEFT, LEFT... NOW RIGHT A LITTLE... NOW LEFT...

...A DEPUTY SHERIFF...

...THE ASSISTANT WARDEN OF A TEXAS PRISON...

MORNING, MEN.

MORNING, WARDEN.

...A LAWYER...

LADIES AND GENTLEMEN OF THE JURY...

...A CHILD-CARE EXPERT...

...A NEWSPAPER EDITOR...

...AND A CANCER RESEARCHER...

...TO NAME A FEW.

TEACHING SCIENCE WAS ONE OF HIS FAVORITE CAREERS, AND HE WAS GOOD AT IT.

TROUBLE WAS, HIS ENTHUSIASM BROUGHT HIM ATTENTION--AND ATTENTION INVARIABLY GOT HIM CAUGHT.

IT DOESN'T MATTER HOW GOOD YOU ARE. YOU HAVE TO BE SOMEBODY WHO REALLY EXISTS!

I'VE GOTTA TAKE YOU IN.

HERE'S HOW I FIGURE IT. YOU TAKE ON NEW IDENTITIES TO GET YOU INTO NEW WORLDS. YOU EXPECT LIFE TO BE RICHER THAN IT IS.

YOU'RE WRONG.

EVERY TIME I TAKE A NEW IDENTITY, SOME PART OF ME DIES.

A GOOD BIT OF HIM MUST HAVE DIED, THEN, BY THE TIME HE LEFT THE CAYUGA IN 1951.

THE ENSUING PUBLICITY FINISHED HIM OFF.

LIFE — THE GREAT IMPOSTOR

FERDINAND WALDO DEMARA

LIFE — THE GREAT IMPOSTOR

FAME FORCED HIM INTO A SINGLE, REAL IDENTITY.

THE GREAT IMPOSTOR
HE WAS A MONK, A SURGEON, A DENTIST, A LAWYER, A TEACHER...
THE TRUE STORY OF FERDINAND WALDO DEMARA

ROBERT CRICHTON

Meet the most charming fraud who ever pulled the wool over a man's eyes...

GREAT IMPOSTOR

I'LL HAVE TO BE...ME.

HIS CRAMPED STYLE DEPRESSED HIM. WHEN HE DIED AT 60 IN 1982, HE WAS A MINISTER TO PATIENTS IN A CALIFORNIA HOSPITAL.

DURING HIS LAST YEARS, HE'D FINALLY LIVED AS HIMSELF... ALMOST.

IN THE END, HE USED THE NAME "FRED" DEMARA.

43

IDI AMIN

KNOWN TO THE WESTERN PRESS AS BIG DADDY, UGANDA'S CLOWNISH STRONGMAN WAS A POPULAR CHAP -- UNTIL HIS PEOPLE GOT TO KNOW HIM.

AMIN WAS BORN IN 1925 NEAR SUDAN, AND REARED BY HIS MOTHER, A LUGBARA WOMAN WHO PRACTICED WITCHCRAFT.

LIKE MANY A PEASANT'S SON, AMIN TOOK THE ONLY OPPORTUNITY AROUND: IN 1946 HE JOINED THE BRITISH COLONIAL ARMY AS AN ASSISTANT COOK.

AT SIX-FOUR AND 240 POUNDS, AMIN FOUND A VOCATION IN THE RING AND WAS UNDEFEATED NATIONAL HEAVYWEIGHT CHAMP FOR NINE YEARS.

WHEN THE BRITISH DEPARTED IN 1962, THEY HAD HIGH -- IF CONDESCENDING -- PRAISE FOR AMIN.

IDI WAS A SPLENDID CHAP, THOUGH A BIT SHORT OF THE GREY MATTER.

AYE, JUST A WEE BIT.

AS ONE OF ONLY TWO OFFICERS IN UGANDA'S ARMY, AMIN WAS GUARANTEED RAPID ADVANCEMENT.

WHEN MILTON OBOTE TOOK POWER AFTER INDEPENDENCE, AMIN BECAME THE ARMY'S CHIEF OF STAFF.

THE STRONGMAN NEVER TRUSTED AMIN -- WITH REASON.

OBOTE HAD SEEN AMIN'S BRUTAL SIDE -- AND KNEW THAT IT WAS JUST BARELY CONTROLLABLE.

IN THE MONTHS THAT FOLLOWED, UGANDA THRIVED. MOST PEOPLE THOUGHT THERE WAS ONLY ONE THING WRONG WITH IT:

MILTON OBOTE.

IN 1971, IDI AMIN FIXED THAT.

NOT TO WORRY, PEOPLES. FREE ELECTIONS IN 1974.

THE BIG GUY WITH THE SECOND-GRADE EDUCATION BECAME A REASSURINGLY COMIC FIGURE IN KAMPALA, THE CAPITAL.

I AM 50 OR 60 YEARS AHEAD OF MY TIME, MY SPEED IS VERY FAST!

THEY ALL LAUGHED WHEN HE JUMPED INTO SWIMMING POOLS AT PARTIES.

MY... SPEED... IS... VERY... FAST.

BUT SOON, THE LAUGHTER WOULD STOP.

HIS PARANOIA UNCHECKED, AMIN ORDERED HIS TROOPS TO ROUND UP MILITARY LEADERS WHO HAD FAILED TO SUPPORT HIS COUP.

GENERAL HUSSEIN... YOU MUST COME WITH US, SUH.

THE ACCUSED WERE TRIED SWIFTLY -- AND DECISIVELY.

THWOCK!!

RUMOR HELD THAT AMIN BERATED THE GENERAL'S HEAD AT DINNER, AND KEPT IT WITH OTHERS IN THE FRIDGE AT NIGHT.

DAMMIT, HUSSEIN, I TOLD YOU AND TOLD YOU!

THE PURGE SWEPT UP THE COUNTRY'S CHIEF JUSTICE AND EVEN CABINET MINISTERS.

YOU MAY CALL ME ... PRESIDENT-FOR-LIFE.

HE ADDED 15,000 THUGS TO THE GOVERNMENT ROLLS.

THOUSANDS DIED BECAUSE HIS GOONS WANTED THEIR PROPERTY.

JUST SAY YES.

THE TERROR CONTINUED. BODIES WERE FOUND WITH THEIR LIVERS, NOSES, GENITALS, AND EYES MISSING.

IT ALL LOOKS SO GOOD.

PEOPLE SAID THAT POLITICAL PRISONERS WERE FORCED TO BLUDGEON THEIR FELLOWS -- OFTEN WITH HELP FROM AMIN.

BUT AMIN'S LIFE SEEMED CHARMED. HE SURVIVED 22 ATTEMPTS TO KILL HIM.

FINALLY HE STUMBLED. HE ATTACKED NEIGHBORING TANZANIA AND LOST.

DEFEAT FORCED HIM INTO EXILE IN SAUDI ARABIA, WHERE HE REMAINS TO THIS DAY.

HIS PRIVATE QUARTERS WERE ALL ONE WOULD EXPECT...

CHRIKEE, JUST LOOK 'ERE!

...IN THE PLAYROOM OF A DERANGED, SADISTIC CHILD.

CHAPTER THREE

EVANGELISTS AND PHILOSOPHERS

ODDLY GODLY

"God told me to do it," is the psychotic's first defense — but it's a defense that seldom, if ever, convinces. Juries, and folks in general, never believe that God instructs the actions of truly evil weirdos. Satan, however, is another story. Lots of folks believed Aleister Crowley (*page 63*) when he said he had a direct line to the Lord of Darkness — but God? No way. To convince people you've got the ear of the Lord, you've got to be pure and righteous and honest and spiritual — or at least, like many of the weirdos considered in this section, know how to fake it. Then again, some spiritual weirdos took another approach entirely — like Wilhelm Reich, who dropped the religious pretense altogether and created his own god of sexual energy. Nice work, if you can get it.

RASPUTIN

GRIGORY YEFIMOVICH NOVYKH, A HOLY MAN WITH A REPUTATION FOR HEALING AND A STRANGE KIND OF PERSONAL MAGNETISM, CAME TO THE RUSSIAN CAPITAL OF ST. PETERSBURG (THEN CALLED PETROGRAD) IN 1903.

A SIBERIAN BY BIRTH, HE'D WANDERED THROUGH RUSSIA, GREECE, AND THE HOLY LAND...

...AND FOLLOWED THE TEACHINGS OF THE KHLYSTY MONKS. KHLYSTY MEANS FLAGELANTS.

THEY TAUGHT THAT CONTRITION BROUGHT CLOSENESS TO GOD...

...AND THAT THE SHORTEST PATH TO CONTRITION WAS SIN. LOTS OF IT, FOLLOWED BY A LITTLE FLAGELLATION.

BECAUSE HE PURSUED CONTRITION WITH SUCH ZEAL, GRIGORY WAS GIVEN THE NAME RASPUTIN -- "DEBAUCHED ONE".

IT WILL BRING YOU CLOSER TO GOD, TRUST ME.

UGH! HE'S SO FILTHY, AND HE SMELLS LIKE A GOAT!

BUT... THOSE EYES...

HIS ENTIRE PERSONALITY SHONE FROM THOSE EYES, WHICH HE USED TO HURT -- BUT ALSO TO HEAL.

IN 1905, RASPUTIN WAS SUMMONED TO THE IMPERIAL PALACE, WHERE A TERRIBLE FAMILY SECRET WAS UNFOLDING.

YOU SENT FOR ME, SIRE?

YOUNG ALEXIS, HEIR TO THE THRONE, HAD HEMOPHILIA. A SCRATCH COULD BE FATAL, AND HE WAS OFTEN IN TERRIBLE PAIN.

RASPUTIN EASED THE BOY'S PAIN...

THERE, HE WILL SLEEP NOW.

...AND WON THE UNDYING GRATITUDE OF HIS PARENTS, ESPECIALLY THE EMPRESS ALEXANDRA.

HE IS... A SAINT.

THE LIFE OF YOUR HEIR... YOUR DYNASTY... IS LINKED TO ME NOW.

AFTER RULING RUSSIA FOR SOME 300 YEARS, THE ROMANOVS HAD BEEN CAPTURED BY AN ILLITERATE SIBERIAN MONK.

A SAINT.

AWAY FROM THE PALACE, RASPUTIN CONTINUED TO PURSUE CONTRITION.

AT COURT, HE EASED THE SUFFERING OF ALEXIS AND THE EMPRESS ALEXANDRA.

THE LITTLE ONE WILL NOT DIE, DO NOT ALLOW THE DOCTORS TO BOTHER HIM TOO MUCH.

THE EMPRESS DISMISSED REPORTS OF RASPUTIN'S LICENTIOUS BEHAVIOR.

SAINTS ARE OFTEN CALUMNIATED. HE IS HATED BECAUSE WE LOVE HIM.

STILL, PEOPLE HAD BEGUN TO TALK.

BECAUSE ALEXIS' ILLNESS WAS KEPT A CLOSE SECRET, NO ONE OUTSIDE THE PALACE KNEW WHY RASPUTIN WAS THERE.

IT'S OBVIOUS. ALEXANDRA IS HIS MISTRESS.

RUMORS FLEW. FINALLY, IN 1911, RASPUTIN WAS EXPELLED FROM PETROGRAD.

I SHALL RETURN.

HE DID, IN 1914, AFTER AGAIN HELPING ALEXIS FROM A DISTANCE. BY THE TIME HE RETURNED, RUSSIA WAS AT WAR WITH GERMANY.

MAY GOD BLESS THE IMPERIAL ARMY!

WHEN THE CZAR RODE OFF TO WAR IN 1915, HE LEFT HIS EMPRESS IN CHARGE...

...AIDED BY HER SAINT.

A YEAR LATER, RUSSIA HAD 8 MILLION CASUALTIES...

...AND THE ECONOMY WAS IN RUINS.

BREAD QUEUE

PEOPLE SAID THAT THE GERMANS WERE GETTING STATE SECRETS FROM RASPUTIN'S LOOSE LIPS. THE EMPEROR AND EMPRESS WERE OBLIVIOUS TO SUCH CRITICISMS.

IN THEIR DAILY LETTERS THEY CALLED RASPUTIN "OUR FRIEND."

"OUR FRIEND HAS LOOKED AT THE POOR WOMAN, WHOSE SPINE AND SKULL WERE BADLY INJURED. 'SHE WILL LIVE,' HE SAID, 'BUT AS A CRIPPLE.'"

"...AND AS A SPECIAL PRECAUTION, BEFORE GOING TO YOUR GENERALS, YOU MUST COMB YOUR HAIR WITH OUR FRIEND'S COMB,..."

≡UGH!≡

HE'D BEGUN TO HAVE SECOND THOUGHTS ABOUT THEIR DEBAUCHED ONE.

OTHERS WANTED HIM DEAD.

PRINCE FELIX YUSUPOV DECIDED IT WAS TIME TO ACT. HE CONTACTED SEVERAL OTHER NOBLES WHO FELT THE SAME.

DONE! RASPUTIN IS AS GOOD AS DEAD.

BUT THEY COULDN'T HELP WONDERING: WAS HE?

ON DECEMBER 29, 1916, YUSUPOV WELCOMED RASPUTIN TO HIS PALATIAL HOME.

AH, BROTHER GRIGORY, WELCOME!

YOUR INVITATION RATHER SURPRISED ME.

WE'LL GO TO OUR CELLAR... THEY WON'T, HA HA, HEAR US THERE.

HERE WE ARE, SOME WINE, SOME TEA CAKES... PLEASE HELP YOURSELF.

THE WINE AND TEA CAKES HELD ENOUGH POISON TO KILL A MONASTERY.

CYRUS R. TEED

IN THE LATE 1890S, A STERN LITTLE MAN AND HIS FOLLOWERS FOUNDED ESTERO, A COMMUNITY NEAR NAPLES, FLORIDA...

...A HEAVEN ON EARTH THAT THEY BELIEVED WOULD ONE DAY BE HOME TO TEN MILLION BELIEVERS, THE ABODE OF PEACE AND PROSPERITY.

THEIR CHARISMATIC LEADER: AN UPSTATE NEW YORKER IN HIS LATE 50S NAMED CYRUS R. TEED.

LONG A SCIENTIFIC DABBLER IN THE EXTRAORDINARY, HIS WORK ON WHAT HE CALLED "ELECTRO-ALCHEMICAL RESEARCH..."

CY-RUS TEED...

WHA--?

...LED HIM ONE NIGHT INTO A TINGLING TRANCE AND A VISION.

THE DIVINE MOTHERHOOD!

YES, CYRUS, I BRING SOME BIG NEWS...

YOU ARE THE *MESSIAH!*

JUST AS I SUSPECTED.

NOW IT'S UP TO YOU, CY.

I SHALL APPLY MY SCIENCE TO REDEEMING HUMANITY!

I SHALL TAKE THE HEBREW NAME FOR CYRUS: KORESH!*

*NO RELATION TO DAVID.

BUT FIRST HE WOULD HAVE TO RID THE WORLD OF SOME REALLY DUMB IDEAS, SUCH AS THE COPERNICAN NONSENSE THAT THE EARTH MOVED ABOUT THE SUN.

...OR THAT WE LIVE ON THE SURFACE OF A SPINNING BALL IN SPACE.

TEED BELIEVED THAT CONVENTIONAL COSMOLOGY WAS A FARCE...

...AND THAT HE KNEW WHAT THE UNIVERSE WAS REALLY LIKE.

TEED'S COSMOS WAS CONTAINED IN A SINGLE GOLD-PLATED SPHERE...

...ABOUT 8,000 MILES IN DIAMETER AND ABOUT 25,000 MILES IN CIRCUMFERENCE.

ALMOST EXACTLY THE SIZE OF THE SO-CALLED PLANET EARTH, AS A MATTER OF FACT.

THE BALL WAS HOLLOW...

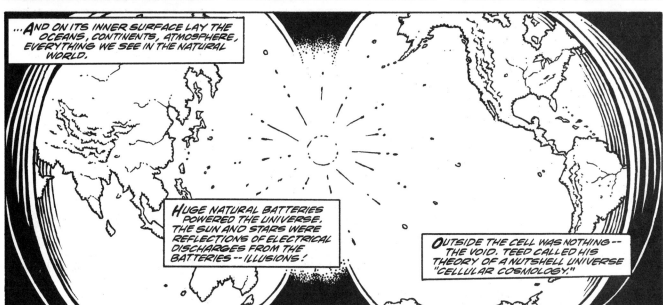

...AND ON ITS INNER SURFACE LAY THE OCEANS, CONTINENTS, ATMOSPHERE, EVERYTHING WE SEE IN THE NATURAL WORLD.

HUGE NATURAL BATTERIES POWERED THE UNIVERSE. THE SUN AND STARS WERE REFLECTIONS OF ELECTRICAL DISCHARGES FROM THE BATTERIES -- ILLUSIONS!

OUTSIDE THE CELL WAS NOTHING -- THE VOID. TEED CALLED HIS THEORY OF A NUTSHELL UNIVERSE "CELLULAR COSMOLOGY."

GRAVITY WAS ANOTHER ILLUSION. THINGS LIKE PEOPLE WERE HELD ON THE CONCAVE SURFACE BY CENTRIFUGAL FORCE!

PEOPLE WHO DO NOT ACCEPT CONCAVITY...

...DENY GOD!

HIS FOLLOWERS CALLED THEMSELVES KORESHANTISTS.

BUT TEED WAS SCIENTIST ENOUGH TO WANT TO PROVE THE BASIS OF KORESHANITY.

WE MUST HAVE PROOF!

AND I BELIEVE I SEE HOW TO GET IT, KORESH.

TEAMING WITH ENGINEER ULYSSES GRANT MORROW, TEED BEGAN A SURVEY ALONG THE PERFECTLY-STRAIGHT OLD ILLINOIS DRAINAGE CANAL.

BY PROJECTING A STRAIGHT HORIZONTAL LINE THROUGH THE AIR, TEED AND MORROW BELIEVED, THEY COULD SHOW THE CONCAVE SURFACE RISING TO MEET IT.

ENCOURAGING, MORROW. VERY ENCOURAGING.

BUT NOT THE PROOF WE SOUGHT, KORESH, WE MUST TRY AGAIN.

A MORE ELABORATE TEST FOLLOWED AT ESTERO...

...WHERE A HUGE SPIRIT LEVEL WAS SLOWLY CARRIED DOWN THE BEACH TO ESTABLISH THE NECESSARY HORIZONTAL LINE THROUGH THE AIR.

THIS WILL PROVE CONCAVITY ONCE AND FOR ALL!

IN SOMETHING OVER A MONTH, THEY ESTABLISHED A LINE FOUR AND ONE-EIGHTH MILES LONG.

EUREKA! LOOK WHERE THE GROUND MEETS OUR LINE!

OF COURSE, DETRACTORS SAID THE KORESHANTISTS HAD MERELY SEEN WHAT THEY'D WANTED TO SEE.

THAT'S WHAT I SAID... $100,000 TO ANYONE WHO PROVES WE'RE WRONG.

THERE WERE NO TAKERS, BUT NOT BECAUSE TEED WAS RIGHT. THE GEOMETRY OF HIS OUTSIDE-IN WORLD WAS THE MIRROR IMAGE OF THE REAL, INSIDE-OUT ONE. WHAT PROVED ONE WOULD ALSO PROVE THE OTHER.

THE LITTLE KORESHAN UNITY SETTLEMENT KEPT ITS MOTTO:

"WE LIVE INSIDE."

OUTSIDE, THEY BEGAN TO DOMINATE LOCAL POLITICS.

REMEMBER, A VOTE FOR OUR CANDIDATE IS A VOTE FOR TRUTH!

IN 1906, AN ENRAGED VOTER SLUGGED THE MESSIAH IN THE FACE.

TEED NEVER FULLY RECOVERED FROM THE INSULT.

TWO YEARS LATER, HE DIED. SEVERAL DAYS LATER, SINCE THE MESSIAH DID NOT RISE, HEALTH OFFICIALS ORDERED TEED BURIED.

THEN, THIRTEEN YEARS LATER, A HURRICANE SWEPT TEED'S REMAINS OUT TO SEA.

CALL IT "AN ACT OF GOD!"

AIMEE SEMPLE McPHERSON

...PRESIDED OVER ONE OF AMERICA'S GREATEST CIRCUSES OF THE SOUL-- AND DREW THOUSANDS OF BELIEVERS TO HER CHURCH OF THE FOUR-SQUARE GOSPEL DURING THE 1920S AND 30S.

HOURS BEFORE THE SERVICE BEGAN, VISITORS -- THE FAITHFUL AND THE CURIOUS -- BEGAN TO LINE UP FOR TICKETS...

I'VE COME ALL THE WAY FROM MONTREAL TO SEE SISTER AIMEE.

...AND AIMEE NEVER DISAPPOINTED.

SHE GAVE THEM JESUS, WHO OFFERED THEM SALVATION...

...AND SATAN, WHO THREATENED THEM WITH DAMNATION.

SHE PREACHED ABOUT HEAVEN UP ABOVE...

...AND HELL DOWN BELOW...

...AND ABOUT THOSE MORTAL PITFALLS HUMANS MUST AVOID --JAZZ MUSIC. ALCOHOL. SEX.

AND IMPLICIT IN ALL HER SERMONS WAS A NONE-TOO-SUBTLE PLEA FOR CASH FOR HER MINISTRY.

GOOD FRIENDS, WE NEED YOUR DONATIONS.

...WE NEED YOUR DONATIONS...

HER SERMONS WERE TRANSMITTED TO LOUDSPEAKERS OUTSIDE THE THEATER FOR THOSE WHO HADN'T BEEN ABLE TO GET SEATS...

...AND WERE BROADCAST OVER HER OWN RADIO STATION, KFSG.

AIMEE WAS AMONG THE FIRST TO RECOGNIZE THE MEDIUM'S POTENTIAL TO INFLUENCE...

...DONATIONS.

I'D GIVE ANYTHING TO SEE HER.

ME TOO.

YOU HAD TO SEE AIMEE IN ACTION TO BELIEVE HER.

SISTER AIMEE LIKED ALLEGORIES. ON STAGE SHE SOMETIMES WORE AN ADMIRAL'S UNIFORM...

...TO DEMONSTRATE HOW EASILY THE LAUNCH OF PLEASURE...

...IS OVERTAKEN BY SATAN'S POWERBOAT.

AND HOW ATTACKS BY THE SUBMERGED FOES OF THE CHURCH OF THE FOURSQUARE GOSPEL WOULD ALWAYS FAIL.

YOU SEE? YOU SEE?

HALLELUJAH, AIMEE!

SINK THE U-BOAT!

WITH HER COSTUMED ACTORS AND ELABORATE SETS, SHE STAGED SUCH SUCCESSES AS THE UNEVEN COMBAT BETWEEN DAVID AND GOLIATH.

FROM 1923 TO 1926, AIMEE DID HER THING 9 TIMES DAILY.

HALLELUJAH!

BUT WHAT IS FAITH IF IT BE NOT TESTED?

IN 1926, A SHATTERING SURPRISE.

SISTER AIMEE...SHE'S DISAPPEARED!

THE BAY WAS DRAGGED FOR HER BODY.

...AND GIVE US BACK OUR DIVINE SISTER AIMEE...

BESIDES PRAYER, THE FAITHFUL PUT UP A $25,000 REWARD.

A WEEK LATER, AIMEE STAGGERED ONTO A REMOTE HIGHWAY OUTSIDE OF DOUGLAS, ARIZONA...

HELP!

IT WAS TERRIBLE! I WAS KIDNAPPED! THEY WANTED $500,000 RANSOM...

MIRACULOUSLY ...I ESCAPED.

THE AUTHORITIES DIDN'T BELIEVE HER.

THEY KNEW THAT AIMEE HAD FALLEN INTO ONE OF THOSE MORAL PITFALLS SHE ALWAYS TALKED ABOUT. HER "KIDNAPPING" HAD BEEN A SECRET WEEK WITH HER RADIO OPERATOR, KENNETH ORMISTON.

SHE WAS CHARGED WITH PERJURY, CONSPIRACY, AND OBSTRUCTING JUSTICE.

I AM LIKE A LAMB LED TO THE SLAUGHTER.

AN ENTERPRISING D.A. --WHO LATER WENT TO JAIL FOR BRIBERY -- SAW THAT SHE WAS ACQUITTED.

BUT NONE OF THIS DENTED HER VAST POPULARITY.

SISTER AIMEE, SISTER AIMEE, SISTER AIMEE,

EVEN WHEN AN OVERDOSE OF SLEEPING PILLS ENDED 54-YEAR-OLD AIMEE McPHERSON'S LIFE IN 1944, 50,000 PEOPLE CAME TO SEE HER CASKET.

FACTOID BOOKS

GEORGES IVANOVICH GURDJIEFF,

ARMENIAN MYSTIC, SCOURED THE WORLD TO TAP THE ENORMOUS, SECRET RESOURCES HIDDEN IN THE HUMAN BRAIN--AND, MANY BELIEVE, FOUND AVENUES TO EXTRAORDINARY MENTAL POWER. INDEED, TO SOME, HE MAY HAVE SEEMED INDESTRUCTIBLE...

Hmm, ZE OLD MAN FINALLY DIED AFTER ALL.

QUELLE OLD MAN?

"THAT ACCIDENT I HAD FIVE MONTHS AGO? I TOTALLED A LITTLE COUPE."

MON DIEU!

"I KNEW I HAD KILLED THE DRIVER.

"BUT THIS LITTLE OLD MAN GOT OUT... AND WALKED AWAY.

"I FOLLOWED HIM."

WHY WASN'T HE KILLED?

YOU'LL FIND OUT.

SO... WHO WAS HE?

GEORGES GURDJIEFF, THAT'S WHO.

GURDJIEFF? GURDJIEFF? NEVER HEARD OF HIM.

HE WAS LIKE... LIKE A MESSIAH.

IT SOUNDS LIKE RUBBISH TO ME.

IT WOULD.

YOU'RE THE FELLOW WHO JUST KILLED ME.

I...

"HE KNEW WHAT I WAS THINKING."

"HE FIXED ME WITH SUCH A LOOK..."

I SHALL TELL YOU WHAT YOU WANT TO KNOW.

"HE TOLD ME."

GURDJIEFF BEGAN LIFE IN ARMENIA IN 1872. HE AND HIS FAMILY WERE VERY POOR...BUT NOT UNHAPPY.

"EVEN AS A CHILD, HE FELT IN TOUCH WITH THE PARANORMAL."

"WHEN HIS FATHER TOLD SUCH STORIES AS THE LEGEND OF KING GILGAMESH, GURDJIEFF SENSED THE MIND'S POWER FOR CREATING AND CONTROLLING REALITY."

I AM, THEREFORE I THINK, THEREFORE I AM...

"HE SET OUT TO EXPLORE TRUTH WHEREVER HE COULD FIND IT."

"HE WAS MECHANICALLY ADEPT AND PAID HIS WAY BY FIXING THINGS."

IT WILL BE AS GOOD AS NEW, NO...

...BETTER.

"HE SEARCHED FOR TRUTH IN TEMPLES AROUND THE WORLD AS HE PROBED THE NATURE OF REVELATION.

"HE SAT AT THE FEET OF REMARKABLE TEACHERS."

61

"HE TOOK HIS NEW POWER BACK TO RUSSIA."

"WHEN THE COMMUNISTS TOOK OVER IN 1917, GURDJIEFF AND HIS FOLLOWERS FLED TO FRANCE..."

"...AND SET UP HIS FAMOUS INSTITUTE AT FONTAINEBLEAU, OUTSIDE PARIS."

INSTITUTE FOR THE HARMONIOUS DEVELOPMENT OF MAN

LIFE IS SLEEP. TO BE TRULY ALIVE, WE MUST TURN THAT SLEEP INTO A HIGHER STATE, WHERE THOUGHT HAS THE CLARITY AND FORCE OF PURE LIGHT...

...THROUGH RIGOROUS AND PRECISE EXERCISE... THROUGH DANCE... THROUGH MEDITATION.

"HIS FOLLOWERS INCLUDED HIS FAMOUS LOVER, AUTHOR KATHÉRINE MANSFIELD... AND A HOST OF OTHER PROMINENT PEOPLE."

PURE LIGHT.

PURE LIGHT.

THE INSTITUTE CLOSED IN 1933, BUT GURDJIEFF CONTINUED TEACHING...

TEACHING RUBBISH.

I THINK HIS POWERS WERE REAL. I THINK HE KEPT HIM- SELF ALIVE FOR FIVE MONTHS AFTER THE ACCIDENT JUST BY FORCE OF WILL.

BUT HE WAS A FINE TEACHER...

...TO THE END.

Aleister Crowley

CALLING HIMSELF THE GREAT BEAST, EDWARD ALEXANDER CROWLEY--ALEISTER TO THE WORLD--HELPED BRING BLACK MAGIC INTO THE 20TH CENTURY.

HE CALLED IT MAGICK--THE OLD SPELLING--NOT TO BE CONFUSED WITH STAGE MAGIC.

BORN INTO A FUNDAMENTALIST SCOTTISH HOME IN OCTOBER 1847, CROWLEY RESENTED THE CONFINES PLACED UPON HIM.

EDWARD, IF YE VALUES THY SKIN, LAD, THA'LL NOT LAG BACK SO MUCH.

AYE, EDDIE--IT'S THY SOUL WE'RE CONCERNED WITH.

EDWARD, COME ON, IT'S TIME FER CHURCH.

NOT FOR ME IT ISN'T, FATHER.

THERE WAS MORE FOR HIM, HE BELIEVED, WITH SATAN.

HE BEGAN TO DABBLE IN WHAT IS CALLED HIGH, OR GREAT, MAGIC--

--THE MAGIC THAT COMES FROM ALL THE ANCIENT, DARK MYSTICISM OF THE WORLD...

HEAR ME, SATAN, HEAR ME, OSIRIS AND ANUBIS...

...FROM ANCIENT EGYPT, FROM THE JEWISH CABALA, FROM EONS OF WITCHCRAFT AND BLACK, BLACK MAGICK.

ERIKISEPHEARARARA...

CROWLEY BEGAN HIS QUEST FOR THE TRUTH OF EVIL.

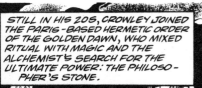

STILL IN HIS 20S, CROWLEY JOINED THE PARIS-BASED HERMETIC ORDER OF THE GOLDEN DAWN, WHO MIXED RITUAL WITH MAGIC AND THE ALCHEMIST'S SEARCH FOR THE ULTIMATE POWER: THE PHILOSO-PHER'S STONE.

PIERRE THOUGHT MY ELIXIR TASTED QUITE GOOD...

THEN WHAT'S THE PROBLEM --?

WELL, IT MADE HIS HAIR AND FINGERNAILS FALL OUT.

IDIOT.

WHEN THE HERMETIC ORDER FALTERED ABOUT 1900, CROWLEY WAS SENT TO TAKE OVER THE LONDON LODGE...

...AND WAS SWIFTLY REJECTED BY THE DYING ORDER.

IDIOTS.

WHEN HE WAS THROUGH WITH THE GOLDEN DAWN, HE'D BEGUN TO DISCOVER THAT MAGIC -- MAGICK -- WASN'T ABOUT CHEMISTRY.

MAGIC IS ABOUT DRUGS, AND SEX.

CROWLEY BOUGHT A HOUSE NEAR THE MONSTER-RIDDEN DEPTHS OF LOCH NESS...

...AND BEGAN HIS EXPERIMENTS IN SEXUAL MAGIC.

GOOD GOD, THA'S NA BOOT A MONSTER...

THE SUMMONED DEMONS, IT WAS SAID, DROVE CROWLEY'S SERVANT INTO A MURDEROUS INSANITY. VILLAGERS WHISPERED OF... HUMAN SACRIFICE.

CROWLEY ROAMED THE WORLD, ADDING TO HIS REPERTOIRE OF THE SEXUAL AND OCCULT -- AND TO HIS IDENTITIES.

AS A YOGI, FOR EXAMPLE, HE WAS KNOWN AS MAHATMA GURU SRI PARAMAHANSA SHIVAJI.

THE POWER... THE POWER.

HE BECAME IRRESISTIBLE (TO HIS ACOLYTES).

THERE...

HAVE NO FEAR...

HIS MOTTO: DO WHAT THOU WILT SHALL BE THE WHOLE OF THE LAW.

HE FOUNDED AN ORDER OF HIS OWN -- ARGENTINUM ASTRUM, THE SILVER STAR.

HEAR ME, HEAR THE GREAT BEAST...

THE GREAT BEAST...

...THE ANTICHRIST... SATAN... OR, PERHAPS, JUST ANOTHER PSYCHOPATH.

IN 1920, CROWLEY ESTABLISHED AN ABBEY IN SICILY...

...WHERE HE AND HIS FOLLOWERS CONTINUED THEIR OCCULT JOURNEY OF SEXUAL EXPLORATION.

DO AS THOU WILT.

WITHIN A YEAR HE BECAME TOO MUCH EVEN FOR SICILY, AND WAS SENT BACK TO ENGLAND.

TURN THEM INTO FROGS!

THE BRITISH PRESS BOTH LOVED AND HATED CROWLEY.

LONDON'S ANTICHRIST RETURNS

IDIOTS.

I AM THE GREAT BEAST.

Evening News
CREEPY CROWLEY BACK IN TOWN!
Wickedest man in world returns to

BUT WHEN THE STOCK MARKET CRASH OF 1929 CAME, THE GREAT BEAST WENT BUST, LIKE EVERYBODY ELSE.

CROWLEY WAS BANKRUPT. THE GOOD TIMES WERE FINISHED.

MASTER? ARE YOU THERE?

BUT HE KEPT TEACHING.

COME IN, MY DEAR. DO...WHAT...THOU...WILT.

THERE IS NOTHING TO BE AFRAID OF...

HE WAS ALWAYS A DANGEROUS MAN.

DANGEROUS, EVEN AFTER HIS DEATH IN 1947, WITNESS THE PASADENA GARAGE OF CALTECH ROCKET PROPULSION SCIENTIST JACK PARSONS, JUNE 1952.

BAH-ROOMP!

A MYSTERIOUS EXPLOSION KILLED PARSONS.

HE MUST'VE MIXED CORDITE AND FULMINATE OF MERCURY.

HARD TO BELIEVE, HIM A CHEMIST AND ALL.

HARD TO BELIEVE, INDEED.

IT WAS THE HOMUNCULUS!

JACK WAS TRYING TO MAKE CROWLEY'S HOMUNCULUS!

THE HOMUNCULUS -- THE TINY ARTIFICIAL MAN WHO WOULD IMPART VAST MAGICAL POWERS TO HIS CREATOR.

OR NOT.

CROWLEY HAD PLANTED "BOOBY TRAPS" IN ALL HIS PUBLISHED MAGICAL TEXTS. THROUGH THESE MEANS, AND OTHERS...

...THE GREAT BEAST LIVES ON.

MARCELLO · CRETI

To his followers, Marcello Creti is something between a messiah and a second Leonardo da Vinci -- a blend of mysticism and invention.

His followers pursue both in a monastery north of Rome they call *Sapienta* -- wisdom.

Creti believes that a race of superior beings ruled the earth in prehistoric times -- beings he calls the *Antalidei*.

He detects their spirits still in the hills around Sapienta.

Recognizing themselves, perhaps, in him, these spirits of the Antalidei have given Creti special powers -- to find precious minerals, for example.

When he enters a trance-like state, they give him philosophy...

WORM COLONIES ARE BETTER ORGANIZED THAN MANKIND NOWADAYS.

...and tell him what to invent.

A BETTER MOUSETRAP, MARCELLO.

OF COURSE!!!

QUICKLY, PENCILS, PAPER, SLIDE RULE!

CRETI PAINSTAKINGLY JOTS DOWN THE REVEALED DIAGRAMS, FORMULAS, AND DRAWINGS...

...WHICH HIS FOLLOWERS USE TO BUILD THE NEW THING.

THE MASTER SAYS IT CONNECTS TO THIS...

NO, NO, IF YOU'LL JUST READ HIS DIAGRAM...

DON'T THINK LIKE CABBAGES, MY CHILDREN.

THE ANTALIDEI HAVE LED CRETI TO 118 "SCIENTIFIC REVELATIONS" THUS FAR...

...INCLUDING A DEVICE FOR TRIMMING NOSE HAIR, INVENTED WHEN HE WAS JUST 7.

AMONG HIS OTHER INSPIRATIONS:

AN ELECTROSHOCK APPARATUS...

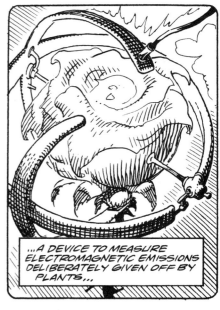

...A DEVICE TO MEASURE ELECTROMAGNETIC EMISSIONS DELIBERATELY GIVEN OFF BY PLANTS...

...DON'T FORGET THE CANCER CURE.

...AND A CURE FOR CANCER.

YOU JUST HAVE TO FREE YOURSELF FROM THE MUD OF CONVENTION.

ERGOS

CRETI'S MOVEMENT IS CALLED ERGOS -- ENERGIA RADIANTE GOVERNANTE OGNI SCIENZA, OR RADIANT ENERGY GOVERNING ALL SCIENCE. HIS FOLLOWERS ARE CALLED ERGONIANS.

MASTER, MASTER, SEE WHAT WE HAVE DONE!

I'LL BE GLAD WHEN THE ANTALIDEI GIVE US THE BICYCLE...

TRUE, MANY OF THE INVENTIONS THE SPECTRAL ANTALIDEI REVEAL TO CRETI ARE OLD NEWS. NO PROBLEM -- UNLESS, OF COURSE, YOU'RE STUCK IN THE MUD OF CONVENTION.

WILHELM REICH

AUSTRIAN PSYCHIATRIST, ACHIEVED EARLY DISTINCTION IN 1922 WHEN, HAVING GRADUATED FROM THE UNIVERSITY OF VIENNA MEDICAL SCHOOL, HE ENTERED THE NEW FIELD OF PSYCHOANALYSIS.

HE WORKED WITH SUCH GIANTS AS SIGMUND FREUD, AND BEGAN TO LOOK LIKE A GIANT HIMSELF.

MOST INSIGHTFUL OF YOU, VILLIE.

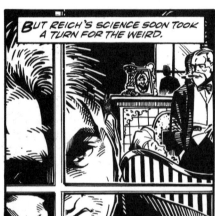

BUT REICH'S SCIENCE SOON TOOK A TURN FOR THE WEIRD.

A MARXIST, REICH THOUGHT HE UNDERSTOOD THE PLIGHT OF THE UNDERCLASS.

IT ISN'T CHUST MONEY....

...IT'S INCOMPLETE SEXUAL RELEASE!

SOCIETY HAS BEEN CRRRIPPLED BY MONOGAMY, A BAN ON PREMARITAL SEX, AND ALL SUCH HANGUPS.

IN 1934 HIS BELIEFS GOT HIM EJECTED FROM THE INTERNATIONAL PSYCHOANALYTIC ASSOCIATION.

EUNUCHS!

HE FLED TO SCANDINAVIA WHEN THE NAZIS CAME TO POWER.

REPRESSED NEUROTICS!

HE WAS ON THE VERGE OF DISCOVERING THE MEANING OF EVERYTHING -- OR SO HE BELIEVED.

IN EXILE IN NORWAY, REICH TURNED TO BIOLOGY -- SOMETHING HE KNEW VERY LITTLE ABOUT.

PHYSICS HAS ELEMENTARY PARTICLES -- WHY NOT LIFE?

HE DECIDED THAT LIFE'S FUNDAMENTAL PARTICLE WAS SOMETHING CALLED THE BION.

BIONS, HE DEDUCED, AROSE SPONTANEOUSLY FROM NON-LIVING STUFF.

MORE IMPORTANT, HE DISCOVERED THE UNIVERSAL FORCE: ORGONE ENERGY...

...THE ENERGY OF ORGASM.

REICH'S UNIVERSE, LIKE HIS POLITICS, RAN ON SEX.

THIS IS THE FUNDAMENTAL POWER SOURCE OF THE UNIVERSE!

ORGONE ENERGY WAS IN EVERYTHING, EVERYWHERE, ESPECIALLY IN THINGS COLORED BLUE: THE SEA, THE SKY, WATER.

IT IS ZO OBVIOUS!

ORGONE GIVES US THE WEATHER!

GRAVITY IS A MYTH! ORGONE HOLDS THE COSMOS TOGETHER!

FOR REICH TO BE RIGHT, EVERYBODY ELSE HAD TO BE WRONG. HE DIDN'T MIND.

IN 1939, HE BROUGHT WHAT HE CALLED ORGONOMY TO AMERIKA.

HE BUILT HIS FIRST ORGONE ACCUMULATORS, BOXES BUILT BY ALTERNATING ORGANIC AND INORGANIC MATERIALS.

REICH SAID THAT SITTING IN THE ACCUMULATOR WOULD COUNTER THE ILLNESSES OF SEXUAL REPRESSION--ULCERS, CANCER, OBESITY, ALCOHOLISM, COMMON COLDS.

WILL IT DO CELLULITE?

REICH MADE HIS LIVING BY SELLING AND RENTING ACCUMULATORS TO THE FAITHFUL. HE BECAME FATHER OF REICHIAN PSYCHOANALYSIS.

IN 1954, THE U.S. GOVERNMENT CALLED THE ACCUMULATORS A FRAUD, AND ORDERED REICH TO STOP PEDDLING THEM. BUT HE WAS BUSY WITH OTHER THINGS...

THEY CALL THEMSELVES THE GOVERNMENT, BUT I KNOW VAT THEY RRREALLY ARE...

...AND I AM RRREADY FOR THEM!

"THEY" WERE EXTRA-TERRESTRIALS.

BUT NOT TO WORRY. A COLLECTION OF HOLLOW PIPES--HIS CLOUDBUSTER--WOULD ROB THEIR SAUCERS OF THE ORGONE ENERGY THEY RAN ON.

BOY, THIS CLOUD-BUSTER REALLY MAKES IT RAIN!

REICH WOULD GO TO JAIL IN 1956 FOR CONTINUING TO SELL HIS ACCUMULATORS.

MAYBE I SHOULD TURN IT OFF FOR A WHILE.

HE WOULD DIE IN PRISON, BROKEN AND ALONE, A MARTYR TO REICHIANS...

OKAY, NOW, I'VE TURNED IT OFF. THAT SHOULD DO IT...

...AND A BELIEVER IN HIS ORGONE-POWERED UNIVERSE TO THE END.

72

CHAPTER FOUR

NOVELISTS AND POETS

THE WRITTEN WEIRD

Writing — like suicide — is a solitary pursuit. Long hours spent in quiet seclusion, waiting for inspiration to strike, and praying it does before the rent is due. All that thinking! All that worrying! It's no wonder writers sometimes drop over the edge into the realm of the weird. Each of the peculiar writers covered in this chapter embarked on a journey of self-discovery that led to revelations which ultimately took control of their lives. The affection Guy de Maupassant (*page 78*) had for prostitutes brought him to a madness that found voice on paper. The brilliantly paranoid observations of Franz Kafka (*page 82*) haunted his every waking moment. Ambrose Bierce (*page 88*) came to believe his own cynical social criticism so strongly that he was compelled to abandon society. If our examination of weird writers teaches us one thing, it's that it IS possible to think TOO MUCH....

Edgar Allan Poe

...CHARMED AND TERRIFIED THE EARLY 19TH CENTURY WITH HIS POEMS AND STORIES OF ROMANCE, DEATH, AND THE OCCULT, AND BECAME THE FIRST AMERICAN AUTHOR TO BE INTERNATIONALLY RENOWNED.

AND YET, HIS LIFE WAS A CONSTANT STRUGGLE -- AGAINST POVERTY, AND AGAINST THE EVIL HE SENSED HOVERING ABOUT HIS SOUL.

THE GENTLE, AFFECTIONATE, RELIABLE POE WAS BORN IN BOSTON IN 1809, AND GREW TO BE A SOBER FAMILY MAN.

THE OTHER POE INSIDE HIM WAS A MAN OF NIGHTMARISH VISIONS, A COMPULSIVE GAMBLER...

... A MAN FOR WHOM ALCOHOL WAS LIKE A DEADLY POISON.

ADOPTED AFTER THE EARLY DEATHS OF HIS ACTOR-PARENTS...

TIME TO GO, EDGAR.

YES, AND MORE THAN TIME.

...HE BEGAN HIS IMPRESSIVE LIST OF FAILURES EARLY. THROWN OUT OF THE UNIVERSITY OF VIRGINIA FOR EXCESSIVE GAMBLING DEBTS...

COME NOW, POE, YOU'VE HAD ENOUGH, ADMIT IT.

I HAVEN'T YET BEGUN, OLD SPORT.

...AND EXPELLED FROM WEST POINT FOR MISSING DRILLS AND CLASSES.

NOW I CAN BEGIN.

HE WAS INTERESTED IN ONLY ONE THING: WRITING.

WORKING AS AN EDITOR OF LITERARY MAGAZINES, POE BEGAN THE CAREER THAT WOULD MAKE HIM FAMOUS.

HE MARRIED HIS COUSIN, VIRGINIA CLEMM, WHEN SHE WAS 13...

AH, VIRGINIA, UNFORTUNATE CHILD!

I DO!

...BUT SOON LOST HIS EDITOR'S SPOT, APPARENTLY FOR HIS STEADY, CRAZY DRINKING.

¡DIOTSH!

BUT POE WASN'T JUST ANY LUSH...

... HE SEEMS TO HAVE BEEN ALLERGIC TO ALCOHOL.

I GIVE YOU LONG LIFE AND HAPPINESS...

ONE GLASS OF SHERRY COULD SEND HIM ON A SPREE THAT LASTED FOR WEEKS.

GLAAAH!

HIS WORK PROCEEDED IN SPITE OF HIM.

...FOUND MYSELF, AS THE SHADE OF EVENING DREW ON, WITHIN VIEW OF THE MELANCHOLY HOUSE OF USHER...

I HEAR IT'S OPIUM DOES THAT TO 'IM.

NAW, IT'S SPIRITS, MORE LIKE. POE CAN'T AFFORD OPIUM!

BALTIMORE ST.

PARTLY, IT WAS A LESION ON HIS BRAIN.

75

"...THE BOUNDARIES WHICH DIVIDE LIFE FROM DEATH ARE AT BEST SHADOWY AND VAGUE. WHO SHALL SAY WHERE THE ONE ENDS, AND WHERE THE OTHER BEGINS?..."

POE PIONEERED THE MYSTERY STORY, IN WORKS LIKE MURDER IN THE RUE MORGUE.

YOU SEE, MON AMI, IT IS AS I SAID. THE MURDERER IS NOT A MAN.

HE EXPLORED HALLUCINATION... MADNESS... VIOLENT DEATH.

AS A NEWSPAPER EDITOR, HE ALSO LIKED THE OCCASIONAL PRANK.

WE'LL GO THE SUN'S HOAX ONE BETTER... THE MIRROR WILL GO ACROSS THE ATLANTIC!

GOD, HOW THEY'LL HATE US AT THE SUN!

HIS TRANS- ATLANTIC BALLOON HOAX SWEPT THE FIELD-- AND SOLD A LOT OF PAPERS.

A YEAR OR SO LATER, HE WROTE HIS MOST FAMOUS POEM.

"...QUOTH THE RAVEN..."

NEVERMORE!

FAME BROUGHT RESPONSIBILITY.

"DEAR MADAM, I MUST APOLOGIZE-- I HAVE NO PET RAVEN..."

IT ALSO BROUGHT THE OBSESSED INTEREST OF CERTAIN WOMEN, LIKE POET FRANCES LOCKE.

SHE GOT HIM TO FALL IN LOVE WITH HER -- AND POE'S WIFE, VIRGINIA, DIDN'T MIND.

THEN THE POETESS WROTE ALL ABOUT HER AFFAIR, ADDING TO THE POE SCANDAL.

WITH ME, POETRY HAS BEEN NOT A PURPOSE, BUT A PASSION....

HE LIKED HIS AIR OF AUTHORITY, AND PRESENTED HIMSELF AS A MAN WHO WAS ENTIRELY ORIGINAL, HIGHLY ORGANIZED, AND ALMOST MECHANICALLY PRECISE.

IN FACT, BOTH PHYSICALLY AND MENTALLY, HE WAS AS FRAIL AS ONE OF HIS FRAGILE PROTAGONISTS.

"TO THE TINTINABULATION THAT SO MUSICALLY WELLS...

FROM THE BELLS, BELLS, BELLS, BELLS, BELLS, BELLS, BELLS

IN 1847 HIS LONG-SUFFERING, BELOVED WIFE, VIRGINIA, DIED.

NEVER-MORE.

AND ALWAYS, ALCOHOL WAITED LIKE DEATH FOR HIM.

OLD DEATH

IN 1849, HE STOPPED OFF IN BALTIMORE ON HIS WAY HOME TO RICHMOND, AND TOASTED A BIRTHDAY GIRL.

...AND MANY HAPPY, HAPPY RETURNS OF THE DAY, MY DEAR GIRL.

HOURS LATER, THE 40-YEAR-OLD WRITER STAGGERED THROUGH THE STREETS OF BALTIMORE'S RED-LIGHT DISTRICT IN A DRUNKEN STUPOR.

SALOON

NEVERMORE.
NEVERMORE.
NEVERMORE.

IT WAS TO BE HIS LAST DRINKING BOUT.

FOUND UNCONSCIOUS IN THE STREET, HE WAS RUSHED TO THE HOSPITAL... AND LIKE ONE OF HIS DOOMED CHARACTERS, ARRIVED JUST IN TIME TO DIE.

FACTOID BOOKS

HE WAS ONE OF THE BEST-KNOWN AND BELOVED WRITERS IN 19TH-CENTURY FRANCE. FOR HIS LONGER WORKS, HE WAS SECOND ONLY TO EMILE ZOLA IN POPULARITY, BUT HE IS ACKNOWLEDGED AS THE ALL-TIME MASTER OF THE SLICE-OF-LIFE SHORT STORY. IN HIS SHORT LIFE HE KNEW GREAT FAME AND FORTUNE, EVEN AS HIS INNER DEMONS BROUGHT HIM GREAT -- AND ULTIMATELY FATAL -- TRAGEDY.

GUY DE MAUPASSANT

MAUPASSANT'S SPARE, IRONIC STYLE WAS PERFECT FOR DESCRIBING THE REALITIES OF WAR AND THE LIVES OF THE PEOPLE OF NORMANDY. HIS SUBJECTS SPANNED THE SOCIAL CLASSES.

HIS CHOICE OF CHARACTERS RANGED FROM THE HIGHEST NOBLES TO THE LOWEST STREET PROSTITUTES...

THOUGH IT MUST BE SAID THAT, IN LIFE AS WELL AS ART, HE PREFERRED THE LATTER.

THE GREAT FRENCH NOVELIST GUSTAVE FLAUBERT HELPED HIM SEE HIS LITERARY POTENTIAL...

OBSERVED DETAIL, MY BOY. OBSERVED DETAIL.

IS IT TRUE THAT YOU ARE MY REAL FATHER?

(RUMOR HELD THAT GUY WAS FLAUBERT'S ILLEGITIMATE SON.)

THE WOMEN OF FRANCE HELPED HIM WITH EVERY-THING ELSE.

SO MANY OF THESE CREATURES. AND SO LITTLE TIME.

BY THE TIME HE WAS IN HIS EARLY 20S, THEY'D ALSO GIVEN HIM SYPHILIS.

I AM A PROMISCUOUS CULT OF ONE.

WHEN MEDICINE CURED THE SORES, MAUPASSANT THOUGHT HE WAS HOME FREE. BUT NO -- THE DISEASE HEADED FOR HIS BRAIN.

BORN NEAR DIEPPE IN 1850, MAUPASSANT HAD BEEN BROUGHT TO HIS SINGLE, PROMISCUOUS LIFE BY WARRING PARENTS.

WHAT A POOR THING YOU ARE, FATHER.

THEN GO, YOU WORTHLESS WORM! GO!

GUY SIDED WITH HIS MOTHER.

AH, GUY, YOU ARE THE PERFECT SON.

I TRY TO BE, MAMA.

BUT HIS FICTION TEEMED WITH WEAK, HENPECKED HUSBANDS AND THE LONELINESS OF FATHERLESS SONS.

AS HIS ILLNESS REAWAKENED IN HIS BRAIN, HIS REALISM WEAKENED.

"I AM AFRAID OF EVERYTHING, OF WALLS, OF FURNITURE, OF FAMILIAR OBJECTS WHICH SEEM TO ME TO ASSUME A KIND OF ANIMAL LIFE.

"ABOVE ALL I FEAR THE HORRIBLE CONFUSION OF MY THOUGHT, OF MY REASON ESCAPING, ENTANGLED AND SCATTERED BY AN INVISIBLE AND MYSTERIOUS ANGUISH.

HIS REALITY ALTERED, MANY OF HIS STORIES BEGAN TO REFLECT THE WRITER'S OWN FEARS AND INSECURITIES. TALES FEATURING MADNESS AND HALLUCINATIONS BECAME MAUPASSANT'S STOCK-IN-TRADE.

IN ONE STORY, LE HORLA, MAUPASSANT CREATED A FICTIONAL ACCOUNT OF A BELIEF THAT HAUNTED HIM IN REAL LIFE --

--THE IDEA OF THE INVISIBLE DOUBLE, ONE WHO TAKES CONTROL OVER THE CHARACTER'S LIFE.

NO MATTER HOW HARD THE MAIN CHARACTER OF LA HORLA TRIES, HE CANNOT ESCAPE HIS EVIL DOPPELGANGER...

...ANY MORE THAN HE CAN ESCAPE HIMSELF.

SEX HELPED MAUPASSANT FORGET HIS DEMONS. SO DID DRUGS, ESPECIALLY ETHER.

AH.... MON.... DIEU...

HE HAD FOUND HIS HELL -- AND, POSSIBLY, HIS DESTINY.

HE BEGAN SUFFERING DEEP CHILLS, AND BECAME TERRIBLY SENSITIVE TO NOISE AND LIGHT.

GUY, MON CHER... ARE YOU ALL RIGHT?

NEVER... BETTER.

MY HEADACHE GRINDS MY SKULL INTO ATOMS.

GOD, ALL THESE SPIDERS.

UNWILLING TO ACKNOWLEDGE HIS MALADY, MAUPASSANT NEVERTHELESS FOUND AN EXPLANATION:

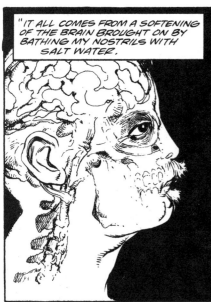

"IT ALL COMES FROM A SOFTENING OF THE BRAIN BROUGHT ON BY BATHING MY NOSTRILS WITH SALT WATER.

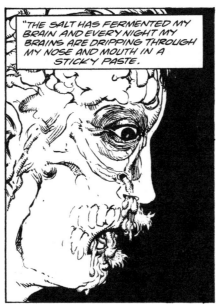

"THE SALT HAS FERMENTED MY BRAIN AND EVERY NIGHT MY BRAINS ARE DRIPPING THROUGH MY NOSE AND MOUTH IN A STICKY PASTE.

"FLIES ARE DEVOURING THE SALT IN MY BRAIN.

"IT MEANS I AM GOING MAD."

FINALLY, HE COULDN'T STAND IT ANYMORE—

GIVE ME THE BULLETS, I TELL YOU! GIVE ME THE BULLETS!

MASTER... I CANNOT.

VERY WELL, DAMN YOU, DAMN YOU...

YEARGGHH!

80

HIS ATTEMPTED SUICIDE IN 1892 BROUGHT HIM TO A PARIS PSYCHIATRIC CLINIC...

...WHERE HE PLAYED OUT HIS FINAL IMAGININGS.

THESE TWIGS WILL GROW...

...INTO LITTLE MALIPASSANTS.

HE RATIONALIZED HIS RAPIDLY DETERIORATING MIND BY COMING TO BELIEVE THAT HIS THOUGHTS HAD TAKEN PHYSICAL FORM AND WERE ESCAPING FROM HIS HEAD...

...AND HE WOULD GO LOOKING FOR THEM.

AH, WHAT PRETTY THOUGHTS.

MON DIEU, HE HAS BECOME AN ANIMAL.

THE FLIES... DEVOUR... THE SALT IN MY BRAIN.

HE SAVED HIS URINE -- IT WAS TOO VALUABLE TO WASTE.

EACH DROP, A DIAMOND.

BUT HE WAS GETTING WORSE.

IN JULY 1893, HE SANK INTO HOURS-LONG FITS OF SCREAMING AND CONVULSIONS...

THE FLIES... THE FLIES...

...DARKNESS.... DARKNESS...,

...UNTIL HIS LAST BREATH SLIPPED AWAY.

81

FRANZ KAFKA

CZECH WRITER FRANZ KAFKA PERSONIFIED THE BEWILDERING IN MODERN SOCIETY. EVEN TODAY, WHEN THINGS ARE SURREALLY NOT WHAT THEY SEEM, WE CALL THEM KAFKAESQUE.

BUT THAT WORLD WAS NOT SOMETHING HE INVENTED.

FOR 40 YEARS, UNTIL HIS DEATH FROM TUBERCULOSIS IN 1924, KAFKA LIVED THERE.

HIS FATHER WAS A DOMINEERING PRAGUE MERCHANT WHOSE LITANY OF ABUSE CRIPPLED YOUNG FRANZ.

WHY DO YOU COWER? WHAT ARE YOU AFRAID OF?

THE CZECH BUREAUCRACY WAS AN OCEAN OF OBFUSCATION.

COME BACK YESTERDAY, UNLESS, OF COURSE, YOU'D PREFER LAST WEEK, DEPENDING OF COURSE, ON YOUR GUILT OR INNOCENCE... 15 CROWNS, PLEASE.

KAFKA'S MIND SWIRLED WITH DISTURBING IMAGES.

HE WROTE OF A CASTLE TO WHICH ONE COULD NEVER GAIN ACCESS BECAUSE OF AN ELABORATE BUREAUCRACY...

...AND OF TRIALS THAT CHARGE A DEFENDANT-- BUT OF UNSPECIFIED CRIMES.

GUILTY!

BUT OF WHAT?

KAFKA'S WORLD WAS A NIGHTMARE.

HE IMAGINED A PRISON MACHINE...

MURDERER
MURDERER
MURDERER

...THAT INFLICTED PUNISHMENT BY INSCRIBING A CONVICT'S CRIMES ON HIS BODY...

...AND A MAN NAMED GREGOR WHO WOKE UP ONE MORNING AS A GIANT TUMBLEBUG.

HE DESCRIBED A BURROWING CREATURE, PROUD OF ITS TUNNELS, BUT LIVING A LIFE OF PERPETUAL FEAR.

I KNOW SOMEONE ELSE IS HERE, I... FEEL ... IT... ... I ... OR MAYBE NOT... BUT, THERE, SOMEONE...

FICTION TO US...

BUT TO FRANZ KAFKA, IT WAS REALITY.

TERRIBLE REALITY.

AS KAFKA HIMSELF PUT IT:

I AM MADE OF LITERATURE.

I AM NOTHING ELSE AND CANNOT BE ANYTHING ELSE.

I AM NOTHING BUT A MASS OF SPIKES GOING THROUGH ME.

WILLIAM S. Burroughs

HEIR TO A BUSINESS MACHINE FORTUNE, WILLIAM S. BURROUGHS IS RANKED BY SOME SCHOLARS AS ONE OF THE GREAT INNOVATIVE WRITERS IN ENGLISH, ALONG WITH SUCH GIANTS AS JAMES JOYCE.

FROM THE BEGINNING, HE WAS ... DIFFERENT. BORN IN ST. LOUIS, MISSOURI, IN 1914 ...

¿GULP!¿

...HE DISCOVERED HALLUCINATIONS LONG BEFORE HE DISCOVERED DRUGS. HE SAW LITTLE MEN AMONG HIS ALPHABET BLOCKS...

...AND BELIEVED THAT ANIMALS LIVED IN THE WALLS.

HIS SLEEP WAS FILLED WITH TERRIFYING NIGHTMARES.

NO! NO!

OH....JUST... A DREAM.

HE GRADUATED FROM HARVARD IN 1936 ...

...AND, AFTER SOME GRADUATE WORK, WENT INTO THE ARMY WHEN WORLD WAR II BEGAN.

THINK WE CAN SCORE?

HOW CAN WE NOT?

BY 1944, HE WAS A HEROIN ADDICT.

JUST ONE MORE.

BURROUGHS WAS TOO MUCH FOR ARMY SHRINKS. HE WAS RESTORED TO CIVILIAN LIFE.

ARMY SHRINK'S OFFICE

OXYGEN.

FOOD.

DRINK.

SMACK.

SMACK.

SMACK.

AS A WRITER, HE HAD THE ADDICT'S DARK, PARANOID VISION.

IN HIS MIND, TECHNOLOGICAL CARTELS OF POWER WOULD RULE THE WORLD...

...AND DESTROY IT.

BECAUSE HE LIVED IN THIS DANGEROUS PLACE, HE ALWAYS PACKED A GUN.

YOU CAN'T BE TOO CAREFUL.

SOMETIMES HE DROVE AROUND THE COUNTRYSIDE, SHOOTING CHICKENS FROM HIS CAR.

HE ONCE BLAZED AWAY AT A MOUSE IN A SALOON.

BLAM BLAM BLAM

HE SURVEYED ALL HIS POTENTIAL TARGETS ON THE STREETS...

...EVEN AS HE BECAME A TARGET OF THE POLICE.

COPS WEREN'T VERY TOLERANT OF JUNKIES-- EVEN BRILLIANT ONES.

AFTER AN ESPECIALLY TOUGH ARREST IN NEW ORLEANS, HE DECIDED TO LEAVE THE STATES.

MEXICO.

IN 1949, BURROUGHS AND HIS FAMILY MOVED SOUTH OF THE BORDER.

ARE THEY REALLY MORE TOLERANT DOWN HERE, BILL?

THESE PEOPLE GROW THE STUFF, JOANIE, WE'LL SCORE SOME *NATURAL* HALLUCINOGENS...

HE DRANK THE BITTER TEA OF PEYOTE...

...AND DISCOVERED THAT, FOR HIM AT LEAST, IT MADE EVERYTHING LOOK LIKE PEYOTE PLANTS.

WOO!

THEN, ON SEPTEMBER 6, 1951, BURROUGHS DID SOMETHING REALLY CRAZY -- EVEN FOR HIM.

JOAN...?

YES?

I GUESS IT'S ABOUT TIME...

...FOR OUR WILLIAM TELL ACT.

BLAM BLAM!

JOAN!

JESUS, BILL, WHAT'VE YOU DONE?

TALK TO ME.

TALK TO ME!

SOMEHOW HE HAD MISSED THE GLASS AT CLOSE RANGE. HIS WIFE DIED INSTANTLY.

WHY I DID IT, I DON'T KNOW. SOMETHING TOOK OVER.

THE JUDGE'LL NEVER BELIEVE THAT WILLIAM TELL STORY. SAY THE GUN WENT OFF ACCIDENTALLY.

THE COURT BELIEVED THEM. BURROUGHS WAS FINED $2,312 FOR CRIMINAL IMPRUDENCE -- AND, BEFORE MEXICO COULD DEPORT THE "PERNICIOUS FOREIGNER," BURROUGHS HAD FLOWN.

HE ROAMED THE WORLD, SCORING HALLUCINOGENIC YAGE IN THE SOUTH AMERICAN RAINFOREST...

...AND EVERYTHING ELSE IN PARIS, LONDON, AND TANGIERS.

AND AFTER ALL THIS, HIS WILDLY FUNNY, WEIRD BEST WORK -- NAKED LUNCH, AND THE SOFT MACHINE, AMONG OTHERS --

--WERE STILL AHEAD OF HIM.

FACTOID BOOKS

Ambrose Gwinnett Bierce

...BECAME FAMOUS AFTER THE CIVIL WAR AS THE "WICKEDEST MAN IN SAN FRANCISCO" AND ALSO HAPPENED TO BE THE BEST-KNOWN WRITER IN THE WESTERN U.S.

SOME RANKED HIM WITH EDGAR ALLAN POE -- ALTHOUGH HE WAS MORE CYNICAL.

IN BIERCE'S MACABRE STORIES, CHILDREN GET EATEN BY DOGS -- ANYTHING COULD HAPPEN.

HIS DEVIL'S DICTIONARY, PUBLISHED IN 1906, SET THE TONE FOR HIS LIFE.

CYNIC: A BLACKGUARD, WHOSE FAULTY VISION SEES THINGS AS THEY ARE, NOT AS THEY OUGHT TO BE.

BIERCE BEGAN HIS WANDERING CAREER AT 15, WHEN HE WALKED AWAY FROM HIS OHIO FARM TO JOIN THE UNION ARMY.

HE WAS A DRUMMER BOY AT SHILOH.

BY NASHVILLE, HE'D MADE LIEUTENANT.

BUT A SEVERE HEAD WOUND IN THE FIGHT FOR ATLANTA CHANGED HIM -- FOREVER.

OH, MY GOD!

AS HE RECUPERATED HE BECAME BAD-TEMPERED AND FULL OF PARANOID SUSPICIONS -- PERFECT FOR A REPORTER.

HE MOVED TO SAN FRANCISCO, AND BECAME ONE OF THE CITY'S BEST-KNOWN JOURNALISTS BY USING HIS CAUSTIC WIT LIKE A WHIP ON PUBLIC FIGURES.

SAINT: A SINNER, REVISED AND EDITED.

DOESN'T MINCE WORDS, DOES HE?

A.G. BIERCE, ALL RIGHT... FOR ALMIGHTY GOD.

IN 1871, HE AND HIS BRIDE, MOLLIE, MOVED TO LONDON.

MARRIAGE: A COMMUNITY CONSISTING OF A MISTRESS, A MASTER, AND TWO SLAVES, MAKING IN ALL, TWO.

THERE HE BEGAN A FAMILY AND PUBLISHED THREE CYNICAL BOOKS.

I SAY, ISN'T THAT OLD BITTER BIERCE?

I GUESS IT'S TIME WE WERE BACK IN SAN FRANCISCO.

BIERCE SETTLED DOWN TO JOURNALISM -- OR TRIED TO.

ACHIEVEMENT: THE DEATH OF ENDEAVOR AND THE BIRTH OF DISGUST.

BUT HIS LIFE BEGAN TO SOUR.

IN 1889, HIS ELDER SON GUNNED DOWN A RIVAL FOR A WOMAN'S AFFECTIONS, THEN SHOT HIMSELF.

A DECADE LATER, HIS OTHER SON WENT ON A COLOSSAL DRINKING SPREE -- AND DIED OF PNEUMONIA.

POOR MOLLIE FOLLOWED A FEW YEARS LATER. BIERCE WAS LEFT ALONE.

IN 1909 HE HIRED A SECRETARY AND WENT TO WASHINGTON TO ASSEMBLE HIS COLLECTED WORKS ...AND TO BROOD.

MY LIFE IS ABOUT TO TAKE A DRASTIC TURN, MY DEAR. A DRASTIC NEW TURN.

IN 1913 HE MADE HIS MOVE.

I'M OFF, MY DEAR.

SAFE JOURNEY, MR. BIERCE.

HE VISITED HIS OLD BATTLEFIELDS...

BY GOD, I WAS HAPPY THEN. WHAT HAPPENED?

...BUT LONGED FOR A NEW ONE.

IF YOU HEAR OF MY BEING STOOD UP AGAINST A MEXICAN STONE WALL AND SHOT TO RAGS, PLEASE KNOW THAT I THINK THAT A PRETTY GOOD WAY TO DEPART THIS LIFE.

TO BE GRINGO IN MEXICO, AH, THAT IS EUTHANASIA.

IN DECEMBER 1913 HE SLIPPED ACROSS THE BORDER...

...AND JOINED UP WITH THE RUTH-LESS BANDIT-REVOLUTIONARY PANCHO VILLA.

PRAY FOR ME NOW, REAL HARD.

"I AM HEADING NORTHWARD TO OJINAGA, WHERE HEAVY FIGHTING IS EXPECTED..."

AFTER THIS LAST MESSAGE, BIERCE VANISHED.

SOME SAY HE WAS MURDERED BY VILLA, OTHERS THAT HE WAS THE OLD GRINGO WHO REPORTEDLY DIED IN THE FIGHT FOR OJINAGA.

BUT MANY BELIEVE THE OLD DEVIL DISAPPEARED ON PURPOSE AND, SOMEWHERE IN THE SOUTH AMERICAN JUNGLE, LIVED ON, LAUGHING AT HUMANITY TO THE BITTER END.

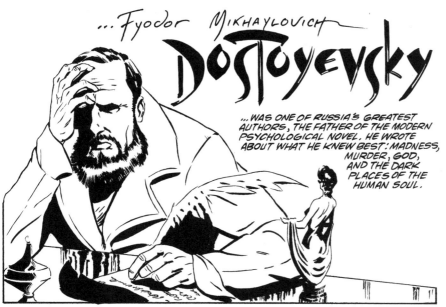

...*Fyodor* Mikhaylovich

DOSTOYEVSKY

...WAS ONE OF RUSSIA'S GREATEST AUTHORS, THE FATHER OF THE MODERN PSYCHOLOGICAL NOVEL. HE WROTE ABOUT WHAT HE KNEW BEST: MADNESS, MURDER, GOD, AND THE DARK PLACES OF THE HUMAN SOUL.

MADNESS, MURDER, AND GOD. YES, THAT WAS FYODOR, ALL RIGHT.

I MET HIM IN 1849... RIGHT HERE, IN FACT.

HE'D BEEN CHARGED WITH SUBVERSION; UNDER CZAR NICHOLAS I, THAT COULD MEAN ANYTHING.

I THINK FYODOR MAY HAVE DONE SOME SOCIALIST WRITING.

"THEY SENTENCED US TO DIE BEFORE A FIRING SQUAD. THEY CAME AND GOT US...

"...AND DRAGGED US TO THE WALL."

READY... AIM...

"BUT THE FIRING SQUAD WAS JUST THE CZAR'S LITTLE JOKE.

"THEY GAVE US FOUR YEARS' HARD LABOR AT OMSK, INSTEAD. FYODOR DIDN'T MIND. HE BELIEVED YOU HAD TO BE PUNISHED FOR YOUR CRIMES."

"MAYBE HE LEARNED THAT AT HOME...

"...WHEN THEIR SERFS BEAT HIS FATHER TO DEATH."

SOMETIMES I THINK POOR FYODOR WOULD RATHER BE TERRIBLY UNHAPPY THAN SLIGHTLY HAPPY.

"HE STUDIED MILITARY ENGINEERING, BUT THAT WASN'T HIS REAL VOCATION.

"HE DID A BOLD, FOOLISH THING; HE LEFT SCHOOL TO BEGIN WRITING FULL-TIME."

THAT WAS IN 1844. HE MUST'VE WRITTEN SOME SOCIALIST STUFF, TOO, BECAUSE I MET HIM HERE IN 1849.

"OMSK FAILED TO KILL US. FYODOR WAS THEN SENTENCED TO 4 YEARS AS A SOLDIER IN SIBERIA. NEVER MIND ABOUT ME.

"IN SIBERIA, HE MARRIED MARYA DMITRIEVNA ISAYEVA -- A CONSUMPTIVE WIDOW WITH A YOUNG SON. OF COURSE, IT WAS A DISASTER.

"SO, 10 YEARS AFTER HE LEFT, HE RETURNED TO MOSCOW WITH A DYING WIFE, A STEPSON...

"...AND SOMETHING FROM HIS PRISON DAYS -- TERRIBLE FITS. EPILEPSY, PERHAPS. OR RAGE."

"HIS WIFE DIED IN 1864, AND A GOOD THING... IT WAS A TERRIBLE MARRIAGE.

"THREE MONTHS LATER, HIS BROTHER DIED.

"HE INHERITED THE WIDOW AND HER CHILDREN.

"CHRIST, THE POOR DEVIL COULDN'T SUPPORT HIMSELF."

AND HE HAD ANOTHER KIND OF SICKNESS...

"...GAMBLING.

"WHEN HE WAS DOWN AND OUT, HE'D BORROW MONEY TO GAMBLE. HE BELIEVED HE'D WIN BIG, PAY HIS DEBTS, AND STOP."

DOUBLE-ZERO! OH, GOD!

I AM SORRY, FYODOR MIKHAYLOVICH. WE CAN EXTEND NO MORE CREDIT.

BUT I'M CLOSE TO WINNING... I SENSE IT!

SORRY, NO.

"OF COURSE, ALL GAMBLERS BELIEVE THAT. IT IS PART OF THEIR ILLNESS.

"HIS STRANGE FITS BECAME WORSE.

"THEN HE MET ANNA GRIGORYEVNA SNITKINA, FIRST HIS STENOGRAPHER...."

"GOOD AND EVIL ARE SO MONSTROUSLY MIXED IN MAN...."

"...THEN HIS ADORING WIFE."

93

ANNA WAS FYODOR'S TICKET BACK TO LIFE.

"SHE COULD ENDURE ANYTHING, THE GRINDING POVERTY..."

"...THE CRAZY GAMBLING..."

GOD, IF I WIN, ANNA CAN HAVE A NEW DRESS AND MY DAUGHTER CAN HAVE ONE TOO. PLEASE, GOD, LET ME WIN!

I'M SORRY, SIR.

"...THE FITS... EVEN THE DEATH OF HER BABY GIRL."

"SHE KNEW HE WAS A GREAT NOVELIST."

WHERE WERE WE?

IVAN WAS SITTING DOWN WITH ALYOSHA AND THE OTHER KARAMAZOV BROTHERS.

"HE KEPT GOING, DESPITE EMPHYSEMA AND THE LINGERING DEATH OF HIS YOUNGEST SON,"

HAK-AKK-AKK!

ANNA MADE CERTAIN THAT HIS WORK WAS PUBLISHED AND COLLECTED. SHE MADE CERTAIN THAT HER GREAT LOVE BECAME A GREAT NOVELIST.

ONE KNOWS HOW HE LEARNED ABOUT MADNESS AND GOD. BUT WHAT ABOUT MURDER? HA HA. MAYBE FROM PEOPLE LIKE ME.

FYODOR MIKHAYLOVICH DIED IN 1881 – JUST 59 YEARS OLD. I EXPECT TO SEE HIM SOON, THIS EXECUTION IS NO JOKE.

94

CHAPTER FIVE

PERFORMERS AND PLAYWRIGHTS

CURTAIN-CALL CRACKPOTS

Call it what you will: nerve, guts, *cajones*... but it takes a certain something for a person to get up on stage and present his or her talents to the world. All performers are exhibitionists at heart, and the weirdos contained in this chapter are no exception. From escape artists and magicians like Harry Houdini (*page 104*) and Chung Ling Soo (*page 102*) to "'dancin' fools" Isadora Duncan (*page 110*) and Vaslav Nijinsky (*page 114*), these performers let it all hang out. In public. On stage. What their wildly appreciative audiences saw them do made them great. But what the public never saw, never even DREAMED, made them immortal. From Edward Askew Sothern (*page 100*) and his obsession with practical jokes, to Sarah Bernhardt (*page 96*) and her love affair with half of Europe, these weirdos led double lives: public and private, upstanding... and bizarre.

SARAH BERNHARDT.

THE DAUGHTER OF AN UNWED JEWISH-DUTCH COURTESAN, FRANCE'S SARAH BERNHARDT BECAME THE GREATEST ACTRESS OF HER TIME -- AND THE FIRST INTERNATIONAL THEATRICAL STAR.

SHE RULED THE WORLD'S STAGES FOR HALF OF THE LATE 19TH CENTURY. OSCAR WILDE CALLED HER THE INCOMPARABLE. OTHERS CALLED HER THE DIVINE.

SHE HAD A STRANGE, COMPELLING, CAT-FACED BEAUTY.

HER MAGNIFICENT VOICE MADE HER PETITE BODY REVERBERATE --SHE COULD PLAY ANYTHING.

EVEN MEN.

DYING WONDERFULLY WAS HER SPECIALTY.

PENSEZ À MOI... ‡gasp!‡ ‡rattle!‡ HORATIO...

IMPRESARIO VICTORIEN SARDOU KNEW HER WELL.

AH. THERE SHE GOES, VICTORIEN.

IF THERE IS ANYTHING MORE REMARKABLE THAN WATCHING SARAH ACT, IT IS WATCHING HER LIVE.

SHE DEMANDED MUCH FROM HER MEN. ONCE SHE WATCHED, EXCITED, AS RIVALS FOR HER FAVORS DUELED.

SHE PUSHED ONE SUITOR FROM A SECOND-STORY WINDOW, AND HORSE-WHIPPED ANOTHER.

BUT LOVE WAS NOT BERNHARDT'S REAL OBSESSION.

SHE WAS FASCINATED BY DEATH.

SHE LIKED TO BE PHOTOGRAPHED IN HER LITTLE ROSEWOOD AND SATIN COFFIN...

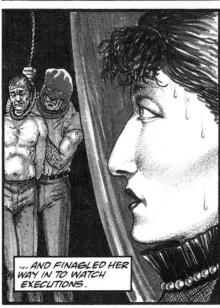

... AND FINAGLED HER WAY IN TO WATCH EXECUTIONS.

ON AN AMERICAN TOUR, SHE EVEN WENT TO WATCH THE SLAUGHTER AT CHICAGO'S FAMOUS STOCKYARDS.

NOT THAT SHE DIDN'T LIKE ANIMALS—ESPECIALLY BIG FELINE ONES. THEY WERE ONE OF HER MAJOR WEAKNESSES.

AH, MA PETITE.

FRENCH NOVELIST ALEXANDER DUMAS ONCE FOUND HER PUMA EATING HIS STRAW HAT.

UH, SARAH...

MONEY ALSO OBSESSED HER. SHE TOOK HER PAY IN GOLD COINS, AND CARRIED THEM IN BAGS EVERY-WHERE SHE WENT.

SHE PURSUED A GRAND LIFE-STYLE OF HUGE PARTIES IN LUSH SURROUNDINGS.

CAN I HELP YOU, MADAME ?

CHAMPAGNE FOR ME -- A RAT FOR MY LIZARD.

ENORMOUS SUMS OF GOLD WENT INTO HER BEJEWELED DRESSES.

I BELIEVE I'LL TAKE THEM ALL!

ALTHOUGH VASTLY POPULAR, BERNHARDT WAS AN EXPENSIVE ACT.

SETS! FOOD! LODGINGS! HOW CAN I TURN A PROFIT?

IT IS WHAT I REQUIRE!

I WILL COVER ALL COSTS, MADAME-- EXCEPT COSTUMES.

POOR MAN, OF COURSE I SHALL BUY MY OWN COSTUMES! DO I CARE? MAIS NON!

THIS SELFISH LITTLE PERSON HAD A HEART AS BIG AS THE LOUVRE.

WATCH OUT, GARÇON!

DIEU!

SHE COULD EVEN FORGIVE SOMEONE FOR DROPPING HER GOLD INTO A PARIS STREET.

THERE, DON'T FRET. DON'T FRET.

BUT THE SIMPLE TRUTH WAS THAT FRANCE COULD NOT AFFORD HER. SHE TOURED EUROPE...

...THEN HEADED FOR THE HIGH-ROLLING AUDIENCES IN THE AMERICAS.

GIVE ME YOUR GOLD EAGLES!

FIRST NORTH...

OR, FOR THAT MATTER, YOUR NUGGETS.

THEN SOUTH...

OR, FOR THAT MATTER, YOUR ORO.

98

THEN, HALF WAY AROUND THE WORLD, TO THE AUSTRALIAN OUTBACK.

G'DAY.

THE WORLD ADORED BERNHARDT.

BUT SHE WAS WEARING OUT.

BON DIEU, BUT... ONE MUST PRESS ON.

WHEN SHE WAS 70, SHE SUFFERED AN INJURY...

AHH.

FETCH THE DOCTOR, QUICKLY!

WE MUST TAKE THE LEG.

EXTRAVAGANCE CURED ANYTHING. THE DIVINE HIRED A GOLD AND WHITE SEDAN CHAIR AND ATTENDANTS TO CARRY HER ABOUT.

CRUTCHES ARE FOR CRIPPLES.

BUT SHE WAS DOOMED. BERNHARDT DIED FOR THE LAST TIME–OFFSTAGE–IN PARIS IN MARCH, 1923...

OH, MADAME! MADAME!

... AND 30,000 PEOPLE WATCHED THEIR IDOL POSE FOR THE LAST TIME IN HER LITTLE COFFIN.

HER GRAVE IN PARIS' PÈRE LACHAISE CEMETERY IS AS AUSTERE AS HER LIFESTYLE WAS EXTRAVAGANT.

SARAH

BERNHARDT

Edward Askew Sothern

HA HA HA HA HA HA HA HA HA

..., WAS A WELL-KNOWN BRITISH ACTOR, FAMOUS FOR HIS PORTRAYAL OF A SATIRICAL STEREOTYPE OF AN ENGLISH ARISTOCRAT. BUT IN HIS DAY, SOTHERN WAS KNOWN -- AND FEARED -- FOR HIS OFFSTAGE MANIA FOR JOKES - PRACTICAL, THAT IS.

HE WAS THE QUINTESSENTIAL -- SOME SAID PATHOLOGICAL -- PRANKSTER.

HA HA HA

BORN ON APRIL FOOL'S DAY, WITH ASKEW AS MY MIDDLE NAME -- HOW COULD I BE ANYTHING ELSE?

FOR SOTHERN, THE WHOLE WORLD WAS A STAGE FOR MISCHIEF.

I SAY...A TRAY OF LETTERS!

"I SHALL BRING THE PYTHONS ON THURSDAY."

HA HA HA HA HA

PYTHONS?... THURSDAY?... WOT TH'... I SAY... ARRGHH.

THERE YOU GO, MY GOOD MAN.

OH, BLESS YOU, SIR, FOR A SAINT, SIR...

FOR A DIRTY ROTTEN SCOUNDREL, SIR, FOR GIVING A POOR MAN FALSE SILVER!

HE GAVE COUNTERFEIT MONEY TO THE POOR - WHAT A RIOT! NOT TO MENTION HIS MERRY JESTS AT THE POST OFFICE...,

HA HA HA HA HA HA

ROYAL TELEGRAPH

SOUTHWELL SMALLPOX HOSPITAL

CONTAINS CLOTH SAMPLES: HANDLE WITH CARE!

HOME FOR THE INCURABLE ITCH

ASYLUM FOR CONFIRMED VIRGINS 7 PARK AVE.S YORK, NY100 USA

HA

YOU WILL BE SAD TO LEARN OF THE SUDDEN DEATH OF.... LET'S SEE... JONATHAN DOE IN OSLO STOP YOU SHOULD RECEIVE HIS REMAINS WITHIN THE NEXT SEVERAL DAYS STOP....,

HA HA

HA HA HA?

BUT THE ROYAL MAIL WAS JUST A WARMUP FOR THE IRREPRESSIBLE JOKESTER.

ONE OF HIS FAVORITE WACKY HIJINKS WAS TO BOARD A TRAIN WITH A FRIEND.

REMEMBER, OLD BOY, WE'RE TOTAL STRANGERS.

BY THE TIME THE TRAIN HAD LEFT THE STATION, THE "TOTAL STRANGERS" WERE READY TO FIGHT.

BY GOD, I WON'T HAVE IT!

NOR, BY GOD, WILL I!

PLEASE, GENTLEMEN...

AND STAY OUT!

YOU'RE MAD-MEN, BOTH OF YOU!

I SAY, DO YOU KNOW WHAT THEY'RE TALKING ABOUT, OLD FRUIT?

NO IDEA, OLD CHUM. NONE WHATSOEVER.

ANOTHER OF HIS JOLLY ANTICS WAS TO STOP PEOPLE IN THE STREET —

AGES SINCE I LAST SAW YOU, OLD MAN, HOW'VE YOU BEEN, AND THE FAMILY?

DO... I... KNOW YOU, SIR?

NO, SIR... YOU DO NOT!

WHAT A WILD AND CRAZY GUY!

HA HA HA...

WHILE IN NEW YORK, SOTHERN HIRED ACTORS TO TERRIFY A DINNER GUEST WHO WAS CURIOUS ABOUT THE ROUGH SIDE OF AMERICA.

BEST ARM YOURSELF... THEY'RE ABOUT TO TALK LITERATURE.

BUT HE LOVED IMPROMPTU JOKES BEST.

HERE HE COMES! QUICKLY, EVERYONE UNDER THE TABLE!

STRANGEST THING — WHEN I TOLD THEM YOU'D ARRIVED, THEY ALL DIVED UNDER THE TABLE!

SOTHERN KEPT UP THIS MADCAP FUN UNTIL HIS DEATH IN 1881, THEREBY EARNING HIS ETERNAL FAME AS THE ORIGINAL MERRY PRANKSTER.

WILLIAM ELLSWORTH ROBINSON WAS A STRUGGLING 39-YEAR-OLD NEW YORK MAGICIAN AT THE TURN OF THE CENTURY, AND HIS UNIQUE RELATIONSHIP WITH CHINESE CONJURER...

CHUNG LING SOO

...MADE THEM PARTNERS-FOR LIFE!

ROBINSON DESIGNED WONDERFUL TRICKS--WHAT MAGICIANS CALL "EFFECTS"--FOR OTHERS.

BUT WHEN PERFORMING HIMSELF, HE DIDN'T HAVE MUCH SUCCESS AS JUST PLAIN WILLIAM ELLSWORTH ROBINSON...

...ESPECIALLY AGAINST HIS CHINESE ARCHRIVALS, LED BY THE MASTER MAGICIAN CHING LING LOO.

THEN A VAUDEVILLE AGENT DECIDED TO CASH IN ON THE CHINESE MAGICIANS' POPULARITY.

NINE MONTHS AT THE FOLIES BERGERE IN PARIS, BILLY... BUT ADD A PIGTAIL.

THEY'LL NEVER SEE ME AGAIN.

A PIGTAIL, ORIENTAL MAKEUP, A COSTUME, AND PRESTO --

--CHUNG LING SOO, THE MARVELOUS CHINESE CONJURER, WAS BORN.

CHUNG LING SOO WAS AN IMMEDIATE SENSATION.

William Ellsworth Robinson

WILLIAM ELLSWORTH ROBINSON DISAPPEARED.

THERE *WAS* NO ROBINSON NOW. OFFSTAGE AND ON, THERE WAS ONLY CHUNG LING SOO.

HE USED AN INTERPRETER WHEN DEALING WITH THE MEDIA.

CHUNG LING SOO SAY, THANK YOU EVER SO, GENTLE-MENS, AND NOW, GOOD DAYS.

EVEN HIS WIFE, OLIVE, WENT ALONG. SHE BECAME SUEE SEEN.

HIS EFFECTS HAD A DEFINITE ORIENTAL FLAVOR...

...ESPECIALLY HIS MOST FAMOUS STUNT:

THE DEATH-DEFYING BULLET CATCH, WHICH HE SAID HE USED TO ESCAPE EXECUTION DURING THE BOXER REBELLION.

AFTER VERIFYING THAT THE RIFLE WAS INDEED LOADED, THE VOLUNTEER WOULD FIRE IT AT THE MAGICIAN...

KPOW

...WHO WOULD SEEM TO CATCH THE BULLETS IN MID-AIR BEFORE THEY COULD HARM HIM.

BUT THE RIFLE HAD A SECRET COMPARTMENT THAT RETAINED THE BULLETS WHEN THE GUN FIRED.

ON MARCH 23, 1918, CHUNG LING SOO REALLY CAUGHT A BULLET--IN HIS CHEST.

KPOW

THE FALSE CHAMBER FAILED AND LET THE BULLET FLY.

MY GOD-- I'VE BEEN SHOT!

THEY WERE THE FIRST ENGLISH WORDS HE'D SPOKEN ON STAGE IN 18 YEARS--AND HIS LAST EVER.

HARRY HOUDINI

...WAS A MAGICIAN'S MAGICIAN, A MAN WHO LOVED TO MYSTIFY WITH CARDS, WITH SLEIGHT OF HAND, VANISHINGS, AND IMPOSSIBLE ESCAPES.

HIS REAL NAME WAS ERIK WEISZ, BORN IN BUDAPEST IN 1874.

WHERE ARE WE GOING, PAPA?

TO AMERIKA.

AROUND THE TURN OF THE CENTURY, RABBI WEISZ TOOK HIS FAMILY TO NEW YORK...

...WHERE, BORROWING A NAME FROM A FRENCH MAGICIAN, ERIK WEISZ BECAME HARRY HOUDINI...

ROBERT HOUDIN

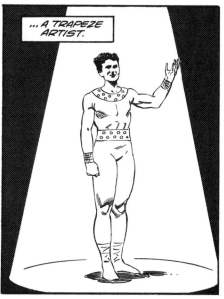

...A TRAPEZE ARTIST.

WHILE NOT VERY BIG, HE WAS POWERFULLY BUILT, AND HAD A HIGHLY DEVELOPED CONTROL OF HIS BODY--

--HE COULD MAKE IT DO ANYTHING.

AT 20, HOUDINI MARRIED WILHELMINA RAHNER. HARRY AND BEATRICE--BESS--HOUDINI BECAME AN ACT THAT WAS TO LAST ALL THEIR LIVES...

HARRY HOUDINI FIRST PREMIER

...AND, SOME SAY, BEYOND.

I SEE... THE ACE... OF SPADES!

FROM BURLESQUE HOUSES TO THE COUNTRY'S FINEST THEATERS, THE HOUDINIS AMAZED AUDIENCES WITH EVERYTHING FROM MATERIALIZING CARDS...

A NINE... OF DIAMONDS!

...TO DISAPPEARING PACHYDERMS, THE MAGIC SEEMED SOMETHING MORE THAN MERE EFFECTS --- IT FELT LIKE THE REAL THING.

AND NOW, TANTOR-- GO!

NOT EVEN THE ELEPHANT KNOWS HOW IT'S DONE!

BUT HOUDINI BECAME MOST FAMOUS FOR HIS DARING ESCAPES.

HANGING UPSIDE DOWN 75 FEET ABOVE THE SIDEWALK...

...HE COULD EXTRICATE HIMSELF FROM SHACKLES AND A STRAITJACKET.

HE HAD HIMSELF SEALED IN A METAL CASKET IN LOCKED SHACKLES...

THIS MAY TAKE A WHILE, LADIES AND GENTLEMEN.

...AND THROWN INTO THE RIVER.

CONTROLLING HIS BREATHING LIKE A DEEP-DIVING SEAL, HE COULD STAY IN THE COFFIN FOR MORE THAN AN HOUR... AND SURVIVE.

DON'T TRY THIS AT HOME.

HE AND BESS ALSO HAD A SUCCESSFUL MIND-READING ACT.

MASTER, WHAT IS THE WORD?

BEGINNING. THE WORD IS... BEGINNING.

HIS HIGHLY TUNED BODY COULD SEND SECRETS BY THE ALMOST IMPERCEPTIBLE TWITCHING OF AN EAR...

AN OLD SWEET SONG, MASTER...

ROSABELLE!

THEY USED SONGS LIKE "ROSABELLE" TO COMMUNICATE SECRETLY IN CODE.

♪ ROSABELLE, SWEET ROSABELLE, I LOVE YOU MORE THAN I CAN TELL. ♪

MAGIC OF HOUDINI

WHEN HOUDINI PRETENDED TO SPEAK WITH THE VOICE OF A MURDER VICTIM...

...AND NOW I WANDER THROUGH ETERNITY, SEEKING THAT REST WHICH I SHALL NEVER FIND...

...SOME MEMBERS OF THE AUDIENCE FLED IN TERROR.

BUT AFTER A WHILE, HOUDINI GREW UNEASY WITH HIS CROWD-PLEASING FORAYS INTO THE "SPIRIT WORLD..."

YOU KNOW, BESS, I HATE FOOLING PEOPLE THAT WAY.

YOU MEAN THE MENTALIST ACT?

YES, FROM NOW ON, IT'S STRAIGHT MAGIC FOR US.

BUT MORE THAN UNEASY, HOUDINI'S EXPERIENCE AS A "MENTALIST" MADE HIM SKEPTICAL OF OTHER SPIRITUALIST ACTS.

AHA!

HE WOULD ATTEND SEANCES AND EXPOSE THE FAKES.

A STEADFAST BELIEVER IN THE SUPERNATURAL, HOUDINI'S FRUIT-LESS SEARCH FOR TRUE CONTACT WITH THE SPIRIT WORLD MADE HIM AN EXPERT AT DEBUNKING FRAUDS.

HIS BOOK, "A MAGICIAN AMONG THE SPIRITS," REVEALED SUCH SCAMS AS SPIRIT WRITING AND THE MANIFESTATION OF ECTOPLASM.

BUT, INJURED ACCIDENTALLY BY A FAN, HOUDINI HIMSELF WAS ABOUT TO JOIN THE SPIRITS.

HEY, THAT STOMACH'S GOIN' A LITTLE SOFT, HARRY.

AGH!

THE FRIENDLY PUNCH HELPED KILL HOUDINI, WHO DIED OF PERITONITIS IN 1926.

EVEN IN DEATH, HIS OWN BELIEF IN THE SUPERNATURAL WAS NEVER QUITE FORGOTTEN.

HE PROMISED HE'D TRY TO SEND ME A MESSAGE IN OUR SPECIAL CODE...

NO SOONER WAS HOUDINI DEAD THAN BESS WAS BESIEGED BY PSYCHICS WITH MESSAGES FROM THE DECEASED.

HE SAYS HE WANTS YOU TO SELL, SELL, SELL.

NO, BUY, BUY, BUY.

IF IT ISN'T IN OUR CODE, IT ISN'T HARRY.

WHEN BESS ACCIDENTALLY FELL DOWN THE STAIRS, SHE ASKED A HAUNTING QUESTION.

HARRY, DEAR, WHY DON'T YOU COME BACK TO ME FROM THE OTHER SIDE?

A SPIRITUALIST INVITED HER TO A SEANCE.

IT IS THE VOICE OF HOUDINI'S SPIRIT!

ROSABELLE, ANSWER, TELL, PRAY, ANSWER, LOOK, TELL, ANSWER, ANSWER, TELL...

THE WORDS WERE FROM THE SONG "ROSABELLE" --THEIR OLD MIND-READING CODE.

OHHH....

HAD HOUDINI POSTHUMOUSLY VERIFIED THE VERY SPIRITUALISM HE'D TRIED TO DISCREDIT?

A FINAL DILEMMA NOT EVEN HOUDINI CAN ESCAPE.

ALFRED-HENRI JARRY

FOUNDER OF THE THEATER OF THE ABSURD, HE SPOKE A ROBOTLIKE LANGUAGE ALL HIS OWN CALLED "UBU," AND STROLLED LEASHED LOBSTERS THROUGH THE STREETS OF TURN-OF-THE-CENTURY PARIS.

A BRILLIANT STUDENT IN HIS NATIVE BRITTANY, IN PARIS JARRY QUICKLY EARNED A REPUTATION AS A MASTER OF THE BIZARRE.

A VIRTUAL DWARF, JARRY FAVORED ROOMS WITH CEILINGS TOO LOW FOR PEOPLE OF NORMAL HEIGHT...

ALFRED-HENRI.... ARE YOU HERE?

HE CALLED HIS APARTMENT A "MURDERED MAN'S CALVARY" AND FILLED IT WITH OWLS, WHO WERE NOCTURNAL, AS HE WAS.

I AM WRITING A GREAT PLAY. I CALL IT... UBU ROI.

THREE YEARS AFTER HE ARRIVED IN PARIS, A FLU EPIDEMIC KILLED HIS FATHER.

EXACTLY ON SCHEDULE.

SO GRIEVED WAS JARRY THAT HE QUICKLY SQUANDERED HIS INHERITANCE ON THE LEFT BANK'S SLEAZY TEMPTATIONS.

HE ABUSED HIS SMALL BODY SPECTACULARLY.... AND BECAME ADDICTED TO BOTH THE LIQUEUR CALLED ABSINTHE AND ETHER.

AH... HOLY WATER.

HIS ANTI-ROYALIST ABSURDIST PLAY, UBU ROI -- KING UBU -- OPENED IN 1896 AND CREATED A DELICIOUS SCANDAL.

OUTRAGEOUS! THE ENTIRE PRODUCTION IS AN OBSCENITY!

AT 23, JARRY WAS A COUNTER-CULTURE HERO.

TO UBU-ROI!

AUTHOR, AUTHOR!

TO PERE UBU!

BUT UBU ROI CLOSED AFTER ONE PERFORMANCE.

JARRY DIDN'T CARE. HE JUST WANTED TO DESTROY HIMSELF...

...AND EVERY CIVILIZED CONVENTION. HE OSTENTATIOUSLY ATE HIS MEALS BACKWARD, FROM DESSERT TO SOUP.

HERE'S YOUR APPETIZER, SIR.

HE EXPRESSED HIMSELF INDIRECTLY.

WILL THAT WHICH BLOWS PREVENT MY USING MY EXTERNAL SKELETON, THAT WHICH ROLLS? *

* TRANSLATION: WILL THE WIND KEEP ME FROM RIDING MY BIKE?

HE ROAMED PARIS, ARMED TO THE TEETH.

YOU'LL KILL MY CHILDREN!

I SHOULD BE DELIGHTED TO GET SOME NEW ONES WITH YOU!

SKASH

BLAM

LIFE MAY END, BUT THE BRAIN GOES ON.

NO ONE COULD SURVIVE THE ABUSE JARRY GAVE HIS LITTLE BODY. IN 1907 THE 34-YEAR-OLD SANK INTO PARALYSIS, EN ROUTE TO DEATH.

LIFE MAY END, BUT THE BRAIN GOES ON.

I AM DYING, PLEASE... BRING ME A TOOTHPICK.

ABSURDIST TO THE END!

FACTOID 100% TRUE BOOKS

ISADORA DUNCAN

THE IRREPRESSIBLE ISADORA DUNCAN FREED DANCE FROM THE BONDS OF CLASSICAL BALLET FOREVER, AND MADE THE ONE WORD, ISADORA, A SYNONYM FOR ARDENT NONCONFORMITY.

BUT BY 1927, THE 49-YEAR-OLD SEEMED TO BE SETTLING DOWN IN THE FRENCH CITY OF NICE.

AN AMERICAN PUBLISHER HAD COMMISSIONED HER TO WRITE HER MEMOIRS...

MY LIFE
ISADORA DUNCAN

...AND SHE WAS THINKING OF WAYS TO SPEND THE HEFTY ADVANCE.

SHE'D THOUGHT OF BUYING A CAR.

SHE'D HAD HER EYE ON A SPIFFY AMILCAR ROADSTER...

DL-9743

...AND ALSO ON THE YOUNG FRENCH FLYING ACE WHO HAD THE LOCAL DEALERSHIP.

THEY BOTH FATALLY ATTRACTED HER.

ISADORA WAS A SAN FRANCISCO GIRL, BORN THERE IN 1877 AND REARED BY HER MOTHER IN BOHEMIAN GENTILITY.

MAMA, I WANT TO BE A DANCER.

THEN, DARLING, THAT IS WHAT YOU SHALL BE.

SHE REBELLED IMMEDIATELY.

MISS DUNCAN— IF YOU DON'T MIND.

SHE BELIEVED DANCE SHOULD BE NATURAL, IMPROVISED RHYTHM AND BODY MOTIONS.

LIKE THE ANCIENT GREEKS DID IT.

YES, YES!

HER FAVORITE EXPRESSION.

AMERICANS FOUND HER MERELY WEIRD.

NO TASTE WHATSO- EVER!

SHE SHOULD TRY BURLESQUE.

UNDETERRED, ISADORA HEADED FOR EUROPE— —AND FAME.

THE SIGHT OF A PRETTY, BAREFOOTED, SCANTILY CLAD YOUNG FEMALE DANCER DREW ADMIRING CROWDS...

...AND CROWDS OF ADMIRING LOVERS. DANCE WAS NOT THE ONLY CONVENTION SHE'D REJECTED.

TWO DIFFERENT MEN GAVE HER A SON AND A DAUGHTER OUT OF WEDLOCK.

THE SCANDAL ADDED PIQUANCY TO HER FAME.

THEY STILL DIDN'T LIKE HER IN THE STATES. BUT NOW IT WASN'T JUST HER DANCING.

...AND SOMETIMES SHE WAS SHOCKING!

WHY PROVOKE THEM THAT WAY?

OH, PIPE DOWN, YOU!

GO BACK TO RUSSIA!

SHAME-LESS!

SHE DANCES LIKE A COMMUNIST, ALL RIGHT.

WHAT IS THEIR PROBLEM?

SHE'D BECOME PART OF THE SO-CALLED "RED MENACE"...

SHE AND YESENIN FOUGHT CONSTANTLY. WHEN THEY RETURNED TO EUROPE, THEY SEPARATED.

A YEAR LATER, THE SOVIET POET KILLED HIMSELF.

FOR A TIME, HER LIFE BECAME ALMOST MORE THAN SHE COULD BEAR. SHE LIVED IN DEBT, DESPAIR, AND AN ALCOHOLIC HAZE.

BUT IN NICE, THINGS HAD TURNED AROUND— THE MEMOIRS, THE MONEY.. THE CAR.

YOU MAY NEED MY LEATHER COAT, MADAME.

ON A COOL SEPTEMBER DAY IN 1927, SHE ARRANGED A TEST DRIVE.

GOODBYE, MY FRIENDS, I GO TO GLORY!

THANK YOU, BUT I HAVE MY SCARF.

INDEED.

BUT NOT WITH THE FLYING ACE.

CAUGHT IN THE AMILCAR'S REAR WHEEL, HER SHAWL BECAME A NOOSE THAT SNAPPED HER NECK, KILLING HER INSTANTLY.

VASLAV NIJINSKY

FROM THE MOMENT HE STEPPED ON STAGE IN MOSCOW IN THE EARLY 1900'S, THE BALLET WORLD KNEW THAT VASLAV NIJINSKY WAS ONE OF HISTORY'S GREATEST DANCERS.

HIS ATHLETIC, ABANDONED STYLE UTTERLY CHARMED-- AND CHANGED-- THE WORLD OF BALLET.

BUT HE WAS POSSESSED BY MORE THAN TALENT.

WITHIN HIS QUIET, INARTICULATE SHELL, THERE BREWED A TERRIBLE MADNESS.

A LONELY, SILENT FIGURE OFFSTAGE, AND TERRIBLY SHY, HE WAS INCAPABLE OF EXPRESSING HIMSELF...

...EXCEPT THROUGH DANCE.

THERE HE COULD SAY ANYTHING.

HE'D BEEN BORN TO DANCE.

TO FLY.

HIS POLISH-BORN PARENTS WERE DANCERS WHO EARNED THEIR LIVING TOURING RUSSIA WHEN HE WAS BORN IN 1889.

ABANDONED BY HIS FATHER, HIS MOTHER TAUGHT YOUNG VASLAV AND HIS BROTHER TO DANCE.

A FALL LEFT THE OLDER BROTHER CRIPPLED.

SOMEHOW, VASLAV'S MOTHER MANAGED TO ENROLL HIM IN THE IMPERIAL BALLET SCHOOL...

...WHERE HE DAZZLED HIS MASTERS...

...AND ANNOYED HIS COMRADES, WHO THOUGHT HIS SHY SILENCE WAS ARROGANCE.

WE'LL SEE HOW HE LIKES DANCING ON SOAP.

THEIR PRANK PUT HIM IN THE HOSPITAL WITH HEAD INJURIES.

I WILL FLY THAT MUCH HIGHER.

THE REMARKABLE DANCER CONTINUED TO DAZZLE.

PERFECT. I MUST HAVE HIM...

...FOR MY BALLET RUSSE.

HE CAUGHT THE EYE OF IMPRESARIO SERGEY DIAGHILEV, WHO WAS PUTTING TOGETHER A TOURING COMPANY OF RUSSIAN DANCERS.

IN 1909, THE 20-YEAR-OLD DANCER DEBUTED IN PARIS, PLAYING A SLAVE IN ARMIDE'S PAVILION.

PARIS ADORED IT.

THEY ADORE ME.

NIJINSKY!

VASLAV! VASLAV!

BUT IT DIDN'T PLAY WELL IN RUSSIA.

GO BACK TO PARIS!

WHERE ARE HIS CLOTHES?

NIJINSKY WAS EJECTED FROM THE IMPERIAL BALLET.

SUCH SETBACKS ONLY SERVED TO INTENSIFY NIJINSKY'S BROODING OFFSTAGE CHARACTER.

THEY HATED ME, SERGEY.

DON'T WORRY, VASLAV. IT WILL COME RIGHT.

BESIDES, I DON'T HATE YOU.

NEITHER WOULD ALL OF EUROPE, WHICH SWOONED OVER NIJINSKY'S NEXT PERFORMANCE --

-- THE SCANDALOUSLY EROTIC ROLE OF THE SATYR IN AFTERNOON OF A FAUN.

DRUNK WITH SUCCESS, NIJINSKY INSISTED ON BECOMING HIS OWN CHOREOGRAPHER.

BUT MY DEAR BOY, YOU'VE NO FORMAL TRAINING.

HOW WILL YOU TELL THEM WHAT TO DO?

LIKE ME, YOU COW! DANCE LIKE ME!

HE COULD ONLY TEACH BY EXAMPLE-- WORDS, AS ALWAYS, FAILED HIM.

DIAGHILEV WATCHED AND SAID NOTHING, BUT SOME-ONE ELSE HAD BEEN WATCHING HIM:

A HUNGARIAN SOCIALITE NAMED ROMOLA PULSZKY.

I CAN MAKE YOU HAPPY, VASLAV.

IN 1913, HIS PARIS DEBUT OF IGOR STRAVINSKY'S *FAR-OUT RITES OF SPRING* FLOPPED HORRIBLY...

GO BACK TO RUSSIA.

BOO

...EVEN THOUGH DIAGHILEV HAD HIRED A CHEERING SECTION.

NIJINSKY SAILED FOR A SOUTH AMERICAN TOUR.

ROMOLA PULSZKY WAS ABOARD.

MARRIED TODAY IN BUENOS AIRES...

YOU BASTARD! YOU'RE FIRED!

ROMOLA ARRANGED A U.S. TOUR. THE HIGH POINT: A DAY WITH CHARLIE CHAPLIN, WHOM NIJINSKY ADMIRED -- BUT WHO RARELY BROUGHT A SMILE TO THE TROUBLED DANCER'S FACE.

YOU DON'T MAKE IT EASY, VASLAV, MY BOY.

BY 1917 NIJINSKY WAS AGAIN DANCING FOR DIAGHILEV -- BUT ONLY BRIEFLY.

I'M SO GLAD YOU'RE BACK, MY BOY.

BUT THAT WAS A BAD YEAR FOR RUSSIANS. THE WAR. THE REVOLUTION. NIJINSKY CAME UNDER THE INFLUENCE OF TOLSTOY MYSTICS.

RENOUNCE EVERYTHING.

FORGET DANCING. FORGET SEX.

LIFE IS... LIFE IS...

SENSING HIS SUSCEPTIBILITY TO THE MYSTICS'S SUGGESTIONS, ROMOLA TOOK NIJINSKY TO ST. MORITZ, SWITZERLAND.

HOW COULD I HAVE CAUSED SUCH A HORRIBLE WAR?

BUT IT WAS TOO LATE. HE STARTED TO BECOME DELUSIONAL, UNHINGED...

I AM WHAT CHRIST FELT. I AM BUDDHA AND EVERY KIND OF GOD.

HE DANCED ONLY ONCE IN ST. MORITZ.

I WILL DANCE YOU THE WAR.

HIS MIND WAS GONE.

HIS DIARIES KEPT TRACK OF HIS DISINTEGRATION.

"My ideas don't have any direction."

"They change all the time. My existence is ruined."

"I am a clown... a lunatic... a monster..."

I FEAR HE IS CATATONIC, MADAME NIJINSKY.

HIS LIFE BECAME A SEARCH FOR CURES.

LOURDES PROVIDED NO MIRACLE...

... NOR DID ELECTROSHOCK THERAPY, OR INSULIN.

WHEN WORLD WAR II BEGAN, ROMOLA TOOK HIM HOME TO HUNGARY.

LOOK AT THIS DEFECTIVE. PUT HIM DOWN FOR EXTERMINATION.

BUT SIR, HE IS THE GREAT NIJINSKY, THE GREATEST DANCER THE WORLD HAS EVER KNOWN!

WHEN SOVIET SOLDIERS CAPTURED BUDAPEST, THE DANCER HAD A LAST CLEAR-MINDED MOMENT.

COMRADES! WELCOME!

FOR A BRIEF INTERVAL HE COULD SPEAK AND UNDERSTAND RUSSIAN.

THEN HIS MADNESS SEALED HIM OFF AGAIN.

AFTER HE DIED IN 1950, ROMOLA TOOK HIM BACK TO PARIS WHERE, FOR A BRIEF MOMENT YEARS BEFORE, HE HAD TOUCHED HAPPINESS.

118

CHAPTER SIX

ENTERTAINERS AND ARTISTS

Society allows — perhaps even encourages — outrageous behavior by "creative types." We go to extra lengths to tolerate their fetishes and compulsions, so long as the heights of their genius exceed the depths of their weirdness. For most of the weirdos in this section, meeting this criterion was no problem and so, with society's blessing, they played up their individual eccentricities to the max. Salvador Dali (*page 138*), Andy Warhol (*page 135*), and Erich von Stroheim (*page 124*) all became as famous for their peculiar personalities as for their artistic contributions to the worlds of fine art and cinema. But for every high there's a low, and here you'll also find artistic casualties like Clara Bow (*page 126*), Ed Wood, Jr. (*page 128*) and even Vincent van Gogh (*page 131*). To an unsympathetic public, they were just too weird to be understood.

As he climbed to the top of a new profession during the 1920s, Avlin Anthony Kelly perched his way into—and out of—America's heart as...

SHIPWRECK KELLY

...the man who made flagpole-sitting a national fad.

His prior job was supposed to keep him on his FEET.

He was a boxer, and fought under the moniker of "Sailor" Kelly.

But "Sailor" spent so much time sitting down that fans began to call him...

..."Shipwreck."

But in 1924 the 39-year-old fighter's luck changed.

HEY, YOU... SHIPWRECK...

CALL ME...

A studio wanted him to help promote a new film.

TEN HOURS?

PIECE 'O CAKE!

KELLY

Kelly stayed up for 13 days, 13 hours, launched a national craze...

HOLLYWOODLAND

...and carved out a profitable new career for Shipwreck.

120

BY 1928, OF WHICH HE SPENT 145 DAYS ON A FLAGPOLE, SHIPWRECK KELLY WAS EARNING $100 PER DAY WITH HIS SEDENTARY SENSATION.

5 MONTHS X $100 PER DAY EQUALS $14,500 IN 1928 MONEY!

HE DESIGNED A SEAT WITH HOLES INTO WHICH HE ANCHORED HIS THUMBS WHEN HE SLEPT.

TILT!!

IF HE TEETERED, THE PAIN IN HIS THUMBS WOKE HIM UP.

HE'D SIT ON ANY FLAGPOLE...

...ANYWHERE.

HOW'S HE EAT?

YEA, AND...

IN 1930, HE SPENT MORE THAN 49 DAYS ON ATLANTIC CITY'S STEEL PIER FLAGPOLE, TO THE DELIGHT OF 20,000 GAWKERS.

IT WAS THE LAST BIG STUNT OF HIS CAREER BECAUSE, LIKE THE STOCK MARKET...

...SHIPWRECK WAS ON HIS WAY DOWN.

IN DESPERATION, HE TRIED TO REPRISE HIS FIRST SIT.

NOTE— SHIPWRECK IS HERE!

13 DAYS, 13 HOURS, AND 13 MINUTES ON THE FLAGPOLE OF NEW YORK'S PARAMOUNT HOTEL. THE STUNT EARNED $13.

ON FRIDAY, OCTOBER 13, 1939, KELLY ATE 13 DONUTS WHILE STANDING ON HIS HEAD ON A PLANK JUTTING FROM THE 56TH FLOOR OF A SKYSCRAPER.

IT WAS HIS LAST MAJOR PERFORMANCE.

DOWN AND OUT FOR ANOTHER DOZEN YEARS, KELLY CLUNG TO HIS NEWSPAPER CLIPPINGS.

WHEN SHIPWRECK WAS FOUND DEAD IN 1952, HE STILL CARRIED HIS SCRAPBOOKS— HIS MEMORIES OF A TIME WHEN, LITERALLY, HE'D BEEN AT THE TOP.

TO MANHATTANITES, THE BLIND MAN IN A VIKING COSTUME WAS JUST A CHARMING MUSICAL ECCENTRIC, CHANTING HIS LYRICS AND HUMMING HIS SONGS. EVERYBODY CALLED HIM...

MOONDOG

THEY CONSIDERED HIM A NEW YORK LANDMARK.

BORN LOUIS T. HARDIN IN KANSAS IN 1916, MOONDOG GREW UP IN WYOMING...

...WHERE A DYNAMITE CAP BLEW UP IN HIS FACE, DESTROYING HIS VISION WHEN HE WAS 16.

TANGIER EXPLOSIVES

AT A SCHOOL FOR THE BLIND IN IOWA, HE LEARNED ABOUT MUSIC --PLAYING IT, COMPOSING IT, HEARING IT.

MUSIC BECAME HIS LIFE.

IN 1943 HE CAME TO NEW YORK, WHERE THE NEW YORK PHILHARMONIC LET HIM DEVELOP HIS TALENT FOR COMPOSITION.

WONDERFUL TOWN.

BUT HE WAS ALSO DRAWN TO THE SOUNDS AND SOULS OF THE RISING BEAT GENERATION.

BEAT POETS

HE TOOK THE NAME MOONDOG, ADOPTED VIKING DRESS, AND MADE HIS WAY RECITING POETRY AND SINGING HIS MUSIC.

WEST 57

HE LOOKED LIKE JUST ANOTHER IMPOVERISHED DROPOUT.

FEW KNEW HE HAD A SECRET LIFE.

HE RECORDED HIS MUSIC FOR THE CBS, MARS, AND PRESTIGE LABELS.

IN 1974, HIS SECRET LIFE TOOK OVER. HE DISAPPEARED.

MOONDOG'S GONE.

YEAH, I HEARD HE DIED.

IN A WAY, HE DID. MOONDOG SURFACED IN A SMALL TOWN IN GERMANY, WHERE HE'D BEEN INVITED TO DO A RADIO SHOW -- AND HAD DECIDED TO SETTLE DOWN.

SINCE THEN, HE'S COMPOSED MORE THAN 40 JAZZ SYMPHONIES...

DUM-DE-DE-DUM...

...AND TOURED EUROPE AND THE U.S.

AND NOW... MOOOON... DOG...!

HE CONDUCTED THE BROOKLYN PHILHARMONIC.

FRIENDS SAY HIS IDEAS COME TOO FAST FOR HIM TO SET THEM ALL DOWN IN BRAILLE. MOONDOG IS ONE OF MUSIC'S BUSIEST MEN.

IT'S NOT THE SAME WITHOUT OLD MOONDOG.

YEAH.

BUT FOR MANY, THERE WILL ALWAYS BE A PECULIAR EMPTY SILENCE ON THE SIDEWALKS OF NEW YORK.

FACTOID BOOKS

ERICH VON STROHEIM

ERICH VON STROHEIM WAS ONE OF THE GREAT FILM DIRECTORS TO EMERGE AFTER THE FIRST WORLD WAR... A TALENT THAT SHAPED THE WAY PEOPLE WOULD MAKE MOTION PICTURES FOR A GENERATION!

BENEATH HIS STERN EXTERIOR, HOWEVER, HE WAS JUST A BOY FROM VIENNA WHOSE REAL NAME WAS HANS ERICH MARIA STROHEIM VON NORDONWALL...

CHUST CALL ME VON!

HE ARRIVED IN AMERICA IN 1914...

...AND BECAME AN ASSISTANT TO FILM GREAT D.W. GRIFFITH ON SUCH CLASSICS AS...

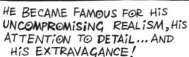

CIVIL WAR SOLDIERS

FOOTLOCKER

..."THE BIRTH OF A NATION"!

STROHEIM'S OWN MASTERPIECE WAS CALLED "GREED," A BLEAK, REALISTIC TALE OF THE CORRUPTING POWER OF MONEY THAT RAN FOR 10 HOURS!

Bleak! Realistic! Long...

HE BECAME FAMOUS FOR HIS UNCOMPROMISING REALISM, HIS ATTENTION TO DETAIL...AND HIS EXTRAVAGANCE!

EVERYTHING MUST BE CHUST RIGHT!

WHEN HE TOOK A HAND AS AN ACTOR, HE USUALLY PLAYED A SADISTIC PRUSSIAN OFFICER...

...SOME SAID HE PLAYED THE PART TOO WELL!

FOR FILMS LIKE "THE MERRY WIDOW," STROHEIM RECREATED OLD VIENNA-PROSTITUTES, ORGIES, AND ALL-WITH HIS CUSTOMARY EYE TO REALISM!

IT SOMETIMES TOOK **20** HOURS TO SHOOT A BORDELLO ORGY-ALWAYS ON A CLOSED SET...

THE "EXTRAS" DINED ON SQUAB AND **REAL** CHAMPAGNE - IN THE HEART OF PROHIBITION!

OK, EVERYBODY... ONE MORE TAKE PLEASE!

YES, ERICH!!!

GEE!... IT'S MORNING!

REMEMBER, GIRLS... NOT A WORD!

STUDIO B

OH WOW!... LOOK AT **THAT!** HOT DOG! LOOK AT **HER!**

PHEW! THAT VON STROHEIM MUST BE **CRAZY!**

HAYS OFFICE

NO ONE DARED **SHOW** SUCH STUFF, HOWEVER! THE HAYS OFFICE CENSORS MADE SURE STROHEIM'S **BIG** SCENES STAYED ON THE CUTTING-ROOM FLOOR!

THEN THE HOLLYWOOD ESTABLISHMENT WENT AFTER HIM...

WORKING WITH STROHEIM IS LIKE SHOVELLING MONEY INTO A WELL!

YEAH... I GUESS I'LL PASS...

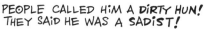

PEOPLE CALLED HIM A **DIRTY HUN!** THEY SAID HE WAS A **SADIST!**

WHO? MOI??

TINSELTOWN WON...

HOLLYWOOD KILLED ME...

YEAH... ME TOO...

IN THE MID-1930's, ERICH VON STROHEIM WENT HOME TO EUROPE...

... WHERE SOME **REAL** SADISTS WERE **JUST GETTING STARTED!**

FACTOID BOOKS 100% TRUE

CLARA BOW

...WAS THE HOTTEST JAZZ BABY IN MOTION PICTURES, THE ACTRESS EVERYONE WANTED TO LOOK LIKE WHILE THE 1920s ROARED.

THE BROOKLYN-BORN BEAUTY WAS MAKING IT IN SILENT FILMS BEFORE SHE TURNED 20.

THEN, IN 1927, SHE PLAYED THE LEAD IN THE FILM "IT"-- AND WAS SOON FAMOUS AS THE IT GIRL...

...A ROLE SHE BEGAN TO PLAY OFF-SCREEN, AS WELL AS ON.

PEOPLE WATCHED FOR THE RED-HAIRED FLAPPER IN HER ATTENTION-GRABBING RED KISSEL CONVERTIBLE WITH TWO MATCHING CHOW DOGS.

SHE NEVER DISAPPOINTED. THERE WAS THE FAMOUS "LOVE BALM ROMANCE" WITH DOC PEARSON...

...THAT COST HER $30,000 FOR ALIENATING HIS AFFECTIONS FROM MRS. PEARSON.

CLARA DIDN'T CARE. THERE WAS PLENTY MORE DOUGH WHERE THAT CAME FROM.

CLARA'S LAS VEGAS GAMBLING WAS FRONT-PAGE NEWS...

...AS WAS HER SEX LIFE, THANKS TO PRIVATE SECRETARY DAISY DE VOE...

...WHO TATTLED ON HER EMPLOYER'S FOUR-YEAR ORGY WITH EVERYBODY, INCLUDING THE UNIVERSITY OF SOUTHERN CALIFORNIA'S TROJANS.

TROJANS

STUNG, CLARA ELOPED TO VEGAS WITH COWBOY ACTOR REX BELL...

...THEN EMBARKED ON A SERIES OF NERVOUS BREAKDOWNS.

WHEN SHE TRIED A TALKIE...

HELLO, EVERYBODY...

...HER VOICE CAME OUT LIKE A BRONX CHEER AND SHATTERED THE VACUUM TUBES IN THE STUDIO.

TROUBLE WAS, PEOPLE FOUND THE DEPRESSION MORE INTERESTING THAN YESTERDAY'S IT GIRL.

CLARA NEVER QUITE GOT OVER BEING A RELIC OF A VANISHED ERA...

SANITORIUM

...EVEN AT AGE 60, WHEN SHE DIED IN NEUROTIC SECLUSION.

ED WOOD JR.

...DIRECTED SOME OF HOLLYWOOD'S MOST UNFORGETTABLE FILMS -- FILMS THAT OFFERED A CRAZY PARODY OF LIFE...

...FILMS TOO AWFUL, TOO CHEAP, TO IGNORE.

WOOD SHOWED UP IN HOLLYWOOD IN 1947, WITH STORIES TO TELL.

HE'D BEEN A MARINE AT TARAWA...

POW!

...AND HAD GONE ASHORE WEARING WOMAN'S UNDERWEAR UNDER HIS FATIGUES.

YOW!

HE SAID HE'D BEEN A CARNIVAL GEEK...

SQUAWK!

GRRR!

R.I.P.

WOOOSSH!

FLASH!

POP!

...AND HAD GONE UNDERCOVER TO ROOT FOREIGN AGENTS FROM THE ICE CAPADES. (GO FIGURE.)

WITH A CAMERA HIS DAD HAD GIVEN HIM, HE SHOT THE HINDENBERG --

OH, BOY!

-- ON HER FINAL FLIGHT.

AT LAST HE REALIZED HIS DREAM OF MOVING TO HOLLYWOOD. AT FIRST HE WORKED AS AN EXTRA...

HEY, YOU IN THE ANGORA SWEATER...

...AND STUNT DOUBLE.

TOOT TOOT

POW!!

RUMBLE

SCREECH

IN 1948, HE DIRECTED HIS FIRST FILM: CROSSROADS OF LAREDO.

ACTION!

IT WAS NEVER RELEASED--OR EVEN SOUND-TRACKED.

THEN, JUST AS HE RECEIVED HIS FIRST REAL DIRECTORIAL ASSIGNMENT IN 1953, WOOD MET HIS GREAT HERO.

MY GOD! IT'S BELA LUGOSI!

THE WORLD'S MOST FAMOUS DRACULA BECAME WOOD'S CLOSE FRIEND.

I NEVAH DRINK ... VINE ...

WOOD MADE HIS FIRST FEATURE FILM A SHRINE TO THE AGING OPIUM ADDICT'S TALENTS.

HE CAST LUGOSI AS AN OMNISCIENT, GODLIKE NARRATOR.

SANDBURG

GLEN OR GLENDA

THE FILM WAS CALLED GLEN OR GLENDA. IT WAS A PLEA FOR UNDERSTANDING OF THE STRANGE WORLD OF TRANS-VESTISM AND TRANSSEXUALITY.

IT STARRED WOOD HIMSELF, IN BOTH PARTS.

I JUST CAN'T DECIDE.

THE FILM ESTABLISHED WOOD AS A MAKER OF REALLY BAD MOVIES.

PERHAPS THE WORST EVER.

BRIDE OF THE MONSTER CONFIRMED THOSE SUSPICIONS.

THEN CAME 1956, AND THE WATERSHED OF WOOD'S CAREER: PLAN 9 FROM OUTER SPACE...

F/X!

...WHICH HAD TRADEMARK ED WOOD SPECIAL EFFECTS...

GREETINGS, MY FRIEND. WE ARE ALL INTERESTED IN THE FUTURE, FOR THAT IS WHERE WE ARE GOING TO SPEND THE REST OF OUR LIVES...

...AND TRADEMARK ED WOOD THOUGHTS.

WOOD'S LATER FILMS, LIKE ORGY OF THE DEAD...WELL, THEY WERE NO PLAN 9.

WOOD WAS ON THE SKIDS.

HE WAS FORCED TO WRITE PORNOGRAPHY, MAKE SEXPLOITATION FILMS, AND TO DRINK. MOSTLY, HE DRANK.

ED WAS MARRIED TO KATHY WOOD FOR 20 YEARS.

THAT DAY IN 1978....I WAS SITTING HERE WITH MY FRIEND BEULAH, AND ED HAD GONE INTO MY BEDROOM. HE'D BEEN DRINKING, AS USUAL. SO I SAID, WHY DON'T YOU GO AND SEE HOW HE'S DOING?

"I STILL REMEMBER WHEN I WENT INTO THAT ROOM THAT AFTERNOON AND HE WAS DEAD, HIS EYES WERE WIDE OPEN. AS LONG AS I LIVE, I'LL NEVER FORGET THE LOOK IN HIS EYES."

IT LOOKED LIKE HE'D SEEN HELL. WHAT DO YOU SUPPOSE HE SAW IN THOSE LAST FEW MOMENTS? WHAT DO YOU SUPPOSE HE SAW?

JUST A GUESS: ORGY OF THE DEAD? TAKE IT OUT IN TRADE? PLAN 9?

VINCENT VAN GOGH

...THE DUTCH IMPRESSIONIST PAINTER OF THE 19TH CENTURY, IS RANKED WITH HIS FAMOUS COMPATRIOT REMBRANDT AS ONE OF THE GREATEST ARTISTS OF ALL TIME.

FEW HAVE SEEN THE WORLD MORE VIVIDLY.

HIS ROUGH STROKES, HIS VIBRANT COLORS, WERE PART OF HIS SPECIAL VISION...

...ONE THAT SAW THE WORLD THROUGH A LENS OF MADNESS.

WITH EACH LEAP IN BRILLIANCE ON HIS CANVAS, HOWEVER, HE MARKED ANOTHER STEP ON HIS OWN AGONIZING JOURNEY TOWARD UTTER, FINAL DESPAIR.

HE WAS BORN IN HOLLAND IN 1853, THE ELDEST OF SIX CHILDREN...

...AND THE LONELIEST.

HE BECAME SOLITARY EARLY ON, AS HE SEARCHED FOR WHAT HE WOULD DO WITH HIS LIFE.

I WANT TO HELP. BUT,...HOW?

HE TRIED TO BE A MISSIONARY TO THE POOR COAL MINERS OF BELGIUM.

THEIR POVERTY BROKE HIS HEART.

HERE, TAKE WHAT I HAVE... IT'S NOT MUCH, BUT IT'S YOURS. HERE...

VAN GOGH WAS FIRED WHEN HE GAVE AWAY ALL HIS EARTHLY GOODS.

YOU'RE JUST TOO CHRISTIAN FOR US, VINCENT.

IN A WAY, IT WAS SALVATION.

VAN GOGH BEGAN TO TEACH HIMSELF TO DRAW...

...AND DRAW, AND DRAW.

I CAN'T DO THIS ALONE. I'LL NEED TO GO TO SCHOOL.

BY 1886, HE'D BECOME AN ACCOMPLISHED, BUT STILL ORDINARY, PAINTER.

HE VISITED HIS BROTHER, THEO, A MARGINALLY SUCCESS-FUL ART DEALER.

AH, MY ARTISTIC OLDER BROTHER, WELCOME TO PARIS, VINCENT.

I CAN'T TELL YOU HOW EXCITING IT IS TO BE HERE, THEO.

IN PARIS, VINCENT MET THE GREAT IMPRESSIONISTS OF THE DAY: TOULOUSE-LAUTREC, PISSARRO, SEURAT, GAUGUIN...

GAUGUIN, HIS FRIEND...

...AND NEMESIS.

IN 1888, THE YEAR HE MOVED TO ARLES, IN THE SOUTH OF FRANCE, VAN GOGH BEGAN TO PAINT HIS MASTERPIECES.

YES.... YES!

SPONTANEOUS, INTUITIVE, ALIVE...

...THE WORLD HE SAW WAS VISIBLE ONLY TO HIM.

HE WAS A CAMERA...

...THAT LOOKED THROUGH THE LENS OF MADNESS.

HELLO, PAUL....

HELLO, VINCENT. WHAT KIND OF CRAZINESS ARE YOU CAPTURING FOR US TODAY?

REALLY, VINCENT, YOU'VE GOT TO GET HOLD OF YOURSELF.

YES, PAUL... YES... I SHALL ...I'M FEELING BETTER ...

I MUST GET HOLD OF MYSELF. THANK GOD FOR PAUL.

THE HELL WITH THIS STINKING HOLE. I'M OFF TO THE SOUTH SEAS.

GAUGUIN'S DEPARTURE WAS A TERRIBLE BLOW.

COME HERE, I'LL BUY YOU A DRINK.

I DON'T DRINK WITH MAD DUTCH-MEN.

NOT EVEN AT CHRISTMAS? WELL.... I'LL SEE THAT YOU GET SOMETHING VERY SPECIAL THIS YEAR.

VERY SPECIAL!

THE SEVERED EAR LOBE HE SENT THE SCORNFUL PROSTITUTE BECAME AS FAMOUS AS HIS ART.

NOW HIS DEMONS TURNED UP THE VOLUME.

SOME SAY HIS MADNESS CAME FROM TOO MUCH ABSINTHE, OR FROM A FORM OF EPILEPSY, OR A CRIPPLING DISORDER OF THE INNER EAR.

WHATEVER THE CAUSE, THE MADNESS TERRIFIED VAN GOGH.

IT WILL KEEP ME... FROM WORKING... FROM BEING IN TOUCH WITH... REALITY.

HE ENROLLED IN AN ASYLUM FOR EPILEPTICS FOR 12 MONTHS.

I'M VAN GOGH. PLEASE LET ME IN.

IN THAT STATE, HE PAINTED FEVERISHLY, AND CREATED...

STARRY STARRY NIGHT...

...WORK THAT WILL LIVE FOREVER.

AFTER HIS RELEASE, HE RETURNED TO PARIS...

GOD, HOW I'VE MISSED YOU, THEO.

ARE YOU REALLY BETTER, VINCENT?

OH YES, THEO, NEVER BETTER.

BUT HE HAD BEEN BETTER. HE COULDN'T SILENCE HIS DEMONS, WHO DROVE HIM TOWARD DESPAIR.

I ... CAN'T...

ON JULY 29, 1890, THE 37-YEAR-OLD ARTIST SHOT HIMSELF.

OF MORE THAN 800 OIL PAINTINGS AND 700 DRAWINGS, HE'D SOLD ONLY ONE, AND HE'D NEVER HAD A SHOW OF HIS OWN.

THE MIRACLE IS THAT IT TOOK HIM SO LONG TO SURRENDER TO ETERNITY.

ANDY WARHOL

...THE *ENFANT TERRIBLE* AND GURU OF AMERICAN STYLE IN THE 1960s, BECAME WEALTHY AND FAMOUS BY TURNING THE EVERYDAY JUNK OF LIFE INTO SOMETHING CALLED POP ART -- AND BY BEING STEADILY OUTRAGEOUS.

ANDREW WARHOLA WAS BORN IN PITTSBURGH IN 1927, THE SON OF CZECH EMIGRES.

DURING THE 1950s, HE LABORED ANONYMOUSLY AS A DESIGNER OF CHRISTMAS CARDS, RECORD ALBUM COVERS, AND THE LIKE.

PISTOLS FOR TWO

DEALING WITH DESIGN FROM A COMMERCIAL STAND-POINT SEEMED TO INSPIRE HIM.

ART!

IN 1962, WARHOL BECAME INSTANTLY FAMOUS FOR A NEW KIND OF ART WITH HIS FAMOUS PAINTING OF A CAMPBELL'S SOUP CAN.

Campbell's CONDENSED TOMATO SOUP

HE SAID HIS ART WAS MORE THAN MECHANICAL REPLICAS OF HOUSEHOLD ITEMS.

WOULD YOU SAY YOU WERE DOCUMENTING THE BANALITY OF AMERICA'S COMMERCIAL CULTURE?

Brillo.

WHY NOT?

A KIND OF APOTHEOSIS OF OUR TASTELESS SOCIETY--?

POP ART.

WARHOL'S ART BROUGHT FAME, MONEY, SEX..., AND DRUGS.

LOTS OF DRUGS.

FAME BROUGHT ARDENT FOLLOWERS TO THE NEW YORK STUDIO-CUM-CLUB-CUM-TEMPLE THAT WARHOL CALLED THE FACTORY.

PEOPLE WHO LONGED TO BE ANDYS THEMSELVES.

PEOPLE WHO LONGED TO PLAY PEOPLE LIKE THEM-SELVES IN ANDY'S MOVIES.

TOUCH ME... FEEL ME... KNOW ME.

HIS FILMS WERE AS ECCENTRICALLY NON-CONFORMIST AS HIS ART,

PLOTLESS, ANGRY, AND EROTIC, THEY CELEBRATED A FUNNY BRAND OF DRUGGED EROTIC HORROR.

ONE FILM WAS 25 HOURS LONG.

HIS LIFE BEGAN TO BE AS UNUSUAL AS HIS ART.

HE WOULD BINGE ON CHOCOLATES AND THEN EAT NOTHING FOR DAYS.

NOTHING... BUT GARLIC.

NO. 5
PARFUM
CHANEL
PARIS
NEW YORK

HE DRENCHED HIMSELF WITH PERFUME TO CONCEAL THE SMELL.

HE BELIEVED IN THE POWER OF CRYSTALS -- HE WORE THEM, AND PUT THEM IN HIS SOUPS AND TEA.

HE BOUGHT PILES OF HAMBURGERS AT McDONALD'S...

...JUST TO GET THE STYROFOAM CONTAINERS. PERHAPS IT WAS A WORK IN PROGRESS.

WARHOL BECAME SO FAMOUS THAT, IN 1968, WHEN OTHER FAMOUS PEOPLE WERE BEING SHOT...

...HE WAS SHOT TOO.

VALERIE!

WARHOL GROUPIE VALERIE SOLANIS FAILED. UNLIKE THE OTHER FAMOUS PEOPLE SHOT THAT YEAR, THE FATHER OF POP ART SURVIVED.

ANDY'S SO, LIKE, DEAD ALREADY, MAYBE HIS BODY, LIKE, DIDN'T NOTICE THE BULLETS. HEE HEE.

BUT WARHOL WAS NEVER THE SAME. HE BECAME A FRIGHTENED RECLUSE.

HE ONCE FAMOUSLY SAID THAT IN THE FUTURE EVERYONE WOULD BE FAMOUS FOR 15 MINUTES.

HIS 15 MINUTES LASTED FOR A QUARTER CENTURY, UNTIL HIS DEATH IN 1987.

salvador Dali

...THE SURREALIST PAINTER WHO CREATED BIZARRE IMAGES OF THE WORLD AS THE HUMAN UNCONSCIOUS MIGHT SEE IT -- AND MADE HIMSELF A LIVING SYMBOL OF ALL THAT WAS PECULIAR IN THE REALM OF ART.

BORN FELIPE JACINTO IN FIGUERAS, SPAIN, IN 1902, DALI'S ARTISTIC CAREER BEGAN RATHER CONVENTIONALLY...

...PAINTING WHAT EVERYBODY ELSE DID, MORE OR LESS THE WAY THEY DID IT.

BUT WHO WANTS THIS STUFF?

THEN HE DISCOVERED AUSTRIAN PSYCHIATRIST SIGMUND FREUD...

...AND THE EROTICALLY CHARGED LANDSCAPE OF THE UNCONSCIOUS MIND.

THAT WAS THE WORLD TO PAINT.

IN DALI'S WORLD SOLID OBJECTS MELTED LIKE HOT WAX, FLOATED IN THE AIR, CHANGED FORM.

FORGET REASON. OUR SUBCONSCIOUS IS THE GREATEST REALITY.

OF COURSE, STRANGE ART IS HELPED BY STRANGER BEHAVIOR.

WE ACHIEVE THE GREATER REALITY BY ENTERING A HALLUCINATORY STATE...

...THE PARANOIAC CRITIC.

WHATEVER *THAT* MEANT!

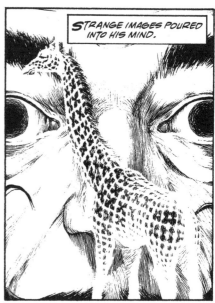

STRANGE IMAGES POURED INTO HIS MIND.

BURNING GIRAFFES.

DEAD ANIMALS. UNSPEAKABLE THREATS.

THE DIMENSION OF TIME, OMINOUSLY TRANSFORMED.

HE TOOK THE GREATER REALITY OF THE PARANOIAC CRITIC TO PARIS...

...AND JOINED THE RANKS OF THAT CITY'S FAMOUS ARTISTS.

IN PARIS, HE ALSO PUT THE FINAL TOUCHES ON HIS FINEST CREATION: HIMSELF.

AH, MY MUS-TACHE...

...IT IS LIKE THE ANTENNAE OF INSECTS, IT PULLS IDEAS OUT OF THE AIR...

ART WAS NOT ENOUGH FOR DALI. HE MADE FILMS...

...DESIGNED THEATER SETS...

MY MUSTACHE... IT IS THE RADAR WITH WHICH I PLUCK IDEAS FROM THE VOID.

...AND DESIGNED JEWELRY.

IN 1941, LIVING IN NEW YORK, HE TOLD THE WORLD HE WAS CHANGING.

FROM NOW ON, I SHALL BECOME CLASSIC.

AND, INDEED, HIS PAINTINGS BEGAN TO LOOK RELIGIOUS.

BUT DALI JUST MAY HAVE BEEN IN IT FOR THE MONEY. HIS "SIGNED LIMITED EDITIONS" WERE PRINTED BY THE THOUSANDS ON BLANK PAPER HE HAD SIGNED.

CALL IT A ...LITHOGRAPHIC INTERPRETATION...YEAH, A LITHOGRAPHIC INTERPRETATION.

THESE "AUTHORIZED GRAPHICS" SOLD BY THE THOUSANDS, FOR UP TO $5000 EACH.

IF PEOPLE WANT TO PRODUCE POOR REPRODUCTIONS OF MY WORK AND OTHER PEOPLE WANT TO BUY THEM...

...THEY DESERVE EACH OTHER.

HE DIED IN 1989, AT AGE 83. HIS LEGACY: THOUSANDS OF SIGNED DALIS, ALMOST WORTH THE PAPER THEY'RE PRINTED ON.

ALMOST.

140

CHAPTER SEVEN

INVENTORS AND SCIENTISTS

What's amazing about the scientific process is that sometimes it isn't a process at all. Sometimes, ideas come from thin air. Without precedent, without reason, ideas drop into the minds of inventors, scientists, and even a naturalist or two. We call it inspiration — it takes shape in the subconscious and bursts into the light of day fully formed and ready to change the world. It's a light bulb. It's an assembly line. It's a lobotomy. It's truly amazing things, thought up by truly amazing people. But inspiration has its price. Not *all* ideas are *good* ideas — and the ability to distinguish the difference, to act on the good ideas while discarding the bad, is what separates the average inventor/ scientist from the weird genius in this chapter.

Thomas Edison

...WAS THE WORLD'S MOST PROLIFIC INVENTOR, AND AN AMERICAN FOLK HERO. BUT HE WAS ALSO A ROUGH, ECCENTRIC MAN WITH LITTLE FORMAL TRAINING, WHOSE BITE WAS AS BAD AS HIS BARK.

EDISON IS PROOF THAT, IN AMERICA, ANYTHING CAN HAPPEN.

BORN IN OHIO, HE WAS A YOUNG HUSTLER--SELLING NEWSPAPERS AND SNACKS ON THE RAILROADS AS A BOY...

Chicago Tribune

...AND WORKING AS A TELE-GRAPH OPERATOR BY THE AGE OF 16.

IN BOSTON, HE REINVENTED THE STOCK MARKET TICKER, AND EARNED $40,000 DOING IT-- A FORTUNE AT THE TIME.

GAD, EDISON! HOW CAN WE THANK YOU!

MAYBE A TICKER TAPE PARADE...

EDISON PUT HIS MONEY INTO A RESEARCH LAB AT MENLO PARK, NEW JERSEY. BY 1876, HE'D ACQUIRED SCORES OF PATENTS.

A YEAR LATER HE INVENTED THE PHONOGRAPH, AND BECAME WORLD FAMOUS.

THEY AIN'T HEARD NOTHIN' YET.

THEN HE BEGAN HIS QUEST FOR AFFORDABLE ELECTRICITY. THE LIGHT BULB WOULD MAKE HIM FABULOUSLY WEALTHY.

FABULOUSLY WEALTHY.

BUT THE MAN THE PRESS CALLED THE WIZARD OF MENLO PARK HAD HIS DARK SIDE, TOO.

BORN IN MILAN, OHIO IN 1847, EDISON WAS ONE OF 7 CHILDREN. HE TOLERATED ONLY ABOUT 3 MONTHS OF GRADE SCHOOL...

...BUT COMPENSATED BY READING VORACIOUSLY.

A SEVERE CASE OF SCARLET FEVER LEFT HIM WITH PROGRESSIVE DEAFNESS.

YOU'RE GOING TO GO DEAF!

WHAT?

BY AGE 12, HE COULD HEAR A SHOUT -- BUT THE REST WAS SILENCE.

THOMAS!

THOMAS!

WHAT?

WHAT?

AS TIME WENT BY, EDISON FOUND THAT HIS DEAFNESS ALLOWED HIM TO CONCENTRATE ON SOLVING SCIENTIFIC PROBLEMS.

HE CANNOT POSSIBLY SUCCEED-- HE HAS NO FORMAL TRAINING IN MATHEMATICS OR SCIENCE!

YOU CAN SPEAK UP-- THE OAF CAN'T HEAR YOU.

EDISON DIDN'T NEED FORMAL EDUCATION; HE DID JUST FINE WITHOUT IT.

PTUI!

TING

YEP, I GOT THE ANSWER..., AND NOT WITH ANY OF THAT LONG-HAIRED THEORETICAL STUFF, NEITHER!

ONE OF THOSE LONG-HAIRS, NIKOLA TESLA, CLAIMED EDISON HAD CHEATED HIM.

BUT, MR. EDEESONE, YOU PROMEESE ME $50,000...

OH, GET OUT OF HERE, TESLA.

EDISON'S STRATEGY HAD LITTLE TO DO WITH SCIENTIFIC THEORY.

FIND A NEED AND FILL IT!

BUT SOMETIMES HE FILLED A NEED WITH SOMEBODY ELSE'S INVENTION...

...THEN SURROUNDED IT WITH A HOST OF PATENTED IMPROVEMENTS.

I AM DEMOCRACY IN ACTION!

AS FOR PEOPLE STEALING HIS STUFF....

...HE DIDN'T LIKE IT.

THOSE NICKELODEON FEATURETTES ARE BEING DONE WITH *MY* PATENTS.

GOTCHA, MR. EDISON.

P.J. McGilliwacky's Nickelodeon

CANDY

HEY! YOU CAN'T...

SEE, AN OPEN-AND-SHUT CASE OF PATENT INFRINGEMENT!

NOBODY MENTIONED THAT IMPOVERISHED BRITISH INVENTOR WILLIAM FRIESE-GREENE HAD PATENTED A MOTION-PICTURE CAMERA IN THE 1890s -- *YEARS* BEFORE EDISON INVENTED THE KINETOSCOPE.

ILL-EQUIPPED TO UNDERSTAND EXACTLY *WHAT* HE WAS INVENTING, EDISON BECAME THE EPITOME OF THE TRIAL-AND-ERROR METHOD.

PREFABRICATED HOUSES MADE OF CONCRETE-- WITH CONCRETE FURNITURE.

IF THAT AIN'T THE WAVE OF THE FUTURE...

IT WASN'T.

NEITHER WAS HIS ATTEMPT AT ANTISUBMARINE WARFARE.

DO YOU WANT TO TRY IT AGAIN?

MAGNETIC EXTRACTION OF METALS, GENTLEMEN, FROM PREVIOUSLY USELESS LOW-GRADE ORE!

IT DIDN'T WORK, BUT IT DID EXTRACT MOST OF THE MONEY HE'D MADE FROM THE LIGHT BULB.

GOLDENROD INTO SYNTHETIC RUBBER, GENTLEMEN! THE WAVE OF THE FUTURE-

-WAS WAVING GOODBYE. ANOTHER IDEA THAT BOMBED.

WELL, IT MIGHT BE INTERESTING TO COMBINE MOTION PICTURES AND SOUND.,.. BUT IRRELEVANT, I SHOULD THINK. I MEAN, WHO NEEDS BOTH?

HE WAS OFTEN WRONG, AND ALWAYS BULLHEADED -- ESPECIALLY WHERE HIS BABY, ELECTRICITY, WAS CONCERNED.

THE TROUBLE WAS, EDISON WAS AN IGNORANT SNOB. HE WAS *PROUD* OF BEING ABLE TO DO WHAT HE DID WHILE KNOWING SO LITTLE.

FROM THE DARKNESS OF MY SO-CALLED "IGNORANCE" SHINES A GENIUS THAT WILL ENLIGHTEN THE EARTH!

HE WAS MOST PROUD OF HIS SCHEME TO ELECTRIFY THE WORLD.

WE'LL NEED GENERATORS, TRANSFORMERS, A WHOLE ELECTRIFICATION SYSTEM .....AND *DIRECT CURRENT'S* THE WAY TO GO!

TESLA, AMONG OTHERS, KNEW IT WAS NOT.

BUT BOSS - THERE'S BIG LOSSES WHEN YOU TRY TO SEND DIRECT CURRENT OVER A MILE OR TWO. MAYBE WE SHOULD TRY ALTERNATING CURRENT?

YOU'RE FIRED!

FOR EDISON, ALTERNATING CURRENT BECAME THE DEVIL.

I KNOW I'M RIGHT, DAMMIT!

HIS COMPETITOR, GEORGE WESTINGHOUSE, THOUGHT NOT, AND WENT FOR A-C.

GENTLEMEN, A-C EMPLOYS DANGEROUSLY HIGH VOLTAGE -- THAT'S WHY IT'S USED TO POWER THE ELECTRIC CHAIR! NO, THE EDISON GENERAL ELECTRIC COMPANY IS STAYING WITH D-C - THE WAVE OF THE FUTURE!

HE CAMPAIGNED AGAINST ALTERNATING CURRENT AS BEING UNSAFE.

WHEN HE LOST, HE LOST BIG.

The New York Times
...STINGHOUSE WINS
...GARA CONTRACT
...DISON'S D-C DEFEATED

I'VE BEEN OUTHOUSED BY WESTINGHOUSE!

UP UNTIL HIS DEATH IN 1931, EDISON CONTINUED TO DISDAIN INTELLECTUALS, THEORISTS, AND HIS DETRACTORS.

TO HECK WITH THOSE LONG-HAIRS!

HE VIRTUALLY INVENTED THE BASIC RESEARCH LABORATORY. SOME SAY HE INVENTED THE MILITARY-INDUSTRIAL COMPLEX.

FIND A NEED...

HE WAS THE FATHER OF INVENTION, CERTAINLY, WITH MORE THAN 1,000 PATENTS. BUT WHAT MIGHT HE HAVE CREATED WITH A BETTER GRASP OF MATH AND SCIENCE?

...AND FILL IT!

WHEN THE ELECTRONIC TWINS, ELECTRICITY AND MAGNETISM, RULED AS NATURE'S MOST INTERESTING MYSTERIES, ONLY ONE MAN REALLY SEEMED TO UNDERSTAND THEM: THE ELECTRIFYING GENIUS NAMED: **NIKOLA TESLA!**

BORN IN 1856 IN SMILJAN IN WHAT WAS ONCE YUGOSLAVIA, THE SERBIAN SAVANT WAS THE SICKLY SON OF AN ORTHODOX PRIEST.

STARS?

YOUNG NIKOLA SAW A LOT OF THINGS... FLASHES OF LIGHT...

...AND INVENTIONS IN PRECISE DETAIL.

IF IT NEVER EXISTED, WHAT DO YOU CALL IT?

HIS PHOTOGRAPHIC MEMORY STORED THESE MENTAL BLUEPRINTS.

TRAINED AS AN ELECTRICAL ENGINEER, HE GOT A JOB WITH A HUNGARIAN TELEGRAPH COMPANY.

A BEAUTIFUL DAY, EH, JACOB? THE SUN SO BRIGHT.

ONE DAY, WALKING IN A BUDAPEST PARK WITH A FRIEND...

THE AIR SO FRESH AND... AND...UM...

QUICK, JACOB... FETCH ME A STICK!

ROTATING MAGNETIC FIELDS... INDUCTION...

...ALTERNATING ELECTRICAL CURRENT...

...IT WILL POWER THE WORLD!

BUT NOT FROM HUNGARY.

IN 1884, TESLA CAME TO THE UNITED STATES WITH FOUR CENTS IN HIS POCKET...

AMERIKA!

...AND SOON FOUND WORK AT INVENTOR THOMAS EDISON'S FAMOUS LAB.

I CAN HELP THIS FELLOW.

WITH GREAT PRIDE, EDISON INTRODUCED TESLA TO HIS DIRECT CURRENT DYNAMO.

MR. TESLA, MEET THE FUTURE.

THE FUTURE? IT IS MORE LIKE ANCIENT HISTORY.

TESLA AND EDISON MIXED. LIKE OIL AND WATER.

YOU PROMISED ME $50,000 TO FIX UP YOUR DYNAMO!

YOU'RE CRAZY!

SOON EDISON WAS ELECTRIFYING NEW YORK WITH DIRECT CURRENT. THE STREETS WERE FULL OF RELAY STATIONS.

BUT TESLA KNEW THE FUTURE BELONGED TO A-C, WHICH COULD BE GENERATED AT HIGH VOLTAGES AND TRANSMITTED OVER LONG DISTANCES.

THAT EDISON IS A SAVAGE!

AND THERE WAS LITTLE LOVE LOST BETWEEN THE TWO INVENTORS.

I QUIT!

YOU'RE FIRED!

MEANWHILE, IN PITTSBURGH, PA, ELECTRICAL TYCOON GEORGE WESTINGHOUSE HAD HIS OWN ELECTRIFYING NOTIONS.

I MUST MEET THIS TESLA CHAP.

WELL, SIR, I GET YOUR ALTERNATING CURRENT PATENT RIGHTS AND YOU GET $70,000-- PLUS $2.50 FOR EVERY HORSE- POWER OF ELECTRICITY WE GENERATE. YOU'RE GOING TO BE A VERY WEALTHY MAN, MR. TESLA.

THE DEAL IGNITED A TITANIC STRUGGLE.

EDISON CLAIMED ALTERNATING CURRENT WAS DEADLY AND ARRANGED FOR IT TO BE USED TO POWER NEW YORK'S NEW ELECTRIC CHAIR.

NOT WESTINGHOUSING! PLEASE DON'T WESTINGHOUSE ME!

WESTINGHOUSE SURVIVED THE ELECTRIC CHAIR ALBATROSS. BY 1896, NIAGARA FALLS HAD BEEN TURNED INTO AN A-C GENERATOR.

THE WESTINGHOUSE DEAL WAS TOO SWEET FOR TESLA TO ENDURE. HE CASHED OUT OF THE DEAL FOR $216,000-STILL A FORTUNE IN THAT DAY.

TESLA LIVED IN AN APART- MENT AT THE WALDORF- ASTORIA HOTEL, WHERE HE'D BECOME FAMOUS IN OTHER WAYS.

AS HIS SCIENTIFIC CONTRIBUTIONS INCREASED, SO DID HIS ECCENTRICITIES.

HE WAS SO AFRAID OF GERMS, THAT HE REFUSED TO SHAKE HANDS.

AH, TESLA! A PLEASURE TO MEET YOU. HOW DO YOU DO?

KEEP IT TO YOURSELF.

HE FEARED WOMEN WEARING PEARL EARRINGS. NO ONE KNOWS WHY.

PREFERRING NUMBERS DIVISIBLE BY 3, TESLA POLISHED EACH MEAL'S SILVERWARE WITH 18 FRESH NAPKINS... AND CALCULATED THE EXACT AMOUNT OF EACH MORSEL OF FOOD BEFORE EATING IT.

BUT HE REMAINED A MASTER SHOWMAN. HIS NEW YORK LAB WAS A SCIENTIFIC CIRCUS.

DON'T TRY THIS AT HOME.

ONE OF HIS INVENTIONS, THE TESLA COIL, IS STILL USED IN MODERN ELECTRONICS.

IN 1898 HE DEMONSTRATED HIS "TELEAUTOMATIC" ROBOT BOAT IN MADISON SQUARE GARDEN.

IN THE FUTURE, ROBOTS WILL DO ALL THE WORK FOR US.

IN HIS COLORADO SPRINGS LAB, TESLA PLAYED WITH HEAVENLY FIRE, CREATING GENERATORS THAT WOULD TRANSMIT ELECTRICITY ACROSS SPACE.

WITH POWER LIKE THIS, WHO NEEDS WIRES?

SOME SAID TESLA HAD INVENTED A DEATH RAY THAT COULD SHOOT DOWN BOMBERS HUNDREDS OF MILES AWAY.

HE TALKED ABOUT COSMIC RAYS BEFORE ANYONE KNEW THEY EXISTED.

AH. A NEW IDEA FOR AN INVENTION COMES TO ME. PERHAPS I SHOULD ATTEMPT TO DEVELOP IT...

HOW DID HE KNOW SO MUCH? SIMPLE, TO SOME WHO SAID HE WAS FROM VENUS.

--OR PERHAPS I'LL JUST PHONE HOME FOR THE SOLUTION.

BACKED BY FINANCIER J.P. MORGAN, TESLA BEGAN TO BUILD THE FIRST TRANS-OCEANIC RADIO TRANSMITTER ON LONG ISLAND.

SORRY, TESLA... I JUST CAN'T PAY FOR ANY MORE OF THIS.

SO...MARCONI WINS.

LOOKS LIKE MARCONI GOT THE JUMP ON YOU.

MARCONI IS A GOOD FELLOW. LET HIM CONTINUE. HE IS USING 17 OF MY PATENTS.

TESLA LATER SUED MARCONI FOR PATENT INFRINGEMENT—AND WON. BUT, IRONICALLY, CREDIT FOR INVENTING RADIO REMAINED WITH THE ITALIAN.

IN FACT, TESLA BECAME THE PRISONER OF HIS OWN ODDNESS. HE STOPPED PATENTING HIS INVENTIONS.

NO LONGER ABLE TO AFFORD THE WALDORF, HE ROAMED THE CITY AT NIGHT, FEEDING PIGEONS.

THE RECLUSIVE INVENTOR SOUGHT DARKNESS IN THE CITY HE HAD GIVEN LIGHT.

IN 1943, THE YEAR THE SUPREME COURT RULED THAT TESLA, NOT MARCONI, INVENTED THE RADIO TRANSMITTER, THE 87-YEAR-OLD VISIONARY DIED IN HIS SLEEP.

HENRY FORD

...THE PIONEER AUTOMAKER, CHANGED THE 20TH CENTURY BY BUILDING THE FIRST AFFORDABLE, GASOLINE-POWERED CAR--HIS VENERABLE, ETERNAL MODEL T.

HE ALSO CHANGED HIS IMAGE, FROM HAYSEED TO GIANT-KILLER--AND BACK AGAIN.

WHEN HE WON THE BATTLE TO BUILD CARS AGAINST COMPETITORS WHO HELD CRUCIAL PATENT RIGHTS, HE LOOKED LIKE A CHAMPION FOR THE COMMON MAN.

YOU CAN'T STOP FREE ENTERPRISE.

TRIMMING SHIFTS TO 8 HOURS AND PAYING $5 A DAY--TWICE THE GOING RATE--FORD LOOKED LIKE ONE OF LABOR'S FOLK HEROES.

WHEN HE BUILT THE BIG ROUGE RIVER PLANT IN 1927, HE SEEMED LIKE A PROPHET OF INDUSTRY.

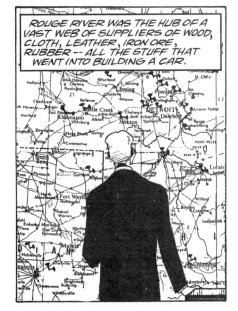

ROUGE RIVER WAS THE HUB OF A VAST WEB OF SUPPLIERS OF WOOD, CLOTH, LEATHER, IRON ORE, RUBBER -- ALL THE STUFF THAT WENT INTO BUILDING A CAR.

AT ROUGE RIVER, RAW IRON ORE ARRIVING ON A BARGE WOULD BECOME PART OF A MODEL T JUST 28 HOURS LATER.

THAT'S RIGHT, EDSEL MY SON. JUST 28 HOURS, HOW ABOUT THAT?

RIGHT ABOUT CARS, FORD BEGAN TO THINK HE WAS RIGHT ABOUT EVERYTHING ELSE, TOO.

HE BECAME INCREASINGLY CON- CERNED ABOUT HOW HIS WORKERS SPENT THEIR FREE TIME.

PLAIN THINGS FOR PLAIN PEOPLE.

FORD THOUGHT SQUARE DANCING COULD SAVE AMERICA FROM THE LOOSE MORALS AND BAD THINKING THAT THREATENED IT.

RABIDLY ANTI-INTELLECTUAL, FORD HAD HIS RADIO STATION AIR SIMPLE ESSAYS FOR THE SIMPLE FOLK HE EMPLOYED.

AND NOW, ANOTHER PLAIN STORY FOR YOU PLAIN PEOPLE...

HISTORY IS MORE OR LESS BUNK.

WITH A VIEW LIKE THAT, IT WAS NATURAL THAT FORD TAKE ON AMERICAN FOREIGN POLICY.

HE WAS VIRULENTLY OPPOSED TO U.S. ENTRANCE INTO WORLD WAR I.

NO WAR IN EUROPE

WILL WE LET A CONSPIRACY OF INTERNATIONAL MONEYLENDERS DRAG US INTO WAR...?

AMERICANS IN AMERICA

STAY OUT OF EUROPE

KEEP OUR BOYS HOME

AND HE HAD A SOLUTION, AS ALWAYS.

WHILE THE BOYS FOUGHT FOR THEIR LIVES IN THE TRENCHES--

--FORD PROPOSED THE DIPLOMATS BE PUT ON A PEACE SHIP, NOT TO RETURN TO SHORE UNTIL A PEACE WAS REACHED.

VERY WELL, BARON. I'LL SEE YOUR REGIMENT AND RAISE YOU A DIVISION.

TOO RICH FOR ME, I'M OUT.

NEIN, YOU IS IN.

THE IDEA WAS WIDELY RIDICULED, ALONG WITH ITS CREATOR.

GOOD GAWD, HAVE YOU READ WHAT THAT HAY- SEED FORD'S UP TO NOW?

THE PEACE SHIP. WHAT NEXT? PUT ALL THE DIPLOMATS IN A CAVE?

HE HATED THE MEN WHO MADE FUN OF HIM. HE HATED THEIR OLD MONEY, THEIR OLD NAMES.

JEALOUS, THAT'S ALL.

BUT THERE WERE THINGS HE HATED EVEN MORE.

HE HATED UNIONS SO MUCH...

...THAT HE THREATENED TO CLOSE HIS DOORS IN 1941, WHEN THEY WERE VOTED IN.

I WON'T HAVE IT, CLOSE THE PLANT.

COOLER HEADS PREVAILED.

BUT MOST OF ALL, HE HATED JEWS.

LIKE HITLER, HE BELIEVED THE WORLD'S ILLS STEMMED FROM A CONSPIRACY OF "INTERNATIONAL JEWS."

The Ford International Weekly

THE DEARBORN INDEPENDENT

Dearborn, Michigan,

| Jewish World Conspiracy Revealed | Protocols of the Elders of Zion |

Fighting the Devil in Modern Babylon

First of a series of articles on New York by Rev. Dr. John Roach Straton

Jewish Jazz—Moron Music—Becomes

Our National Music

Story of "Popular Song" Control in the United States

IN HIS DEARBORN, MICHIGAN, NEWS-PAPER, FORD PUBLISHED THE PROTO-COLS OF THE ELDERS OF ZION, A FALSE JEWISH MANIFESTO CONCEIVED BY THE ANTI-SEMITIC CZAR NICHOLAS MORE THAN HALF A CENTURY EARLIER.

THE OUTCRY WAS SO DEVASTATING THAT FORD HAD TO APOLOGIZE. HE SOLD HIS NEWSPAPER.

I'M SORRY THERE WAS A JEWISH CONSPIRACY. UH, WHAT I MEANT WAS...

IN 1943 HIS ONLY SON, EDSEL, DIED, AND FORD RETURNED TO HIS COMPANY'S HELM FOR A TIME.

WHEN HE DIED AT HOME IN 1947, AGED 84, HE HAD AN AXE NEARBY.

FORD HAD ALWAYS CARRIED THE AXE WHEN HE WALKED AROUND HIS ESTATE. FOR-EVER LOCKED OUT OF THE WORLD HE'D HELPED CREATE...

...HE HAD A PHOBIA ABOUT BEING LOCKED OUT OF HIS OWN HOUSE.

153

EDWARD LEEDSKALNIN

...A LATVIAN EMIGRE, HE BUILT A BIZARRE STRUCTURE IN FLORIDA IN THE 1920s AND '30s - A CASTLE MADE AND FURNISHED ENTIRELY OUT OF SEA CORAL.

HE BEGAN BUILDING HIS DREAM HOUSE IN 1920 NEAR FLORIDA CITY...

...THEN TRUCKED IT ALL TO HOMESTEAD, FLORIDA, WHERE IT STANDS TODAY.

WHAT'RE YOU GONNA DO WITH ALL THIS CORAL?

BUILD A PALACE ACCORDING TO THE ANCIENT EGYPTIAN LAWS OF MAGNETISM, OF COURSE.

LATER, HE WOULD SAY HE'D BUILT IT FOR A MYSTERIOUS WOMAN...

FOR YOU... BELOVED...

BUT WAS SHE REAL, OR JUST A GHOSTLY MUSE?

EITHER WAY, HER MONUMENT WAS SOLID ENOUGH.

WORKING ALONE, HE SOMEHOW QUARRIED SLABS OF CORAL WEIGHING UP TO 3 TONS...

...AND MOVED THEM INTO POSITION.

I ALONE KNOW THE SECRETS OF THE PYRAMIDS.

GRADUALLY, HIS STRANGE EDIFICE ROSE ABOVE ITS 3-ACRE SITE: A CORAL CASTLE.

THE SELF-TAUGHT ARCHITECT AND ENGINEER LIVED AND STUDIED IN A ROUGH SHACK HE BUILT ON THE GROUNDS.

HE EXPERIMENTED WITH MAGNETISM AND ELECTRICITY, KEEPING HIS NOTES IN A CRYPTIC JOURNAL.

HE ALSO RECORDED HIS UNCON-VENTIONAL BUILDING TECHNIQUES.

WAS HE PRACTICING ENGINEERING OR EGYPTIAN MAGIC? MYSTICAL SYMBOLS WERE REPEATED THROUGHOUT THE CASTLE.

THIS SYMBOLISM OBVIOUSLY HELD DEEP MEANING FOR LEEDSKALNIN.

HE BUILT A HUGE CORAL WHEEL — HIS "SUNCOUCH" — TO TRACK THE SUN'S MOVEMENTS.

WITH ITS GIANT THRONES, 8-FOOT-LONG CORAL BEDS, AND A CONFERENCE TABLE CUT IN THE SHAPE OF FLORIDA, THE CASTLE BECAME A TOURIST ATTRACTION.

I AM DELIGHTED TO SHOW VISITORS MY WORK... DELIGHTED...

FOR DECADES, LEEDSKALNIN CONTINUED RECORDING HIS SECRET STUDIES OF MAGNETISM AND MONUMENT CONSTRUCTION

SOMEDAY, MY DISCOVERIES WILL CHANGE THE WORLD!

IN 1951, LEEDSKALNIN DIED OF MALNUTRITION AT THE AGE OF 67.

SHORTLY AFTER HIS DEATH, HIS NOTEBOOKS MYSTERIOUSLY DISAPPEARED. LIKE CORAL CASTLE ITSELF, LEEDSKALNIN'S THEORIES REMAIN INEXPLICABLE.

DURING THE FORTIES AND FIFTIES AN AMERICAN NEUROLOGIST LED THE WAY IN USING *SURGERY* TO CURE *PSYCHOLOGICAL* PROBLEMS. BY SEVERING A NERVE OR TWO IN THE FRONTAL LOBES OF THE BRAIN, HE PERFORMED THE INFAMOUS *FRONTAL LOBOTOMY.* HIS NAME...?

WALTER FREEMAN

THOSE OLD MENTAL DEVILS...

WHIRRRRRRRRRR

BEFORE

...COULD JUST BE *SCRAPED* AWAY.

AFTER!

FREEMAN DIDN'T INVENT THE LOBOTOMY. *THAT* HONOR GOES TO THE *PORTUGUESE* NEUROLOGIST *DR. ANTONIO DE EGAS MONIZ,* WHO GOT THE IDEA IN 1935.

HE FOUND THAT, WITH A ROTATING DEVICE RESEMBLING AN *APPLE CORER,*...

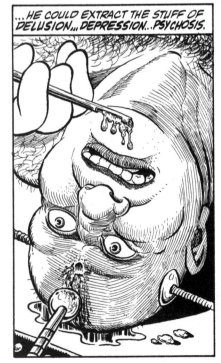

...HE COULD EXTRACT THE STUFF OF *DELUSION....DEPRESSION...PSYCHOSIS.*

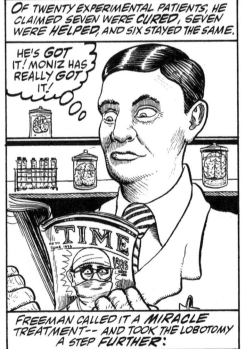

OF TWENTY EXPERIMENTAL PATIENTS, HE CLAIMED SEVEN WERE *CURED,* SEVEN WERE *HELPED,* AND SIX STAYED THE SAME.

HE'S *GOT* IT! MONIZ HAS REALLY *GOT* IT!

TIME

FREEMAN CALLED IT A *MIRACLE TREATMENT--* AND TOOK THE LOBOTOMY A STEP *FURTHER:*

HE REPLACED THE "CORER" WITH WHAT HIS COLLEAGUES CALLED HIS *"GOLD-PLATED ICE PICK"--* A LONG, THIN, POINTED BRAIN-SCRAPER, CARRIED IN ITS OWN VELVET CASE.

Dr. WALTER FREEM

ADMINISTERING A LOCAL ANESTHETIC, FREEMAN *STUCK* HIS ICE PICK...

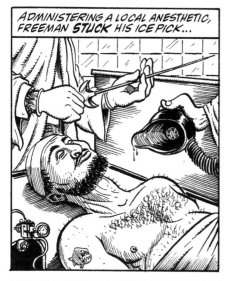

...THROUGH AN *EYE-SOCKET*...

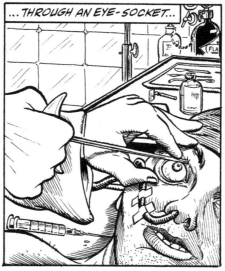

...AND INTO THE *BRAIN*, WHERE HE BLINDLY SCRAPED AWAY.

EACH LOBOTOMY COST ABOUT $1,000-- ALTHOUGH FREEMAN SOMETIMES DID *ASSEMBLY-LINE LOBOTOMIES*--

--FOR $25 BUCKS A *HEAD!*

FREEMAN PERFORMED AT *LEAST* 3,500 LOBOTOMIES. HIS AMERICAN COLLEAGUES, USING VARIOUS CUTTING TECHNIQUES, DID SOME *40,000 MORE!* THOUSANDS MORE WERE DONE ABROAD...

...IT WAS THE *TREATMENT OF CHOICE!*

TROUBLE WAS, LOBOTOMIES LEFT MANY PATIENTS *WORSE OFF* THAN BEFORE!

DEEP APATHY AND MENTAL IMPAIRMENT OFTEN FOLLOWED A LOBOTOMY.

PSYCHOSURGERY FELL FROM FAVOR IN THE LATE 1950s.

AS FOR THE FATHER OF THE LOBOTOMY-- *TWO* GOOD THINGS HAPPENED. IN 1949, ANTONIO DE EGAS MONIZ RECEIVED THE *NOBEL PRIZE*...

...AND IN 1955 HE WAS *BEATEN TO DEATH* IN HIS OFFICE BY A DERANGED *PATIENT!*

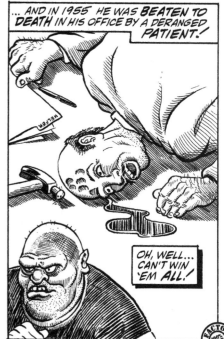

OH, WELL... CAN'T WIN 'EM *ALL!*

IN 1779, ALL PARIS -- WELL, THE RICHER PART OF IT -- WAS *ELECTRIFIED* BY A NEWLY ARRIVED HEALER FROM AUSTRIA, A MAGICALLY GIFTED PHYSICIAN NAMED...

FRANZ ANTON MESMER

IT SEEMED AS IF HE COULD CURE ANYTHING WITH A TOUCH OF HIS WAND.

MY HEADACHE -- IT'S GONE!

I MERELY ACTIVATE A HEALING CURRENT IN THE BODY -- ANIMAL MAGNETISM, AS I CALL IT.

C'EST REMARKABLE!

HIS CLIENTELE WAS THE BEST: QUEEN MARIE ANTOINETTE...

...THE POWER-FUL DUKE OF BOURBON...

EVEN THE AMERICANS' HERO, THE MARQUIS DE LAFAYETTE.

HIS PATIENTS WOULD SIT AROUND A COVERED TUB OF SULFURIC ACID, CALLED A BAQUET, AND GRIP PRO-TRUDING IRON RODS.

A PIANO WOULD PLAY SOFTLY IN THE BACK-GROUND...

...AND THEN MESMER WOULD MAKE HIS ENTRANCE.

CLAD IN A PURPLE ROBE, HE WOULD TOUCH HIS PATIENTS WITH HIS SO-CALLED MAGIC WAND.

HIS PATIENTS WOULD RESPOND WITH SHRIEKS OF LAUGHTER...

OH, DOCTOR... ≥TEE HEE!≥

...OR FITS OF HYSTERICAL TEARS...

IT'S ≥SOB≥ SO WONDERFUL...

...OR SIMPLY WITH CONVULSIONS.

WHEW! I NEEDED THAT, MESMER.

MON PLAISIR M. LAFAYETTE.

TO MANY, IT FELT LIKE A CURE.

BUT NOT TO KING LOUIS XVI.

THE KING BELIEVES ME TO BE A FRAUD.

LOUIS CONVENED A PANEL OF EXPERTS, INCLUDING AMERICAN AMBASSADOR BENJAMIN FRANKLIN, A PIONEER OF ELECTRICITY.

IT IS ALL IN THEIR MINDS.

AS THE PATIENTS OF M. MESMER RESPOND ONLY WHEN THEY ARE PERSUADED THEY HAVE BEEN "MAGNETIZED," WE CONCLUDE THAT ANIMAL MAGNETISM IS MERE-LY SUGGESTIVE -- AND A FRAUD.

IT SLOWED MESMER... BUT DIDN'T BRING HIM DOWN.

HE HAPPILY CONTINUED HIS PRACTICE...,

...BELIEVING THAT WHAT HE WAS DOING WAS PHYSICAL.

WHAT SCIENCE COULD NOT SQUELCH, POLITICS NOW DESTROYED.

MON DIEU!

THE REVOLUTION REMOVED MANY OF THE TETES THAT HAD ATTENDED MESMER'S LITTLE TETE-A-TETES AROUND THE BAQUET.

MESMER FLED FIRST TO ENGLAND, THEN RETURNED TO VIENNA.

BUT HE WAS RUINED.

HIS WEALTHY CLIENTS GONE, HE WAS FORCED TO INTRO-DUCE HIS METHODS TO THE PENNILESS MASSES.

HE ENDED HIS DAYS IN 1815, ON THE SHORES OF LAKE CONSTANCE, WHERE HE'D BEGUN 81 YEARS BEFORE.

WHAT WENT WRONG?

CURIOUSLY, HE NEVER UNDER-STOOD THAT MESMERISM HAD NOTHING TO DO WITH MAGNETISM, ANIMAL OR OTHERWISE, OR WITH HEALING.

WHAT WENT WRONG?

TODAY WE CALL IT HYPNOSIS.

...YOU ARE FEELING VERY TIRED...YOUR EYELIDS WEIGH A METRIC TON...

MESMER DIED NOT KNOWING WHAT THE PHENOMENON HE'D CREATED REALLY WAS.

LORD MONBODDO

...AKA JAMES BURNETT, WAS ONE OF 18TH-CENTURY SCOTLAND'S DISTINGUISHED JUDGES, AMATEUR ANTHROPOLOGISTS, AND CLASSICAL SCHOLARS, A STAR IN EDINBURGH (THE SO-CALLED ATHENS OF THE NORTH).

MONBODDO WAS ONE OF THE FIRST TO FIND SCIENTIFIC SIGNIFICANCE IN THE FACT THAT HUMANS LOOK SOMETHING LIKE APES.

HE'D SEEN TWO ORANGUTANS IN LONDON, AND HAD ONCE GONE TO PARIS TO SEE A STUFFED CHIMP.

BUT... IT'S SO OBVIOUS!

THERE WERE ALSO STORIES OF APES USING TOOLS...

...AND OF ORANGUTANS LUSTING AFTER HUMAN FEMALES.

OOGA! OOGA!

THESE POOR DEVILS ARE SIMPLY TRAPPED FURTHER DOWN THE GREAT CHAIN OF BEING.

THE "GREAT CHAIN OF BEING" WAS A HIERARCHY OF PERFECTION. PROTOZOA WERE THE BOTTOM, HUMANS THE TOP.

THE TROUBLE, MONBODDO DECIDED, WAS THAT RANK ON THE GREAT CHAIN WAS DETERMINED BY LANGUAGE-- AND THE APES HAD NONE.

THEY'RE EQUIPPED TO SPEAK-- BUT THEIR SIMPLE LIFE DOES NOT REQUIRE IT.

ORANGUTAN?

IT'S CLEAR TO ME THAT EVOLUTION MUST TAKE US TOWARD EVER GREATER MENTAL PERFECTION.

ONCE ALL HUMANS WERE PHYSICALLY AND INTELLECTUALLY IDEAL.

IN THE MONBODDO SCHEME OF THINGS, ANCIENT GREEK WARRIOR ACHILLES WOULD HAVE STOOD SOME 14 FEET TALL.

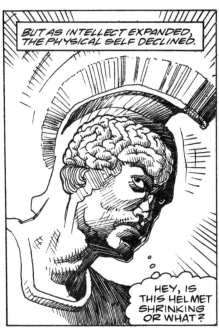

BUT AS INTELLECT EXPANDED, THE PHYSICAL SELF DECLINED.

HEY, IS THIS HELMET SHRINKING OR WHAT?

A PUNY 4-FEET-SOMETHING TALL, MONBODDO SEEMED LIVING PROOF OF HIS THEORY...

...BUT HE TRIED TO STAY PHYSICAL. FOR EXAMPLE, HE DID THE 400 MILES FROM EDINBURGH TO LONDON IN A WEEK, ON HORSE-BACK, NO MATTER WHAT THE WEATHER.

LONDON
350
EDINBURGH
50

WELL, DOBBIN, ONLY ANOTHER 350 TO GO!

CURIOUSLY, A CENTURY BEFORE DARWIN "DISCOVERED" EVOLUTION, MONBODDO'S THEORIES WERE TREATED WITH BEMUSED RESPECT.

WELL, OF COURSE, THE APE THING...

AH, HO HO, THEREBY HANGS A TALE...

STILL, THEY LAUGHED AT HIM.

MONBODDO BELIEVED HE'D STUMBLED UPON MANKIND'S DIRTY LITTLE SECRET. WE WERE BORN WITH TAILS...

...THAT A CONSPIRACY OF MIDWIVES SECRETLY REMOVED.

IN FACT, HUMANS WITH SHORT TAILS ARE BORN ALL THE TIME. MAYBE LORD MONBODDO HIMSELF...

BUT, NO... WE MUST PUT SUCH SUSPICIONS BEHIND US.

IF YOU GOT IT, FLAUNT IT.

TO THE OJIBWA, HIS ADOPTIVE TRIBE, HE WAS "WA-SHA-QUON-ASIA"-- HE WHO FLIES BY NIGHT.

BUT A DOTING WORLD CAME TO KNOW HIM AS THE GREAT NATIVE-AMERICAN NATURALIST CALLED...

GREY OWL

RUMORED TO BE THE BLUE-EYED SON OF A SCOTTISH FATHER AND APACHE MOM, GREY OWL FIRST APPEARED IN THE NORTH WOODS IN 1906, AGED 18.

HE EARNED A LIVING AS A HUNTER AND TRAPPER, TAKING TO IT LIKE A BORN WOODSMAN.

A CLEAN KILL!

HE LIVED FOR YEARS WITH HIS OJIBWA WIFE, ANGELE, UNTIL:

THEY SAY WE'RE AT WAR WITH GERMANY!

THE NEWS WAS ALL THE EXCUSE HIS RESTLESS SPIRIT NEEDED. SOON HE WENT FROM HUNTING GROUND TO BATTLEGROUND.

HE BECAME A HUNTER OF MEN: A SNIPER.

A DIRTY KIND OF JOB.

THE EXPERIENCE OF WAR SICKENED GREY OWL AND, DISENCHANTED WITH THE MODERN WORLD, HE RETURNED HOME.

AT LEAST HERE I KILL TO EAT!

BUT HIS ISOLATED HAPPINESS WAS SHORT-LIVED. WITH HIS SECOND WIFE, THE IROQUOIS WOMAN ANAHAREO, GREY OWL FLED THE ADVANCE OF CIVILIZATION.

WHILE HE HAD ABANDONED CIVILIZATION, CIVILIZATION-- IN THE FORM OF THE MINING AND TIMBER INDUSTRIES-- WAS SLOWLY DESTROYING HIS NATURAL PARADISE.

THEN, IN THE WINTER OF 1928-1929, HE FOUND HIS CALLING.

A BEAVER... MURDERED BY MAN'S CRUELTY.

MEW, MEW.

BUT, AT LEAST I CAN SAVE HER BABIES.

MEW, MEW.

WITHIN MONTHS, THE TWO BEAVER CUBS HAD BECOME PART OF THE FAMILY.

IT'S MONSTROUS TO KILL SUCH CREATURES. I WILL HAVE NO MORE OF IT.

HE VOWED TO RESTORE THE OVER HUNTED ANIMALS TO THE CANADIAN WILDS.

GREY OWL'S WILDERNESS HOME, LIKE HIS NAME, WAS ADOPTED. IN REALITY HE WAS ARCHIE BELANEY, REARED BY HIS AUNTS IN THE BRITISH TOWN OF HASTINGS.

ARCHIE! ARCHIE!

AT 18, ARCHIE HAD PERSUADED HIS AUNTS TO SEND HIM TO TORONTO, TO STUDY FARMING ..., OR SO HE SAID.

DON'T WORRY, AUNT. I'LL BE HOME IN NO TIME.

BUT HE DIDN'T SEE TORONTO. HE HEADED FOR THE NORTH WOODS AND THE OJIBWA INDIANS.

HE NEVER LOOKED BACK. HIS WORK WITH THE BEAVERS MADE HIM WORLD FAMOUS, AND MUCH IN DEMAND AS A SPEAKER.

LET ME TELL YOU ABOUT MY BEAVER COLONY BACK HOME...,

HIS FANS INCLUDED ENGLAND'S FUTURE QUEEN.

OH, DO GO ON!

BUT IT DIDN'T LAST...

WORN OUT, HE DIED IN 1938, AGED 50, OF PNEUMONIA.

A DAY AFTER HIS DEATH, A FELLOW NATURALIST TOLD THE WORLD THAT GREY OWL HAD BEEN ARCHIE BELANEY ALL ALONG.

FACTOID BOOKS

CHAPTER EIGHT

TYCOONS AND MILLIONAIRES

The old adage says that money is the root of all evil. And perhaps, in rational hands, that's true. But money in the hands of a true weirdo is another thing entirely. There, cash is simply the means to an end... and the end is invariably strange. Take Stephen Tennant (*page 168*) who used his fortune to spend decades literally lying in the lap of luxury. Or newspaper tycoon William Randolph Hearst (*page 178*), an unbridled consumerist who filled his palatial estate with more treasure and art than any museum. Or Sarah Winchester (*page 176*), who spent millions building room after room onto her home to try to avoid the assault of angry spirits. Or the king of moneyed crackpots, Howard Hughes (*page 184*), who spent millions developing a plane that never flew. What's obvious from these weirdos' stories is that money couldn't buy them happiness; but it should also be noted that an excess of cash certainly made their misery more tolerable.

MAD JACK MYTTON!

SQUIRE MYTTON, LORD OF HALSTON MANOR IN SHROPSHIRE, WAS 18TH-CENTURY ENGLAND'S HARDEST-RIDING, HARDEST-DRINKING -- AND HARDEST-HEADED -- WASTREL, HEIR TO A VAST FORTUNE, BUT TOO OPEN-HANDED, AND PERHAPS TOO FOOLISH, TO KEEP IT.

HE WAS KNOWN AS MAD JACK.

HIS EXCESSES WERE LEGEND-- 8 BOTTLES OF PORT WINE A DAY, PUNCTUATED WITH LIBERAL DOSES OF BRANDY... GALLONS OF BRANDY.

IT IS SAID THAT HE HAD 3000 SHIRTS AND 1000 HATS.

HE GAMBLED LIKE HE DRANK-- WITH WILD ABANDON, AND BADLY.

...AND I RAISE YOU A THOUSAND GUINEAS, SIR.

HE LIKED A PRANK NOW AND THEN...

EASY DOES IT, NOW, NELL, MY GIRL, EASY DOES IT.

...EVEN WHEN IT BACKFIRED.

OUCH!

GOOD GOD, NELL!

OUCH!

HE LOVED ALL LIVING THINGS, ESPECIALLY HIS ANIMALS -- HIS BEAR, HIS DOZENS OF CATS, HIS HUNDREDS OF DOGS.

BUT HORSES WERE HIS THING.

HE WAS KNOWN TO HAVE JUMPED HIS HORSE OFF A HOTEL'S SECOND-STORY BALCONY INTO THE STREET.

NOTHING STOPPED MAD JACK.

JACK, MIND THE FENCE!

WOT FENCE?

HIS KIND HEART COULD BE DANGEROUS.

HERE, MY BEAUTY, HAVE THIS MULLED WINE. IT'LL SET YOU BACK TO RIGHTS, IT WILL.

DAMN ME. ONLY TRYING TO HELP...

HE COULDN'T HELP HIMSELF, EITHER. WHEN HE SANK INTO DEBT, HE FLED FOR THE CONTINENT.

COME ON, JACK, PAY UP AND NOTHING NEED BE SAID.

YES, JACK, PAY UP OR BLOODY GO TO BLOODY DEBTOR'S PRISON!

DRINK PICKLED HIS REASON. HE ONCE TRIED TO CURE THE HICCUPS BY SETTING FIRE TO HIS NIGHTSHIRT.

GOOD GOD, JACK!

WELL, THE HICCUP IS GONE, BY GOD!

SO WAS MAD JACK MYTTON. ALCOHOL KILLED HIM IN 1834, AT THE AGE OF 38...

...AND, HIS SINS FORGIVEN, HE BECAME AN ENGLISH LEGEND.

Stephen Tennant

...WAS THE EMBODIMENT OF ENTROPY. ACCORDING TO HIS BIOGRAPHER, PHILLIP HOARE, TENNANT MADE A CAREER OUT OF DOING NOTHING — BUT DOING IT VERY, VERY WELL.

TENNANT WAS BORN IN ENGLAND IN 1906, THE PAMPERED SON OF PAMELA SYNDHAM, A SELF-INDULGENT ARISTOCRAT.

OH, *STEENIE*, YOU'RE *SUCH* A DARLING LITTLE THING!

"STEENIE" WAS SO DARLING THAT HIS MOTHER KEPT HIM IN SKIRTS TILL AGE 8...

...AND SO SENSITIVE! EVERY-THING WAS JUST.....TOO MUCH.

THE SIGHT OF A PANSY BLOSSOM MAKES ME ....GIDDY!

BETWEEN THE TWO WORLD WARS, YOUNG ARISTOCRATS FANCIED DRESSING UP AND PLAYING ROLES...

...BEING PHOTOGRAPHED WITH POETS LIKE SIEGFRIED SASSOON BY FAMED PHOTO-GRAPHERS SUCH AS CECIL BEATON...

SAY "FROMAGE!"

...AND ALWAYS STARTING, BUT NEVER FINISHING, A NOVEL.

I'LL CALL IT *LASCAR*, THE TALE OF A SAILOR.

AUTHOR LYTTON STRACHEY CALLED TENNANT "EXTREMELY BEAUTIFUL, BUT FRAIL BEYOND IMAGINATION."

SIR OSBERT SITWELL SAID TENNANT WAS THE BRITISH ARISTOCRACY'S "LAST PRO-FESSIONAL BEAUTY."

HE MAY ALSO HAVE BEEN THE ARISTOCRACY'S LAST GASP. WORLD WAR II MADE HIS KIND OF SELF-ABSORBED UNIVERSE OBSOLETE. HE RETIRED TO HIS FAMILY HOME, WILSFORD MANOR -- AND WENT TO BED.

BY JOVE! I LOVE THESE SATIN SHEETS!

I LOVE MY OLD *VOGUE* PHOTOS, TOO. I LOOK AT THEM IN A DREAM OF BLISS.

AS TIME PASSED, HIS SEDENTARY LIFESTYLE MADE HIM FAT.

BUT I'M *BEAUTIFUL*, AND THE MORE OF ME THERE IS, THE BETTER I LIKE IT!

NEGLECTED, HIS ESTATE WENT COMPLETELY TO SEED.

I REALLY *SHOULD* ATTEND TO THE PROPERTY... PERHAPS TOMORROW...

AND I SIMPLY *MUST* DO SOMETHING ABOUT *LASCAR* ...OR NOT...

THE LESS HE DID, THE LESS HE WANTED TO DO.

AH, I BEGIN TO FEAR MY GREAT WORK WILL NEVER BE COMPLETE.

EVENTUALLY HE SPENT ALMOST ALL HIS TIME COMPLETELY HORIZONTAL.

FRIENDS CAME TO VIEW STEPHEN IN WHAT HE CALLED HIS "DECORATIVE SECLUSION"-- THE STATE IN WHICH HE SPENT THE LAST 17 YEARS OF HIS LIFE.

IN 1987, AT THE AGE OF 81, THE CURTAIN CAME DOWN ON WHAT BIOGRAPHER HOARE HAS CALLED ENGLAND'S GREATEST WORK OF *NON*-PERFORMANCE ART.

HENRIETTA HOWLAND ROBINSON GREEN WAS ONE OF AMERICA'S RICHEST -- AND CHEAPEST -- WOMEN. IN THE EARLY 1900S PEOPLE WERE CALLING HETTY GREEN...

The WITCH of WALLSTREET

SHE STASHED HER SECURITIES IN BOXES AND TRUNKS, WHICH SHE TRUNDLED FROM ONE MANHATTAN BANK TO ANOTHER.

CHEMICAL·NATIONAL·BANK

HER PURSE RARELY HELD MORE THAN A FEW DOLLARS...

...BUT WITH DOZENS OF HIDDEN POCKETS, SHE WAS A WALKING TREASURE CHEST.

SHE HAD NO OFFICE. SHE DID BUSINESS FROM INSIDE HER VAULT IN THE CHEMICAL NATIONAL BANK.

YOU WILL HAVE TO BID HIGHER THAN THAT, SIR.

FOR LUNCH, SHE BROUGHT OUT A FEW SCRAPS OF FOOD FROM HER PURSE, OR HEATED OLD OATMEAL ON THE BANK'S RADIATOR.

BUT I AM DOING LUNCH, SIR.

HETTY GREEN HADN'T ALWAYS BEEN A WITCH. ONCE SHE'D LED A FAIRY TALE-LIKE EXISTENCE...

HER NEW BEDFORD FAMILY HAD AMASSED A FORTUNE KILLING WHALES.

PAPA!

BUT THE ROBINSONS WERE A FRUGAL LOT. HETTY WAS DOING THE ACCOUNTING BY AGE 8.

THEY'RE SPENDING TOO MUCH ON FRIVOLITIES, PAPA.

HER MOTHER DIED AND LEFT HER SOME REAL ESTATE. HER FATHER MOVED TO NEW YORK, BUT HETTY STAYED IN NEW BEDFORD...

WHAT IS AUNT SYLVIA GOING TO DO WITH HER MONEY?

...TO MAKE SURE HER AUNT SYLVIA KEPT HER FORTUNE IN THE FAMILY -- BY LEAVING IT TO HER.

WHO ELSE WOULD YOU LEAVE YOUR MONEY TO, SYLVIA? NOW...I'M GOING TO JOIN PAPA IN NEW YORK.

SHE MET AND LATER MARRIED THE WEALTHY EDWARD GREEN...

...AND BECAME SUDDENLY RICH HERSELF WHEN HER FATHER AND AUNT DIED ONLY A WEEK APART.

IN 1867, THE COUPLE SAILED FOR ENGLAND...

...WHERE THE FREE-SPENDING MR. GREEN PAID THE BILLS...

...AND HETTY BORE TWO CHILDREN, NED AND SYLVIA -- IN BETWEEN PLAYING THE LONDON MARKET.

SO SUCCESSFULLY DID SHE PARLAY HER FORTUNE, THAT UPON HER RETURN HOME SHE WAS PROCLAIMED THE QUEEN OF WALL STREET.

SHE WAS DEDICATED TO HER CHILDREN...

"...AND THEN THE LITTLE RED HEN SOLD ALL HER PENNSYLVANIA RAILROAD SHARES AND LIVED HAPPILY EVER AFTER OFF THE PROFITS.

NOW GO OUT AND PLAY, CHILDREN

...BUT THE SUBJECT OF MONEY WAS NEVER FAR FROM HER MIND.

PENNSYLVANIA RAILROAD SHARES ? PROFITS? HMm...

NED!

NED!

MAMA!

SAVING ON DOCTOR'S BILLS, HETTY TRIED TO TREAT HER INJURED SON HERSELF -- IT COST NED A LEG.

IT'S.... NOT...MY ...FAULT.

EDWARD GREEN DIED IN 1902, AND HETTY GAVE UP HIS EXTRAVAGANT LIFESTYLE AT ONCE. SHE PUT ON A NEW UNIFORM...

...THAT SHE NEVER WASHED. HETTY BECAME THE MISERLY WITCH OF WALL STREET.

NED, NOW SIX-FOUR AND 300 POUNDS, WENT TO TEXAS TO DIRECT ONE OF HIS MOTHER'S RAILROADS -- LIVING OFF HIS MEAGER ALLOWANCE.

I DON'T FEEL RICH.

HE OFTEN HAD TO BEG HIS MOTHER FOR MORE.

"DEAR MAMA, PLEASE SEND MORE $$$. LOVE, NED."

HER DAUGHTER FINALLY MARRIED. BUT HETTY HAD ALREADY SHATTERED HER SPIRIT.

I DO?

HETTY SUFFERED A STROKE IN 1916 -- SHE'D BECOME OVER-EXCITED WHILE CHIDING A FRIEND'S COOK ABOUT HER EXTRAVAGANCE IN THE KITCHEN.

SKIM MILK, NOT WHOLE... YOU... WASTREL...

NED RETURNED TO NEW YORK IN TIME FOR HIS MOTHER TO DIE IN HIS APARTMENT.

$$$

TRUE TO FORM, HETTY KEPT HER $100 MILLION OR SO IN THE FAMILY.

I'M RICH.

FOR 20 YEARS, NED LIVED LIKE A CALIPH. HE STILL HAD ABOUT $50 MILLION WHEN HE DIED...

$$$

...AND, TRUE TO FORM, HE KEPT IT IN THE FAMILY BY GIVING MOST OF IT TO SYLVIA...

...A CHILDLESS RECLUSE -- BUT NOT A MISER.

NO, MAMA!

AT THE END, SHE BROKE HER FRUGAL MOTHER'S SPELL.

SHE DIED IN 1951, AT 80 -- BUT SHE'D DONE A VERY BRAVE THING.

SYLVIA'S WILL SCATTERED THE GREEN FORTUNE TO DISTANT RELATIVES, STRANGERS, AND CHARITIES.

YIPPEE!!

MISERS ARE MADE, NOT BORN.

BERNARR MacFADDEN

FOR THE FIRST HALF OF THE 20TH CENTURY, BERNARR MACFADDEN, RULER OF A MULTIMILLION-DOLLAR MAGAZINE EMPIRE, BECAME ONE OF THE FIRST GREAT FITNESS FREAKS.

A MAN GIVEN TO PERPETUAL, VIOLENT EXERCISE, BEGINNING AS SOON AS HE AWOKE...

101, 102, 103... 104...

...HE ATE STUFF LIKE NUTS, CARROTS, AND BEET JUICE-- OR FASTED.

ORPHANED AS A CHILD, THE INDEPENDENT-MINDED MACFADDEN IN 1899 TURNED HIS EXPERIENCE--AND HIS FITNESS REGIMEN--INTO A MAGAZINE, PHYSICAL CULTURE.

OTHERS SOON FOLLOWED, AS HE EXPERTLY TAPPED THE PUBLIC'S APPETITE FOR CRIME, HEALTH FADS, AND ROMANCE.

TRUE STORIES

TRUE DETECTIVE STORIES

FICTION

SOME SAID HIS $30 MILLION EMPIRE WAS BUILT ON A FOUNDATION OF SEX AND CARROTS.

NON-SENSE.

HE MARRIED FOUR TIMES, ONCE TO THE WINNER OF HIS "GREAT BRITAIN'S PERFECT WOMAN" CONTEST.

I WANT YOU TO BE AN EXAMPLE OF MY WORK AND A CREDIT TO ME.

AYE, DUCKY.

SHE SOON TIRED OF CALIS-THENICS AT DAYBREAK, FOLLOWED BY A DAILY 10-MILE RUN.

LIKE MANY OFT-MARRIED MEN, HE THOUGHT HE UNDERSTOOD THE INSTITUTION PERFECTLY.

...AND INTERCOURSE IS FOR PROCREATION ONLY.

HE THOUGHT GRAPES CURED EVERY KIND OF CANCER.

AS FOR MONEY, HE THOUGHT IT WAS BEST BURIED.

LEGEND HOLDS THAT SOME $4 MILLION OF HIS MONEY IS STILL BURIED IN AMMO BOXES AROUND THE COUNTRY.

HE GAVE PRESS CONFERENCES STANDING ON HIS HEAD.

GRAPES, GENTLEMEN, GRAPES!

IN HIS 80s, HE BEGAN JUMPING OUT OF AIRPLANES.

GERONIMO!

HE INTENDED TO LIVE TO 120. NO ONE DOUBTED THAT HE'D MAKE IT.

BUT AT 87, IN 1955, HE CONTRACTED JAUNDICE.

IT'S NOTHING... STARVE IT OUT.

HE TRIED TO CURE IT BY FASTING -- BUT FAILED.

175

SARAH WINCHESTER

WIDOW OF WILLIAM WINCHESTER, SHE INHERITED THE FORTUNE EARNED BY HER FATHER-IN-LAW'S INVENTION -- THE WINCHESTER REPEATING RIFLE, THE GUN THAT WON THE WEST. IT MADE HER IMMENSELY WEALTHY...

...AND AFRAID. SO AFRAID THAT SHE WOULDN'T EVEN SHOW HER FACE, BUT WENT EVERYWHERE VEILED.

A SPIRIT MEDIUM HAD WARNED HER:

YOUR LOST INFANT AND YOUR HUSBAND WERE MURDERED BY THE ANGRY GHOSTS OF THOSE KILLED BY WINCHESTER RIFLES.

THOUSANDS OF ANGRY SPIRITS. THEY WILL KILL YOU, TOO, UNLESS...

YOU BEGIN BY BUILDING A HOME... AND NEVER STOP BUILDING.

STRANGE ADVICE, PERHAPS... BUT SARAH BELIEVED THE WOMAN.

SHE STARTED WITH AN 8-ROOM FARMHOUSE ON 6 ACRES NEAR SAN JOSE, CALIFORNIA.

AN ARMY OF CARPENTERS AND CRAFTSMEN WENT TO WORK...

...24 HOURS A DAY, 7 DAYS A WEEK, ANY PAUSE MIGHT LET IN THE ANGRY GHOSTS.

SARAH WAS HER OWN ARCHITECT.

WITH MONEY TO BURN, SHE USED ONLY THE FINEST MATERIALS-- GOLD, SILVER, EXOTIC WOODS AND CARPETING.

WE HAVE SOME NICE IVORY JUST IN, MA'AM.

IT TOOK ONE CARPENTER A WHOLE YEAR TO LAY AN ELABORATELY DESIGNED PARQUET FLOOR.

A STRANGE STRUCTURE EVOLVED... 160 ROOMS... 40 BEDROOMS, 13 BATHS, 40 STAIRCASES... ALL JUMBLED TOGETHER.

FLIGHTS OF 7 AND 11 STAIRS TO COVER 3 VERTICAL FEET...

...DOORS THAT OPENED ON BLANK BRICK WALLS... AND ON OPEN SPACE...

ULP!

...MORE THAN 10,000 WINDOWS, INCLUDING AN ELABORATE CIRCULAR TIFFANY WINDOW THAT WAS SIMPLY SET INTO AN INTERIOR WALL.

BUT SARAH ADDED INTERESTING INNOVATIONS, TOO. FOR EXAMPLE, CALIFORNIA'S FIRST AUTOMATIC ELEVATOR.

IN SEPTEMBER 1922, SARAH WINCHESTER DIED. 38 YEARS AND SOME $5 MILLION AFTER IT BEGAN...

THE FRENETIC BUILDING FINALLY CEASED.

177

WILLIAM RANDOLPH HEARST

...TURNED A MINING FORTUNE INTO A PUBLISHING EMPIRE THAT BROUGHT HIM AN ESTIMATED $12 MILLION A YEAR AND GAVE HIM ENORMOUS POWER.

HE WAS ONE OF THE INVENTORS OF YELLOW JOURNALISM, IN WHICH THE STORY IS MORE IMPORTANT THAN THE TRUTH.

WHAT DO YOU THINK, BOSS?

PUT IN MORE ABOUT THE MARTIAN GIRLFRIEND.

HE EVEN HELPED INVENT THE SPANISH-AMERICAN WAR, CABLING THE ARTIST FREDERIC REMINGTON IN CUBA:

"YOU PROVIDE THE NEWS, I'LL PROVIDE THE WAR, HEARST."

BUT MAINLY HE WAS A BIG SPENDER. AUTO TYCOON HENRY FORD ONCE OFFERED SOME ADVICE:

HAVE YOU ANY MONEY?

I NEVER HAVE ANY MONEY, MR. FORD. I ALWAYS SPEND ANY MONEY THAT I AM TO RECEIVE BEFORE I GET IT.

THAT'S A DARNED SHAME. YOU OUGHT TO GET YOUR-SELF TWO OR THREE HUN-DRED MILLION BUCKS AND TUCK IT AWAY.

BUT HEARST COULDN'T TUCK ANYTHING AWAY. HIS MOTHER UNDERSTOOD.

EVERY TIME WILLIE FEELS BAD, HE GOES OUT AND BUYS SOMETHING.

"SOMETHING" WAS CASTLES AROUND THE WORLD...

I'LL TAKE IT.

...AND A UNIQUELY EXTRAV-AGANT HOME OF HIS OWN DESIGN.

IN THE FILM BASED ON HEARST'S LIFE, *CITIZEN KANE*, ORSON WELLES CALLED IT XANADU.

I'LL CALL IT... SAN SIMEON.

HIS DREAMHOUSE WOULD BE BUILT 200 MILES SOUTH OF SAN FRANCISCO ON 250,000 ACRES, WITH 50 MILES OF OCEAN FRONTAGE.

HEARST'S DEALERS SCOUTED THE WORLD, BRINGING BACK WHOLE CASTLES AND MONASTERIES...

... ALONG WITH TAPESTRIES, SUITS OF ARMOR, STATUARY --EVERYTHING.

SEND IT ALL TO THIS NEW YORK ADDRESS...

MOST OF THE STUFF REMAINED IN HEARST'S BURSTING NEW YORK WAREHOUSE.

I'LL JUST PUT THIS THING WITH THE OTHERS.

BUT SOME WENT ON TO SAN SIMEON, WHICH WAS SLOWLY TAKING SHAPE IN A 123-ACRE COMPOUND.

IT'LL COST A FORTUNE TO MOVE THE MONASTERY, MR. HEARST.

DAMN THE EXPENSE! I WANT IT THERE!

EVERY EXPENSE WAS DAMNED. NEPTUNE, THE OUTDOOR POOL, COST $430,000. THE SALTWATER INDOOR POOL WAS A BARGAIN AT JUST $400,000.

WILD ANIMALS ROAMED THE GROUNDS...

... WHILE DANGEROUS BEASTS LIVED IN A ZOO TO KEEP THEM FROM DEVOURING HEARST'S DISTINGUISHED GUESTS.

NO MATTER WHAT THE SEASON, SAN SIMEON WAS A CONSTANT FLORAL EXTRAVAGANZA.

HEARST HAD HIS GARDENERS WORK THROUGH THE NIGHT...

...SO HIS GUESTS WOULD WAKE UP TO FIELDS OF LILIES ON EASTER MORNING.

BUT MOST OF THE REAL WARMTH IN HIS LIFE CAME FROM HIS "FRIENDSHIP" WITH ACTRESS MARION DAVIES.

AH, AN INTIMATE EVENING AT HOME!

BUT WILLIE BOUGHT TOO MUCH.

MR. HEARST, YOU CAN'T GO ON LIKE THIS.

THE DEVIL I CAN'T!

THE DEVIL HE COULD. IN THE 1930s, HE LOST CONTROL OF HIS EMPIRE.

THEY'VE TAKEN EVERYTHING, MARION! EVERYTHING!

WELL, NOT *EVERYTHING*. HEARST STILL HAD HIS HEALTH ... UNTIL 1947, WHEN A HEART ATTACK INCAPACITATED HIM.

HE WAS FORCED TO MOVE INTO DAVIES' SANTA MONICA BUNGALOW...

...WHERE HE DIED IN 1951.

AS FOR HIS MAGNIFICENT SAN SIMEON...

...IT BECAME A MAJOR ATTRACTION FOR TOURISTS WHO LONG TO LIVE A LIFE OF CONSPICUOUS CONSUMPTION, NEVER REALIZING THE PAIN THAT DROVE HEARST'S OBSESSION WITH OPULENCE.

TICKETS

180

NEW YORK POLICE HAD OFTEN BEEN DRAWN BY THE STRANGE GOINGS-ON AT THE RUN-DOWN BROWNSTONE AT 2078 FIFTH AVENUE -- IT WAS THE HOME OF THE CITY'S MOST FAMOUS RECLUSES, HOMER AND LANGLEY...

THE COLLYER BROTHERS

BUT THE CALL ON MARCH 21, 1947, WAS DIFFERENT.

THEY SAY THERE'S A DEAD BODY INSIDE.

DOOR'S LOCKED TIGHT, SIR -- CAN'T BUDGE IT.

BRING THE BATTERING RAM!

HOLY GOD! LOOK AT THAT!

THE OCEAN OF DEBRIS MADE THE DOWNSTAIRS IMPASSABLE.

NOW... WHERE THE HECK IS --

JESUS!

NAME'S HOMER COLLYER, AGE 65. BLIND AND PARALYZED FOR YEARS... HIS BROTHER, LANGLEY, TOOK CARE OF HIM.

YEAH, BUT WHERE'S LANGLEY?

--WHERE INDEED?

THE SONS OF A NEW YORK DOCTOR, THE TWO BOYS HAD GROWN UP IN THE FIFTH AVENUE BROWNSTONE. HOMER, THE ADMIRALTY LAWYER...

... LANGLEY, THE CHEERFUL ENGINEER AND CONCERT PIANIST.

FOR YOU, MOTHER.

DEAR LANGLEY.

AFTER THEIR PARENTS SEPARATED IN 1909, THE BOYS STAYED WITH THEIR MOTHER, WHO DIED IN 1929.

SO, IN A WAY, DID THE COLLYER BROTHERS.

HOMER LOST HIS SIGHT IN 1933 AND BECAME PARALYZED A FEW YEARS LATER.

LANGLEY THOUGHT HE COULD BRING BACK HIS BROTHER'S SIGHT WITH ORANGES -- AS MANY AS 100 A DAY.

REMEMBER... WE ARE THE SONS OF A DOCTOR.

THEY PAID NO BILLS. SOON THEY HAD NEITHER HEAT NOR LIGHT.

LANGLEY COOKED THEIR SIMPLE MEALS ON A KEROSENE STOVE...

... AND BROUGHT THEIR WATER FROM A NEARBY CITY PARK.

AT NIGHT LANGLEY ROAMED NEW YORK, COLLECTING THINGS.

HE BECAME A RESTLESS PACK RAT.

HE SAVED NEWSPAPERS FOR THE DAY THE ORANGES RESTORED HOMER'S SIGHT.

HE'LL WANT TO GET UP TO DATE.

PEOPLE WHISPERED THAT THE HOUSE CONTAINED AN INCREDIBLE FORTUNE.

I TELL YA, THEY'RE RICH!

THAT WHOLE PLACE IS STUFFED WITH MONEY!

IN FACT, THE HOUSE WAS STUFFED WITH JUNK. LANGLEY WALKED THROUGH NARROW, TUNNEL-LIKE TRAILS...

...THAT HE BOOBY-TRAPPED. ON MORE THAN ONE OCCASION, CURIOUS INTRUDERS HAD SCARED THE BROTHERS.

IT TOOK POLICE 3 WEEKS TO CLEAR 120 TONS OF REFUSE FROM THE COLLYER HOUSE.

AMONG OTHER THINGS, THEY FOUND 14 GRAND PIANOS... MOST OF A MODEL T FORD... 3,000 BOOKS... SEWING MACHINES... GUNS AND SWORDS... TONS OF NEWSPAPERS...

...AND LANGLEY--OR WHAT THE RATS HAD LEFT OF HIM.

ON HIS WAY TO FEED HOMER, HE'D TRIPPED ONE OF HIS OWN BOOBY TRAPS AND BEEN ENTOMBED IN TRASH.

HOWARD·HUGHES

THE PLAYBOY-BILLIONAIRE WHO SWEPT TO FAME IN THE 1930s AS A RECORD-SHATTERING PILOT, AERODESIGNER, AND DARING FILM MAKER.

THE YOUNG TEXAN'S FORTUNE CAME FROM THE HUGHES ROCK-EATER, AN OIL-DRILL BIT INVENTED BY HIS FATHER -- AND STILL AN INDUSTRY STANDARD.

HE BOUGHT OUT RELATIVES TO SEIZE FULL CONTROL OF HUGHES TOOL COMPANY...

NEXT.

...AND HEADED FOR HOLLYWOOD.

A HANDSOME SIX-FOUR, HUGHES WAS SMART, DYNAMIC, AND ELIGIBLE. HE COURTED STARLETS BY THE SCORE.

HOLLYWOOD

HE PUT SEX INTO WESTERNS.

ACTION!

BUT HIS GREAT LOVE WAS AVIATION. PLANES EXCITED HIM.

HIS COMPANY BUILT THEM, AND HE STARTED THE AIRLINE THAT BECAME TWA.

TWA

IN 1935 HE SET A WORLD SPEED RECORD OF 352.4 MILES PER HOUR.

THREE YEARS LATER, HE BROKE THE ROUND-THE-WORLD RECORD-- BY HALF.

THE WORLD GOT USED TO SEEING THE BRAVE YOUNG BILLIONAIRE GRINNING FROM THE COCKPIT OF RECORD-BREAKING PLANES.

BUT BEHIND THE MASK OF DASH AND DARING, HUGHES SPIRALED TOWARD THE TWISTED PREOCCUPATIONS THAT WOULD DESTROY HIM.

HE BUILT THE WORLD'S LARGEST AIRPLANE OUT OF PLYWOOD, FLEW THE SPRUCE GOOSE ONCE, AND PUT IT AWAY IN STORAGE. HUGHES AIRCRAFT LOST LUCRATIVE GOVERNMENT CONTRACTS.

HE LOST INTEREST IN AIRPLANES, STARLETS, FILMS... EVERYTHING BUT HOWARD HUGHES.

HUGHES AIRCRAFT

HIS PARANOIA LED HIM TO HOLD MEETINGS IN OBSCURE LOCATIONS LATE AT NIGHT.

LET'S GET DOWN TO BUSINESS, GENTLEMEN.

HE WORE DISGUISES TO THWART IMAGINED ENEMIES.

HI THERE, MR. HUGHES!

MOST OF ALL, HE DREADED GERMS.

AFTER HIS 1957 MARRIAGE TO ACTRESS JEAN PETERS, HE INSISTED ON SEPARATE QUARTERS TO PREVENT FOOD CONTAMINATION.

IN 1966, THE ERRATIC TYCOON WAS FORCED TO SELL HIS CONTROLLING STOCK IN TWA FOR $546,549,771.

FOR THE REST OF HIS LIFE, HE LIVED IN HOTELS IN LAS VEGAS, LONDON, THE BAHAMAS, AND LATIN AMERICA.

ALWAYS HEAVILY GUARDED...

...AND ATTENDED BY SIX TRUSTED AIDES.

WHAT'RE YOU GOING TO DO ABOUT THIS CLIFFORD IRVING BIOGRAPHY?

HUGHES BROKE HIS SILENCE LONG ENOUGH TO TELL THE WORLD THAT IRVING'S BIOGRAPHY WAS A FRAUD.

YOU RECOGNIZE MY VOICE?

IBM

YEAH, RIGHT, MR. HUGHES.

HE SPENT HIS DAYS IN DARK- NESS, ENDLESSLY WATCHING THE SAME FILMS.

ICE STATION ZEBRA WAS HIS FAVORITE.

HE KEPT EVERYTHING -- HIS URINE WENT INTO JARS, HE NEVER CUT HIS HAIR OR NAILS.

UNNNH!

CONSTIPATION KEPT HIM IN THE JOHN FOR HOURS AT A TIME.

FINALLY, IN 1976, HIS NEUROTICALLY ABUSED BODY GAVE UP. HE DIED FROM KIDNEY FAILURE.

AN AUTOPSY REVEALED A BODY SHOT THROUGH WITH PIECES OF BROKEN SYRINGES. THE HIGH-FLYER HAD BEEN IN A GRAVEYARD SPIRAL FOR A VERY LONG TIME.

CHAPTER NINE

MISCELLANEOUS WEIRDOS

If there's one thing that can be said of all the weirdos in this volume, it's that they were unpredictable. Aside from the Gibbons Twins (*page 195*) and the Marcus Twins (*page 198*), no two acted alike. Each had his/her own individual quirks, eccentricities, and obsessions. And while we've attempted to shoehorn all our subjects into nice, neat categories, the following weirdos are truly one-of-a-kind and therefore defy categorization. So here's one final non-category, a miscellany of mixed nuts who share little in common with one another save for the fact that their lives were enhanced — in some cases, defined — by their weirdness.

MARQUIS DE SADE

DONATIEN ALPHONSE FRANÇOISE, COMTE DE SADE, DID NOT INVENT SEXUAL CRUELTY, BUT HE EXPLORED IT AS THOROUGHLY AS FREUD WOULD LATER EXPLORE THE HUMAN MIND -- AND HE GAVE IT HIS NAME:

SADISM.

HIS FATHER, JEAN-BAPTISTE JOSEPH FRANÇOISE, COMPT DE SADE, WAS NO NOVICE AT CRUELTY, EITHER.

WHAT? BRING MY OWN WHIP?

SINCE HE WAS RELATED TO THE ROYAL HOUSE OF CONDE, MANY SINS COULD BE FORGIVEN.

REMEMBER, DON'T CALL ME AT HOME.

BUT NOT ALL. HE MARRIED A LADY-IN-WAITING IN ORDER TO SEDUCE THE PRINCESS SHE WAITED UPON.

WITH GRAND EXTRAVAGANCE, HE USED UP BOTH HIS FORTUNE AND REPUTATION...

...BY 1870, THE YEAR HIS ONLY SON, DONATIEN, WAS BORN.

LA CAQUE SENT TOUJOURS LE HARENG.

TRANSLATION: WHAT'S BRED IN THE BONE WILL COME OUT IN THE FLESH. OR..., YOU AIN'T SEEN NOTHIN' YET!

AT FOUR, YOUNG SADE WAS SENT TO LIVE WITH HIS RELATIVES. FIRST, TO HIS GRANDMOTHER...

ALLO, GRANDE MERE.

...THEN TO HIS HIGH-ROLLING UNCLE, ABBÉ DE SADE OF EBREUIL.

ALLO, MON ONCLE.

THERE IS SO MUCH TO TEACH YOU, MY BOY.

FINALLY, HE RETURNED TO PARIS, TO BE SENT TO THE JESUIT *LYCÉE LOUIS-LE GRAND.* THERE HE WAS TAUGHT THE THINGS HIS UNCLE HAD OVERLOOKED.

AH, YOUNG SADE.

AH, HOME.

THERE HE STUDIED THE CLASSICS...

...AND DISCOVERED WHAT WOULD BECOME HIS CALLING.

DID I HURT YOU?

YES... BUT DON'T STOP.

AT 14, HE WAS UNLEASHED UPON AN UNSUSPECTING, PURITANICAL WORLD.

MIEUX VAUT TARD QUE JAMAIS.

TRANSLATION: BETTER LATE THAN NEVER.

HE JOINED THE KING'S REGIMENT, AND FOUGHT IN THE SEVEN YEARS' WAR.

HE ALSO BECAME, FAMOUSLY, A LIBERTINE, IN THE ERA THAT INVENTED LIBERTINES.

I WAKE UP EVERY MORNING LOOKING FOR PLEASURE.

AND *SUCH* PLEASURES!

IN 1763, HIS FATHER ENGINEERED A GOOD MARRIAGE FOR YOUNG SADE -- TO A WOMAN WHO SHARED HIS SENSE OF PLEASURE.

THE MATCH ALSO BROUGHT HIM THE MOTHER-IN-LAW TO END ALL MOTHERS-IN-LAW: MME. DE MONTREUIL.

THAT INFERNAL MONSTER...THAT BLOODY TROLLOP OF A MOTHER...

...SENTIMENTS HIS MOTHER-IN-LAW HELD JUST AS STRONGLY FOR DE SADE.

DESPITE BEING UNDER THE CONSTANT SCRUTINY OF HIS MOTHER-IN-LAW, SADE CONTINUED HIS SEXUAL EXPLORATIONS. HE BEGAN AFFAIRS, AND ONCE ASKED TOO MUCH OF A LACE MAKER.

ALL YOU HAVE TO DO IS CRACK THE WHIP, OKAY?

SHE HAD HIM ARRESTED FOR BLASPHEMY, AMONG OTHER THINGS...

...AFTER PROFITING FROM "SERVICES RENDERED."

SADE RETREATED TO HIS "LITTLE HOUSE" IN THE SUBURBS, BRINGING WOMEN, MEN, CHILDREN...ANYONE WHO WOULD HELP HIM EXPLORE HIS FANTASIES OF LUST AND PAIN.

WELCOME, MY PETS... WELCOME!

ONE NIGHT HIS HOUSEKEEPER, ROSE KELLER, ESCAPED HIS ATTENTIONS BY LEAPING THROUGH A WINDOW.

WHAT WAS IT, ROSE? SOMETHING I SAID? OR PERHAPS IT WAS THE HOT WAX?

WHEN SHE SHOWED HER CUTS AND BURNS TO THE POLICE AND CLERGY, AND DESCRIBED WHAT SADE WAS UP TO...

...HE WAS IMMEDIATELY PLACED UNDER HOUSE ARREST.

WELL... IT COULD BE WORSE.

...SORT OF LIKE LOCKING THE BULL INSIDE THE CHINA SHOP.

HIS DEBAUCHERIES WERE SO NOTORIOUS THAT KINGS BURNED HIM IN EFFIGY. HE BEGAN PLAYING AROUND WITH HIS YOUNG SISTER-IN-LAW...

LOOK, IT'S NO BIG DEAL, OKAY?

...AND MANAGED TO BE JAILED FOR POISONING MARSEILLE'S PROSTITUTES WITH AN APHRODISIAC.

WHEN HE HIRED A BUNCH OF UNDERAGE HOUSEKEEPERS, THEIR PARENTS HAD HIM LOCKED UP AGAIN.

WE WERE ONLY HOUSE-KEEPING.

THIS TIME IT'S FOREVER, WICKED BOY.

MME DE MONTREUIL USED A ROYAL "SECRET LETTER" TO HAVE HIM SEALED AWAY WITHOUT A TRIAL.

HE WAS FIRST SENT TO LANGUISH IN THE BASTILLE...

...AND FROM THERE WAS PLACED IN THE LUNATIC ASYLUM, CHARENTON.

I THINK I SHALL BECOME A MAN OF LETTERS.

WHEN THE FRENCH REVOLUTION LIBERATED HIM, HIS WIFE REFUSED TO SEE HIM. SHE'D GIVEN UP SADISM FOR LIFE IN A CONVENT.

THE REVOLUTION AND HIS WIFE HAD LEFT HIM PENNILESS.

FOR A TIME, HE LIVED WITH A YOUNG ACTRESS IN DIRE POVERTY, AND CALLED HIMSELF LOUIS SADE.

MY DARLING, I CANNOT EVEN AFFORD A.... WHIP.

UNDER HIS ASSUMED NAME, HE PUBLISHED HIS MOST FAMOUS WORK.

THE MOST ABOMINABLE BOOK EVER ENGENDERED, BY THE MOST DEPRAVED IMAGINATION.

OTHER CRITICS WERE LESS KIND.

SADE WAS DEMORALIZED BY REACTION TO "JUSTINE: THE DANGERS OF VIRTUE."

MAIS, UN MALHEUR N'ARRIVE JAMAIS SEUL.

TRANSLATION: BUT MISFORTUNES NEVER COME SINGLY.

IN 1801 HIS PUBLISHER ADMITTED TO NAPOLEON'S GOVERNMENT THAT SADE HAD WRITTEN JUSTINE.

IT IS THAT CONFOUNDED SECRET ARISTOCRAT SADE, I TELL YOU.

BACK HE WENT TO CHARENTON...

...AND SEDUCING NURSES.

HE WROTE PLAYS, WHICH HE DIRECTED, USING INMATES AS ACTORS.

NOW, PLACES, PLACES...

THEY ESPECIALLY LIKED TO DO THE MURDER OF FRENCH PATRIOT JEAN-PAUL MARAT BY CHARLOTTE CORDAY.

YES, YES.

SOME HAVE SAID THAT SADE'S INTIMATE KNOWLEDGE OF EVIL CAME FROM HIS BEING EVIL INCARNATE.

YES, CHARLOTTE, THAT'S THE WAY, THAT'S THE WAY.

OTHERS SAY THAT HE MERELY LOOKED INTO THE HUMAN PSYCHE, AS FREUD WOULD DO A CENTURY LATER.

YOU CAN'T MAKE AN OMELETTE WITHOUT BREAKING EGGS.

DR. JAMES BARRY

IN JULY 1865 DR. JAMES BARRY, A MUCH-LOVED --AND WIDELY HATED-- EMERITUS INSPECTOR GENERAL OF HOSPITALS IN THE BRITISH ARMY, DIED IN LONDON.

THE DIARRHEA HAS CARRIED HIM OFF.

WHAT A MAN THE GENERAL WAS!

UH... SIR...

"I FIRST HEARD OF BARRY WHEN THE LITTLE PRODIGY BEGAN MEDICAL SCHOOL IN EDINBURGH AT ABOUT AGE 10...

"...THEN BRIEFLY APPRENTICED TO A LONDON SURGEON...

"...BEFORE TAKING A COMMISSION IN THE ROYAL ARMY MEDICAL CORPS."

HE MIGHT HAVE BEEN SMALL AND BEARDLESS, BUT HE WAS SOMETHING TO SEE!

BUT, SIR...

"THE FACT THAT HE TRAVELLED WITH A MANSERVANT AND PET POODLE MADE SOME QUESTION HIS MANLINESS.

"BUT THOSE QUESTIONS WOULD VANISH WHEN BARRY DREW HIS SABRE... A REMARKABLE SWORDSMAN!"

"AN EXCELLENT PHYSICIAN, TOO. BARRY HAD SMALLPOX VACCINATIONS IN SOUTH AFRICA 20 YEARS BEFORE WE HAD THEM IN ENGLAND.

"BARRY PIONEERED CAESAREAN DELIVERY--

"--WE STILL HAVE TROUBLE WITH THAT ONE.

"HE FOUGHT FOR CLEANLINESS, VENTILATION, HYGIENE--FOR ALL THOSE PEOPLE IN PAIN.

"AND NOT JUST FOR THE ENGLISH, EITHER. LEPERS... CONVICTS... THE OUTCASTS OF SOCIETY... THESE TOO HE CARED FOR.

"BARRY WAS A KIND OF OUTCAST HIMSELF.

"HE DRIFTED AROUND THE OUTPOSTS OF THE EMPIRE --MAURITIUS, JAMAICA, CANADA."

PATIENTS ADORED HIM, BUT HIS ENEMIES FINALLY FORCED THE DOCTOR-GENERAL TO RETIRE.

GOD, WHAT A FINE MAN HE WAS!

ACT-CHULLY, SIR... A FINE WOMAN.

WHAAAT?!

WOT'S MORE, SHE 'AD A CHILD... NO ONE KNOWS WHERE, OR WITH 'OO, BUT A CHILD.

IN 1816 A SHIP'S CAPTAIN HAD NOTED OF CAPE TOWN'S DOCTOR THE "PREVAILING OPINION THAT HE WAS A FEMALE"--

APPARENTLY, SOME HAD SUSPECTED DR. BARRY'S TRUE GENDER ALL ALONG...

FACTOID BOOK!

JUNE AND JENNIFER GIBBONS

A PAIR OF IDENTICAL TWINS, THE GIBBONSES BECAME A CAUSE CÉLÈBRE TO THE PSYCHIATRIC COMMUNITY BECAUSE FOR YEARS THEY COMMUNICATED WITH NO ONE BUT EACH OTHER.

WE TRIED TO SPEAK TO OUR PARENTS, BUT IT WAS MORE COMFORTABLE JUST NODDING OUR HEADS.

...THEY TOLD PSYCHIATRISTS MUCH LATER.

THE PARENTS WERE BARBADAN. THE FATHER WAS A SERGEANT IN THE ROYAL AIR FORCE, AND THE TWINS WERE BORN WHILE HE WAS STATIONED IN ADEN.

THEY'RE LOVELY, AREN'T THEY?

BUT... THEY'RE QUIET, AREN'T THEY?

EXPERTS REASSURED THE WORRIED PARENTS.

THEY'RE JUST SHY.

SHY WASN'T THE WORD FOR IT. EACH GIRL'S UNIVERSE HELD ONLY ONE OTHER IMPORTANT PERSON: THE TWIN. THE SHADOW. THE OTHER HALF.

WHEN THEY SPOKE, IT WAS IN A METALLIC, ARTIFICIAL VOICE.

JENNIFER... LET'SGOUPSTAIRS.

UPSTAIRSNEVER-MIND THEM.

BY THEIR TEENS, THE GIRLS HAD ALMOST FUSED IN SILENCE.

WHEN THEY HAD TO COMMUNICATE, THEY WROTE NOTES.

THEY ATE WHAT THEIR PARENTS LEFT OUTSIDE THEIR BEDROOM DOOR.

LEFT ALONE, HOWEVER, THEY COULD BE ROWDY, AND LOUD.

YOU GIRLS ALL RIGHT?

--- ---

SENT TO A TREATMENT CENTER, THEY BECAME IMMOBILE AND RIGID.

MY GOD, THEY'RE LIKE WOODEN PLANKS.

EVERYONE WHO CAME NEAR THEM FELT THEIR POWER.

THEY WATCHED, SMIRKING SILENTLY, AS WE ARGUED ABOUT THEIR TREATMENT OPTIONS.

BY THE TIME THEY WERE 18, HOWEVER, THEY'D BEGUN TO STEP OUT A LITTLE.

HEY, YOU GIRLS ARE, LIKE, KIND OF WEIRD, KNOW WHAT I'M SAYIN'?

THE SAILORS DIDN'T ANSWER THE TWINS' LETTERS, AND SOON RETURNED TO THE U.S.

PRETTY QUIET.

TOO QUIET BY 'ARF.

SO THEY BEGAN STEALING-- AND SETTING FIRES.

PRETTY ISN'T IT?

PRETTY AS A PICTURE.

THEY WERE ARRESTED AND CHARGED WITH 16 COUNTS OF THEFT AND ARSON.

NOW TELL US ABOUT THE WAREHOUSE FIRE.

"HERE IS WHAT HAPPENED..."

THEY RETURNED TO SILENCE. THEY WOULD WRITE, BUT THEY WOULD NOT SPEAK.

SILENT THEY WERE. BUT NOT UNCOMMUNICATIVE. THEY'D WRITTEN MILLIONS OF WORDS IN THEIR DIARIES.

JUNE HAD PUBLISHED A NOVEL WITH A VANITY PRESS...

PEPSI-COLA ADDICT

JUNE GIBBONS

"WE ARE BOTH HOLDING EACH OTHER BACK. SHE DOES NOT WANT JEALOUSY, ENVY, OR FEAR FROM ME. SHE WANTS US TO BE EQUAL. THERE IS A MURDEROUS GLEAM IN HER EYE..."

"...DEAR LORD, I AM SCARED OF HER. SHE IS NOT NORMAL. SHE IS HAVING A NERVOUS BREAKDOWN. SOMEONE IS DRIVING HER INSANE..."

"IT IS ME."

THEY WERE SENT TO BROADMOOR, BRITAIN'S MAXIMUM SECURITY PRISON FOR THE CRIMINALLY INSANE...

"WITHOUT MY SHADOW, WOULD I DIE? WITHOUT MY SHADOW, WOULD I GAIN LIFE?"

...AND SEPARATED.

LATER THEY WERE PERMITTED TO BE TOGETHER AGAIN...

--- ---

...IN THEIR QUIET WAY.

IN 1993 JENNIFER AND JUNE WERE RELEASED FROM CUSTODY. SHORTLY AFTERWARD, JENNIFER DIED... AND JUNE SUDDENLY SPOKE UP, TELLING THE WORLD OF THE TWINS' SYMBIOTIC RELATIONSHIP.

Stewart and Cyril Marcus

BY THE END OF THE 1960s, IDENTICAL TWINS STEWART AND CYRIL MARCUS HAD BECOME WELL-KNOWN GYNECOLOGISTS ON NEW YORK'S PARK AVENUE.

THEIR RESEARCH INTO INFERTILITY HAD EARNED THEM NATIONAL RECOGNITION.

THEY ACHIEVED SUCCESS AS THEY'D DONE EVERYTHING ALL THEIR LIVES--TOGETHER.

THEY'RE SO CUTE.

AS BOYS, THEY EVEN SUFFERED PUNISHMENT TOGETHER.

SINCE WE CAN'T TELL YOU APART, AND YOU COVER FOR EACH OTHER, YOU'LL BOTH GET A SWITCHING -- JUST TO MAKE SURE.

THE BROTHERS OFTEN SEEMED TO BE A SINGLE, COMPOSITE PERSONALITY-- LIKE SIAMESE TWINS JOINED AT THE HEART, THEY DREW LIFE FROM EACH OTHER.

YOU OKAY, LITTLE BROTHER?

I'M OKAY.

IN 1972, SECOND-BORN CYRIL'S HEALTH BEGAN TO FALTER.

YOU OKAY, LITTLE BROTHER?

I DON'T KNOW...

CYRIL BOLSTERED HIMSELF WITH SEDATIVES AND DRUGS.

AS HE DESCENDED INTO ADDICTION, HE BEGAN TO FRIGHTEN PATIENTS WITH BIZARRE PROPOSALS.

I'VE GOT JUST THE THING FOR YOU, MRS. GROSVENOR. JUST THE THING. HEE-HEE-HEE!

HE BECAME SO DANGEROUS...

...THAT STEWART BEGAN TAKING HIS PLACE WITH PATIENTS.

CYRIL? IT IS CYRIL, ISN'T IT?

OF COURSE. NOW... WHERE WERE WE?

THE IMPERSONATIONS MAY HAVE ERASED THE LAST DISTINCTIONS BETWEEN THE TWINS...

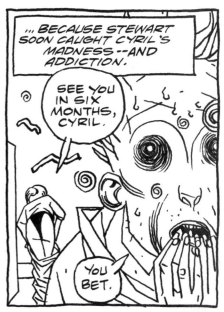

...BECAUSE STEWART SOON CAUGHT CYRIL'S MADNESS--AND ADDICTION.

SEE YOU IN SIX MONTHS, CYRIL.

YOU BET.

STEWART WATCHED HIS BROTHER FALL APART...

...AND, AS HE HAD ALWAYS DONE, JOINED HIM IN THE DESCENDING SPIRAL.

STEWART DISINTEGRATED. CYRIL DIED.

YOU OKAY, LITTLE BROTHER? CYRIL? CYRIL?

ONE HOT JULY DAY IN 1975, TROUBLED NEIGHBORS SUMMONED POLICE.

SURE STINKS!

GOOD THING YOU CALLED!

NO ANSWER INSIDE.

WE'LL BREAK THE DOOR DOWN!

10 H

DO IT!

INSIDE, THEY FOUND CYRIL...

...AND STEWART, WHO'D STAYED WITH HIS TWIN, EVEN IN DEATH.

199

WILLIAM JAMES SIDIS

--NAMED FOR THE FAMOUS PSYCHOLOGIST AND PHILOSOPHER-- POSSESSED WHAT SOME BELIEVE WAS THE FINEST MIND IN HUMAN HISTORY-- WITH AN I.Q. BETWEEN 250 AND 300.

BORN IN 1898, SIDIS COULD TYPE FRENCH AND ENGLISH AT AGE 4, AND KNEW GREEK AT 5.

"THE LIFE WHICH IS UNEXAMINED IS NOT WORTH LIVING." PLATO. HMM.

HE COULD LEARN A NEW LANGUAGE IN A SINGLE DAY.

SIDIS TRIED TO ENROLL AT HARVARD AT 9, BUT THE UNIVERSITY SAID HE WAS TOO YOUNG.

THEY ADMITTED HIM AT 11.

REPORTERS FLOCKED TO HIM WHEN HE GRADUATED AT 16.

I WANT TO LIVE THE PERFECT LIFE.

I PLAN TO TEACH, AND TO CONTINUE MY STUDIES.

WHICH HE DID, ENTERING HARVARD LAW SCHOOL.

HE ALSO BECAME INCREASINGLY ACTIVE IN RADICAL CAUSES.

UNITE! FIGHT OPPRESSION!

DOWN WITH WALL ST

HE WAS ARRESTED IN THE 1914 MAY DAY RIOT IN BOSTON.

HIS FATHER GOT HIM OFF-- BUT IT WAS TOO LATE. WILLIAM SIDIS WAS A CHANGED MAN.

UNTIL THEN, SIDIS HAD BEEN THE PRODUCT OF AN EXPERIMENT BY HIS FATHER, HARVARD PSYCHIATRIST BORIS SIDIS.

SO—I GIVE YOU A SUPERHUMAN INTELLECT AND THIS IS WHAT YOU DO WITH IT!

AFTER HIS ARREST, WILLIAM DROPPED OUT OF HIS FATHER'S MAZE.

I WANT TO LIVE THE PERFECT LIFE—IN SECLUSION—WITHOUT YOU!

HE TOOK WORK THAT REQUIRED NO HIGH INTELLIGENCE AT ALL...

...AND WROTE A BOOK CALLED "NOTES ON THE COLLECTION OF STREET CAR TRANSFERS."

A SERIOUS COLLECTOR, OR PERIDROMOPHILE, SUCH AS MYSELF...

THAT SEEMED TO BE THE LIMIT OF HIS INTELLECTUAL PURSUITS.

THE PRESS HATED SIDIS FOR HIDING HIS GENIUS. WRITER JAMES THURBER SAVAGED HIM IN THE NEW YORKER.

THE NEW YORK

THIS IS TOO MUCH! I'LL SUE!

NEW

HE WON A SMALL OUT-OF-COURT SETTLEMENT.

BUT REPORTERS STILL BLASTED HIM FOR SCORNING THE INTELLECT THEY'D MADE FAMOUS.

YET SIDIS HAD A SECRET. HE HADN'T RENOUNCED HIS INTELLIGENCE—HE'D SIMPLY REMOVED IT FROM PUBLIC VIEW.

YOU THINK YOU KNOW.

IN FACT, HE HAD A RICH LIFE AND MANY FRIENDS...

...WHOM HE DAZZLED WITH FEATS OF MIND-POWER.

OKAY, I THINK I I KNOW.

AFTER A QUICK SCAN HE'D SOLVE THE NEW YORK TIMES CROSSWORD PUZZLE FROM MEMORY.

ONE ACROSS, AIRPLANE-MAKER IN 7 LETTERS, THAT'S DOUGLAS, TWO ACROSS...

HE COULD TRANSLATE 40 LANGUAGES...AND WROTE PRODIGIOUSLY.

SIDIS TOOK THIS SECRET SIDE OF HIS LIFE TO HIS GRAVE IN 1944. BUT 30 YEARS LATER, COLUMBIA UNIVERSITY PSYCHOLOGIST DAN MAHONY EXPLORED THOSE MYSTERIOUS MISSING YEARS.

HE FOUND SCORES OF NEWSPAPER COLUMNS WRITTEN UNDER VARIOUS PEN NAMES, AND EVIDENCE OF A DOZEN UNPUBLISHED BOOKS.

ONLY TWO BOOKS REMAIN: ONE REFERS TO THE COLLAPSED STARS CALLED BLACK HOLES -- DECADES BEFORE THE CONCEPT ENTERED ASTRONOMY.

THE ANIMATE AND THE INANIMATE

William James Sidis 1925—

THE OTHER, A STUDY OF THE INFLUENCE OF INDIAN TRIBAL LAW ON NEW ENGLAND, MAY EXPLAIN SIDIS'S DECISION TO LIE LOW.

THE TRIBES AND THE STATES

THE OKAMAKAMMESSETTS INDIANS TAUGHT THAT ONE'S CONTRIBUTION TO SOCIETY SHOULD BE ANONYMOUS...

THE PERFECT LIFE MUST BE LIVED IN SECLUSION.

...AND SIDIS FOLLOWED THOSE TEACHINGS TO THE END.

JEREMY BENTHAM

...AN 18TH CENTURY BRITISH PHILOSOPHER-ECONOMIST, HE DEVISED THE UTILITARIAN IDEAL THAT SHAPED THE ERA'S NEW DEMOCRACIES: THE GREATEST GOOD FOR THE GREATEST NUMBER OF PEOPLE.

AT THREE HE WAS READING ENGLISH HISTORY. HE READ LATIN AND GREEK WHEN HE WAS FIVE.

HE ENTERED OXFORD AT 12, AND WAS GRADUATED AT 15.

THIS WON'T TAKE LONG.

BUT BENTHAM'S POWERFUL INTELLECT LIVED IN A PUNY LITTLE BODY.

HE DRAGGED HIMSELF UP STAIRS ONE STEP AT A TIME.

COME ON, JEREMY!

WORSE, A DOMINEERING FATHER -- "HONORED SIR" TO JEREMY-- EMBARRASSED THE SHY, FRAIL PRODIGY.

JEREMY! GIVE US SOME OF YOUR LATIN!

YES... I HONORED... SIR.

BENTHAM BECAME AN ATTORNEY, THEN WENT INTO SCHOLARLY SECLUSION TO REINVENT THE BRITISH LEGAL SYSTEM.

AND THERE HE CAME TO THE NOTION OF UTILITY.

THE PURPOSE OF ALL THINGS IS TO AUGMENT HUMAN HAPPINESS AND REDUCE SUFFERING.

THE TROUBLE WAS, BENTHAM COULDN'T STAND HUMANS AND HAD EXPERIENCED VERY LITTLE HAPPINESS.

HE COULD BEAR TO SEE ONLY ONE VISITOR AT A TIME.

NEXT?

HE ONCE FELL IN LOVE -- BUT WAS TOO SHY TO TELL HER.

IF ONLY... IF ONLY...

TOO SHY TO SIT FOR A PORTRAIT, BENTHAM WAS SKETCHED ONLY ONCE -- SECRETLY -- AT A ROYAL SOCIETY MEETING.

AS AN ANTIDOTE FOR LONELINESS, HE TRAINED LITTLE RATS... AND KEPT A NUMBER OF CATS AROUND TOO.

MEOW?

HE TRAINED A PIG TO FOLLOW HIM LIKE A DOG...

HEEL.

...AND GAVE NAMES TO INANIMATE OBJECTS.

HALLO, DAPPLE. IS THE TEA READY?

HE THOUGHT BURIALS WERE A TERRIBLE WASTE OF LAND.

IF STUFFED, ONE'S ANCESTORS WOULD MAKE SPLENDID MORAL EXAMPLES.

WHEN HE DIED, BENTHAM WAS DISSECTED BEFORE A GROUP OF FRIENDS AND RELATIONS AT LONDON'S UNIVERSITY COLLEGE...

GOOD GAWD!

...WHERE HIS REMAINS - PADDED WITH STRAW, FINELY DRESSED, AND TOPPED BY A WAX HEAD - STILL SIT IN A MAHOGANY CABINET.

JOSHUA ABRAHAM NORTON WAS A WEALTHY MAN IN 19TH CENTURY SAN FRANCISCO. BUT HE BECAME REALLY FAMOUS ONLY AFTER HE'D LOST EVERYTHING, AND PROCLAIMED HIMSELF...

Norton I Emperor of the United States (& protector of Mexico)

BRITISH-BORN, NORTON SOUGHT HIS FORTUNE IN SOUTH AFRICA AND BRAZIL BEFORE CALIFORNIA GOLD DREW HIM NORTH TO SAN FRANCISCO.

WORKING IN COMMODITIES, HE PUMPED HIS $40,000 STAKE UP TO $250,000 -- A FORTUNE AT THE TIME.

BUT AN ATTEMPT TO CORNER THE RICE MARKET LED TO FINANCIAL RUIN.

NORTON'S SPIRIT WAS BROKEN...

...BUT ONLY FOR A WHILE.

THREE YEARS LATER, HE EMERGED A NEW AND DIFFERENT MAN.

I, JOSHUA NORTON, DECLARE AND PROCLAIM MYSELF... EMPEROR OF THESE UNITED STATES!

WEARING AN IMPROVISED UNIFORM OF STATE, NORTON BECAME A FAMILIAR FIGURE IN HIS RAMBUNCTIOUS CITY.

GOOD DAY, YOUR EXCELLENCY.

SAN FRANCISCANS BOUGHT HIM FOOD AND DRINKS WHEREVER HE WENT...

HERE'S LOOKIN' AT YOU, EMP.

...PAID FOR HIS "PALACE"-- A LOCAL BOARDING HOUSE...

...AND LET HIM RIDE FREE ON PUBLIC TRANSPORT.

HE EVEN WENT ON TOURS TO OTHER NORTHERN CALIFORNIA TOWNS.

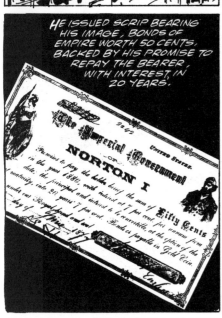

HE ISSUED SCRIP BEARING HIS IMAGE, BONDS OF EMPIRE WORTH 50 CENTS, BACKED BY HIS PROMISE TO REPAY THE BEARER, WITH INTEREST, IN 20 YEARS.

IN RETURN, NORTON GAVE SPEECHES AND INSPECTED CONSTRUCTION SITES.

VERY SOUND, VERY SOUND, INDEED.

NOT THAT HE WAS APOLITICAL.

I SAY THAT WE ABOLISH CONGRESS AND DISSOLVE THE UNITED STATES!

A COMPASSIONATE MAN, HE URGED JEFFERSON DAVIS AND ABRAHAM LINCOLN TO VISIT HIM AND IRON OUT THEIR DIFFERENCES.

DEAR MR. PRESIDENT,...

WHEN FELLOW-ECCENTRIC GEORGE FRANCES TRAIN, SELF-STYLED GREAT AMERICAN CRANK, THREATENED TO INVADE CANADA, NORTON I INTERVENED.

I'LL GIVE YOU VANCOUVER FOR $1200.

AFTER 20 YEARS OF AMIABLE RULE, EMPEROR NORTON I PASSED ON IN 1880. SOME 10,000 SAN FRANCISCANS PAID THEIR LAST RESPECTS.

WHAT A GUY. WHAT A TOWN!

LORD SUTCH

...WAS JUST A MINOR ROCK MUSICIAN UNTIL HE DISCOVERED HE WAS EVEN WORSE AT POLITICS -- AND SHATTERED BRITISH RECORDS FOR THE NUMBER OF UNSUCCESSFUL RUNS FOR THE NATIONAL PARLIAMENTARY OFFICE.

I VOTED LOONY

WITH PRANKS SUCH AS HAVING JOGGERS RUN ON CONVEYOR BELTS TO GENERATE ELECTRICITY, THE SUTCH PLATFORM NEVER CAUGHT ON.

EVEN A CATCHY SLOGAN DIDN'T HELP.

VOTE INSANITY! YOU KNOW IT MAKES SENSE!

VOTE LORD SUTCH

IN MORE THAN 30 RUNS, HIS PARTY FAILED TO CAPTURE A SINGLE SEAT IN PARLIAMENT.

IT'S LONELY AT THE BOTTOM.

VOTE SUTCH

THE SON OF A LONDON POLICEMAN, DAVID SUTCH BEGAN AS A POP SINGER IN THE 1960s, AND STILL WORKS AS A PERFORMER.

JACK... THE... RIPPAH....

SCREAMING LORD SUTCH

MONSTER RAVING

BUT POLITICS CALLED. HE ANSWERED BY STARTING THE NATIONAL TEENAGE PARTY WHICH BECAME THE RAVING LOONIES.

NATIONAL TEENAGE PARTY

BAN THE BOMB

VOTE LORD SUTCH

GIVE 18-YEAR-OLDS THE VOTE... OPEN THE PUBS... LEGALIZE COMMERCIAL RADIO...

MONSTER RAVING LOONY

SOME OF THOSE IDEAS ARE NOW LAW.

IN FACT, THE RAVING LOONIES WON FOUR LOCAL ELECTIONS IN 1990.

CAN SUTCH BE THE WAVE OF THE BRITISH FUTURE?

FACTOID BOOKS

WILLIAM LYON MacKENZIE KING

HE WAS CANADA'S ADORED PRIME MINISTER FOR 22 YEARS. HE LOOSENED HIS NATION'S BONDS TO GREAT BRITAIN, BUILT A SPLENDID CIVIL SERVICE, AND GUIDED HIS COUNTRY THROUGH WORLD WAR II.

BUT INSIDE THIS BRILLIANT, RUTHLESS MAN WAS SOMEONE ELSE -- SOMEONE FOR WHOM CANADIANS MIGHT NOT HAVE VOTED.

THE INNER KING SOUGHT THE SILENCES OF KINGSMERE, A COUNTRY ESTATE SPRINKLED WITH BOGUS ANTIQUITIES.

WELL, PAT, WE MIGHT PUT A SMALL CASTLE JUST THERE. WHAT DO YOU THINK?

A MAUDLIN MAN, HE ADORED HIS IRISH TERRIER, PAT --HE HAD THREE BY THAT NAME.

AH, MY SWEET, SWEET LITTLE BOY. WHAT A DEAR LITTLE SOUL YOU ARE.

HE WORSHIPPED THE MEMORY OF HIS MOTHER, WHO DIED IN 1917.

I LOVE HER WITH ALL MY HEART... SO PURE -- ALMOST HOLY.

I SOMETIMES THINK DEAR MOTHER SENT PAT TO BE A COMFORT TO ME. HE IS FILLED WITH HER SPIRIT OF PATIENT TENDERNESS AND LOVE.

HE OFTEN ASKED HIS MOTHER'S ADVICE.

SHALL I MAKE THIS ONE A RUINED ARCH OR A TOWER, MOTHER?

IF I WERE YOU, BOSS, I'D ASK ABOUT HITLER.

PAT DIED AS KING GUIDED CANADA THROUGH WORLD WAR II.

GIVE MY LOVE TO FATHER AND MOTHER...

THE LITTLE DOG BECAME KING'S MESSENGER TO THE SPIRIT WORLD.

WITH A FEMALE FRIEND, KING EXPLORED THE SPIRIT WORLD AT HIS "LITTLE TABLE" AT KINGSMERE.

THERE HE SOUGHT GUIDANCE FROM THOSE WHO HAD "CROSSED OVER."

LEONARDO? IS THAT LEONARDO DA VINCI?

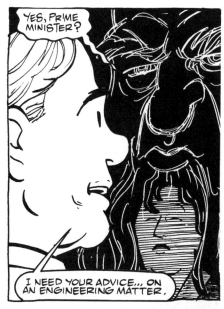

YES, PRIME MINISTER?

I NEED YOUR ADVICE... ON AN ENGINEERING MATTER.

LOUIS PASTEUR...

I HAVE A MEDICAL QUESTION FOR YOU, DR. PASTEUR.

OUI, MONSIEUR... BUT I WARN YOU, I AM A LITTLE OUT OF TOUCH.

LORENZO DE MEDICI...

AN INTERESTING ARCHITECTURAL PROBLEM, MR. KING.

ONLY OCCASIONALLY DID KING ASK ABOUT POLITICS OR AFFAIRS OF STATE.

YOU MUST RUN, BILL, YOU ABSOLUTELY MUST RUN FOR ANOTHER TERM.

SEANCES IN CANADA AND ABROAD PUT HIM IN TOUCH WITH HIS MOTHER, A HOST OF RELATIVES, AND PAT.

WILLIAM...

COUSIN BILL....

WOOF!

WHEN KING "CROSSED OVER" IN 1950, THE WORLD LEARNED HIS SECRET FROM HIS METICULOUSLY KEPT DIARIES...

...THE LOGBOOKS OF A TERRIBLY LONELY MAN WHOSE BEST FRIENDS WERE SPECTERS WHO TOLD HIM WHAT HE NEEDED TO HEAR.

DIARY

J. Edgar Hoover

TRANSFORMED A RAMSHACKLE, CORRUPT FEDERAL BUREAU OF INVESTIGATION INTO THE STRAIGHT-ARROW, SCIENTIFIC CRIME-FIGHTING FBI--THE INITIALS BECAME SYNONYMOUS WITH LAW ENFORCEMENT.

HE WAS FBI DIRECTOR FOR 48 YEARS, UNTIL HIS DEATH, AT 77, IN 1972, WHEN THEN-PRESIDENT RICHARD NIXON CALLED HIM:

...A NATIONAL SYMBOL OF COURAGE, PATRIOTISM, AND GRANITELIKE HONESTY AND INTEGRITY.

HOOVER WAS THE FIRST U.S. CIVIL SERVANT TO RECEIVE A STATE FUNERAL.

BUT EVEN HIS GREATEST ADMIRERS WERE WARY OF HIM.

EHRLICHMAN, WE MAY HAVE ON OUR HANDS HERE A MAN WHO WILL PULL THE TEMPLE DOWN WITH HIM, INCLUDING ME.

THE MAN WHO WOULD BECOME AMERICA'S OMNIPOTENT G-MAN WAS BORN JOHN EDGAR HOOVER IN 1895, AND SPENT ALMOST HIS ENTIRE LIFE IN HIS HOMETOWN-- WASHINGTON, D.C.

MY TOWN.

AFTER GEORGE WASHINGTON UNIVERSITY LAW SCHOOL, HE ENTERED FEDERAL SERVICE IN 1924...

...AND SETTLED INTO A QUIET, DEDICATED, BACHELOR EXISTENCE IN THE CAPITAL.

QUIET, BUT AS THINGS TURNED OUT, NOT THAT QUIET.

AT THE TIME, FEDERAL LAW ENFORCEMENT WAS IN DISREPUTE FROM THE SCANDALS OF WARREN HARDING'S CORRUPT ADMINISTRATION.

PIGS.

HE WAS SOON KICKED UPSTAIRS, INTO A TAILOR-MADE JOB.

SO ATTORNEY GENERAL PALMER WANTS ME TO LIST SUBVERSIVES? BOY, WILL I!

AT THE TIME, THE LIST WAS MOSTLY COMMUNISTS -- WHAT MOST AMERICANS THOUGHT OF AS THE RED MENACE.

WE'LL NEED SOME MUGSHOTS AND FINGERPRINTS, TOO.

PROHIBITION FOSTERED MORE CRIME FOR THE FBI TO WATCH.

THE MOB'S TAKEN OVER THE SPEAKS.

MOB? WHAT MOB?

THE GREAT DEPRESSION BOOSTED CRIME -- AND GAVE HOOVER ANOTHER ANGLE: THE PUBLIC ENEMIES PROGRAM.

WANTED

JOHN HERBERT DILLINGER

$10,000.00

THE FBI WENT AFTER PEOPLE LIKE JOHN DILLINGER...

BRATATA

...BONNIE...

...AND CLYDE.

BARROW THAT IS. THERE WAS ANOTHER, MORE IMPORTANT CLYDE IN HOOVER'S LIFE.

CLYDE TOLSON, HOOVER'S FRIEND AND ROOMMATE -- AND ASSISTANT FBI DIRECTOR, PROMOTED UP FROM THE RANKS.

I MAY GO OUT TONIGHT.

I MAY GO WITH YOU.

AS WORLD WAR II COMMENCED, HOOVER SWITCHED ENEMIES.

WE'RE GOING AFTER THE ENEMY WITHIN, THE SECRET NAZIS IN OUR SOCIETY, GENTLEMEN -- THE FIFTH COLUMN.

AFTER THE WAR, IT WAS BACK TO COMMUNISTS...

...LIBERALS...

WHAT'S NEXT, BOBBY?

JACK, I'M GOING AFTER HOFFA AND THE MOB.

MOB? WHAT MOB?

...CIVIL RIGHTS LEADERS.

ZORRO'S HEADING BACK FOR THE LORRAINE MOTEL.

SOMEBODY SHOT ZORRO IN MEMPHIS.

HOT DAMN! THEY GOT ZORRO!

ZORRO WAS THE FBI'S CODE NAME FOR MARTIN LUTHER KING, JR.

KING WAS THE MOST DANGEROUS MAN IN AMERICA. PEKING WAS IN IT. MOSCOW.

HE'D HATED KING. HE'D BUGGED HIM FOR YEARS, AND HAD SENT HIS FAMILY TAPED EXCERPTS FROM OCCASIONAL TRYSTS.

AND SEX.... SEX WAS IN IT, TOO.

SEX WAS AS BAD AS COMMUNISM.

PERVERSION.

WELL ..., HE WOULD KNOW.

HOOVER'S COINTEL, OR COUNTERINTELLIGENCE PROGRAM, WATCHED EVERYBODY.

CLYDE, WHERE'S MY FILE ON JFK?

COMING UP, CHIEF.

COME LOOK AT THESE SHOTS, CLYDE. MY, THIS IS REALLY RICH... LOOK HERE...

JFK

HOOVER SERVED UNDER 8 PRESIDENTS, NONE GAVE HIM A MOMENT'S TROUBLE.

SOME USED HIM ALL THE TIME.

I WORRY ABOUT THESE ANTI-VIETNAM WEIRDOS, EDGAR.

DON'T, MR. PRESIDENT. WEIRDOS ARE MY...SPECIALTY.

AND THERE'S THE MOB.

MR. PRESIDENT, NO SINGLE INDIVIDUAL OR COALITION OF RACKETEERS DOMINATES ORGANIZED CRIME ACROSS THE NATION.

MOB? WHAT MOB?

FOR A LONG TIME, NOBODY COULD FIGURE OUT WHY HOOVER FOUND THE MAFIA INVISIBLE.

LIBERTINES.

DEVIANTS.

BY THE WAY,... I'M GOING OUT TONIGHT... HONEY.

AH, WELL, EVERYONE HAS HIS LITTLE SECRETS.

ACCORDING TO A 1993 BIOGRAPHY, J. EDGAR'S SECRET WAS NAMED MARY HOOVER.

NO QUESTION, AMERICA'S TOP COP LOOKED GOOD IN BLACK.

ONE ACCOUNT HOLDS THAT, AT THE HOME OF JOE McCARTHY'S FORMER ATTORNEY, ROY COHN, HOOVER HAD APPEARED AS MARY...

ROY...YOU SAID SOMETHING ABOUT BOYS?

THEY'RE WAITING, UH, MARY!

COHN LATER REMARKED TO A FRIEND: "THAT WAS REALLY SOME- THING, WASN'T IT, WITH MARY HOOVER?"

HOOVER HAD SO MUCH ON EVERYBODY ELSE, HE BELIEVED IT DIDN'T MATTER WHAT PEOPLE HAD ON HIM.

ISN'T THAT...?

HUSH, OF COURSE IT ISN'T.

HOOVER WAS RIGHT--HE HAD NOTHING TO WORRY ABOUT...

HOOVER

...WITH ONE EXCEPTION.

THEY'RE ⸘GASP⸘ FROM THE MOB.

MOB? WHAT MOB?

SOME BELIEVE THAT THE MOB'S INCRIMINATING PHOTOS OF HOOVER AND TOLSON HAD KEPT THE FBI OFF ORGANIZED CRIME.

LOOKIT DIS ONE -- J. EDGAR IN ALL HER GLORY!!

KNOW WHAT, HONEY?

NO, WHAT?

I DREAMED ABOUT DILLINGER AGAIN LAST NIGHT.

THOSE G-MEN, ALWAYS TALKING SHOP!

BIO-GRAPHIE

WRITER

CARL A. POSEY
Until about age 20, Carl A. Posey's main ambition was to write and draw a comic strip of his own. Instead, he became an award-winning science journalist, the author of five novels (the latest is *Bushmaster Fall*, 1992), and an editor at DC Comics' corporate cousin, Time-Life Books, in Alexandria, Virginia. He still draws, but not in this volume — his first book-length foray into the world of graphic storytelling.

LETTERER

ROD OLLERENSHAW
Rod has a last name that originates in Derby, England and means "Dweller by the Alder Grove." In real life, he dwells in New Jersey.

ARTISTS

GARY AMARO
Gary enjoys wrassling cassowaries and can navigate the lengths of the Pampas Grasslands in Argentina blindfolded. He draws *The Books of Magic* for DC/Vertigo. *(Page 102)*

MARK BADGER
Mark has drawn lots of comics. Along with the coolest cartoonists in the world, his work appears in *Instant Piano*, a comic done just for the fun of it. *(Page 30)*

RUSSELL BRAUN
I am happy to have survived the experience with both ears, both eyes, and both mouths (you'd need two to talk as much as I do). *(Page 131)*

RICHARD CASE
A collector of things strange, Case is known to have drawn pictures for *Doom Patrol* and *Ghostdancing*, and has recently discovered the joys of coffee. *(Page 142)*

DONALD DAVID
Donald David was imprisoned in the bowels of a Canadian art school for attempting to prove that comics were a valid medium for self-expression. To this day, he is haunted by the experience. *(Page 82)*

AL DAVISON
A black belt in karate who performs his own plays, Al Davison lives in London with his lover, Maggie. Born paralyzed (spina-bifida), he wasn't expected to live/walk. Life's funny sometimes. *(Page 96)*

DAVE DeVRIES
While posing as a popular super-hero, Dave was pummeled silly by angry conventiongoers who were incensed that his costume lacked trousers. *(Page 84)*

D'ISRAELI D'EMON DRAUGHTSMAN
I live in Sheffield, England with my mummy and a nice kitty. If I'm good, doctor says I can stop having the injections. (Page 174).

FELIKS DOBRIN
Feliks was born in Kiev, U.S.S.R. in 1962 and came to the United States two years ago. He is the artist of *Welcome Danger*, the first comic ever produced in the Ukraine. *(Page 154)*

RANDY DuBURKE
Randy is a cover artist for DC Comics, having worked on *Animal Man*, *Darkstars*, *Ms. Tree*, and *The Shadow*. He is also the artist on *Hunter's Heart*, a graphic novel to be published in the Paradox Mystery line. *(Page 8)*

LEO DURAÑONA
Leo Durañona was born in Buenos Aires, Argentina. His past work includes DC's *House of Horrors* and Warren's *Creepy* and *Eerie*, and *Race of Scorpions*, *Indiana Jones*, and *Predator* for Dark Horse. *(Page 88)*

KIERON DWYER
A professional for seven years, Kieron has pencilled, inked, colored and/or painted *Captain America*, *Batman*, *Robin*, *Hellraiser*, and *Lobo*. He is very proud of his work on *The Torch of Liberty*. *(Page 205)*

HUNT EMERSON
Hunt Emerson has drawn "underground" comics for twenty years, including Knockabout Comics' *Lady Chatterly's Lover*, *The Rime Of The Ancient Mariner*, and the highly acclaimed *Casanova's Last Stand*. *(Page 124)*

JIM FERN
Jim started as an inker on various Marvel titles in 1983. He began pencilling in 1987, and has drawn *L.E.G.I.O.N '90*, *Detective*, *Adventures of Superman*, and most recently the *Scarlett* series for DC. *(Page 104)*

SIMON FRASER
Also by the same artist: *Lux and Alby Sign On and Save the Universe,* published by Acme and Dark Horse Comics. Sex, drugs and comics theft. *(Page 20)*

RICK GEARY
Rick's comics and illustrations have appeared in various magazines. His work has been collected in four volumes, including *Housebound with Rick Geary* and *Prairie Moon and Other Stories.* *(Page 53)*

PETER GROSS
Peter lives in Minneapolis. He works monthly on DC/Vertigo's *The Books of Magic,* and Marvel's *Doctor Strange.* He never dodges phone calls from editors when he is behind schedule. *(Page 151)*

REBECCA GUAY
Rebecca's work has appeared in *Cricket Magazine for Children,* Topps' *Star Wars Series II,* and various Marvel and DC Comics. She is currently the regular penciller for DC/Vertigo's *Black Orchid.* *(Page 57)*

CRAIG HAMILTON
J'adore Isadora. My first black-and-white comics story. I'm very pleased with it. I did a lot of research. It was inspirational. J'adore Isadora. Special thanks to Ray Snyder. *(Page 110)*

TONY HARRIS
Penciller, inker, cover painter Tony lives in Georgia with his wife, Stacie, and his two dobermen, Natasha and Cleopatra. He's currently pencilling and painting covers on *Starman* (DC). *(Page 48)*

DANNY HELLMAN
Hail the new dawn! Early next year, Untermensch Hellman will be rocketed to the lunar surface to do battle with Wippy the Two-Headed Death Slarg. Never forget, he gives his life to save us all. *(Page 184)*

GRAHAM HIGGINS
Has contributed to *Punch,* Knockabout Comics, and *Fortean Times.* Taught comic art in college and prison. Owns no cats. *(Page 70)*

ED HILLYER
Ilya "The Terrible" has worked for everyone (Marvel, DC, Dark Horse, Deadline, Tundra, Fleetway, Kodansha) but has returned to self-publishing with *The End of the Century Club.* Go figure. *(Page 16)*

DAVID HINE
A London-based artist, David has been, at various times, editor, artist, writer, and inker on characters ranging from Care Bears to Judge Dredd. His major work: *Strange Embrace* (Tundra/Atomeka). *(Page 166)*

FLOYD HUGHES
Floyd Hughes lives in Red Hook, Brooklyn with his wife Mayleen and daughter Sojourner. He believes all bigots should repent or die painfully. *(Page 200)*

MICHAEL JANTZE
When Michael draws, he thinks animals can talk and people can reason, that men are flexible and women are reasonable. He obviously doesn't make a lot of money at it. *(Page 208)*

DAVID G. KLEIN
David is an illustrator of magazines, books, and comics, including: *Frankenstein, The Scarlet Letter, Darker Than You Think, Batman: Legends of the Dark Knight* #51, and stories for Marvel's 2099 Universe. *(Page 161)*

TEDDY KRISTIANSEN
Teddy lives in Copenhagen with his wife, daughter, two cats, and a huge phone bill from working abroad. He hopes to have more time for painting next year. *(Page 198)*

PETER KUPER
Kuper is co-founder of *World War 3 Illustrated,* and has written and drawn *New York, New York, Life and Death, Bleeding Heart,* and *Wildlife* (Fantagraphics). *(Page 210)*

NGHIA LAM
Nghia was born in a country that no longer exists. He now lives in the deserts of San Diego, where he enjoys the company of blowfish and blond women. *(Page 168)*

ROGER LANGRIDGE
Roger is the artist of *Zoot!,* an obscure black-and-white published by Fantagraphics, and has worked on *Deadline, Judge Dredd,* and for anybody else who will pay the rent. *(Page 74)*

BATTON LASH
Batton Lash is the creator of *Wolf & Byrd, Counselors of the Macabre* and the writer of the *Archie/Punisher* crossovers. His cartooning appears in the other Factoid Big Books. *(Page 176)*

STEVE LEIALOHA
Okay: *Quack, Spiderwoman, The Black Hood, Trypto the Acid Dog,* and *Jack the Lego Boy* are but a few of the titles I have worked on in the past twenty years. *(Page 68)*

STEVEN LIEBER
Steven Lieber hates to write about himself in the third person. He is not related to anyone at Marvel. *(Page 100)*

COLIN MACNEIL
Award-winning Judge Dredd artist Colin MacNeil is a man of many parts: artist, penguin-fancier, carnivore, friend to all dinosaurs, and teller of bad jokes. What a weird guy! *(Page 34)*

GRAHAM MANLEY
On moonlit nights, Graham Manley can sometimes be seen wandering aimlessly among the heather-covered hills and glens of Scotland. His interests include graveyards and dismembering Barbie dolls. *(Page 181)*

ROBERT McCALLUM
I worked on the humor magazine *Electric Soup* while doing design, video, and animation at the Glasgow School of Art. I've worked on *Judge Dredd* and various other comics. *(Page 122)*

CHRIS McLOUGHLIN
Chris was born on November 1, 1971. His work in comics includes other *Big Book* segments, *Mirror, Mirror* by Nick Vance, and phone calls when he should be in bed. *(Page 41)*

LINDA MEDLEY
Little Linda would *still* like to be a housewife when she grows up. *(Page 195)*

TED NAIFEH
Ted is most noted for *The Machine* from Dark Horse's super-hero line. He is currently working on a creator-owned book for Epic called *The Exile of Abra Khan*. *(Page 114)*

MITCH O'CONNELL
Mitch is an award-winning, nationally-exhibited fine artist whose work has appeared in *National Lampoon, Spy,* and *Playboy,* among many publications. *(Page 128)*

MICHAEL AVON OEMING
Boneheads in Ghost Town and sometime *Judge Dredd* artist enjoys Jim Morrison poems, Brady Bunch reruns, and *Star Wars*. He believes in U.F.Os. *(Page 163)*

TAYYAR OZKAN
Tayyar is a Turkish-born Kurd living in New York. His artwork has appeared in *World War 3 Illustrated* and *Heavy Metal*. He is drawing *La Pacifica,* written by Joel Rose and Amos Poe, the first graphic novel in the Paradox Mystery line. *(Page 146)*

JEFF PARKER
Though capable of doing decent, honest work, Parker seems to draw only *Solitaire* for Malibu Comics. He has also inked Bo Hampton on *Uther: The Half-Dead King*. *(Page 91)*

RICK PARKER
Rick is the artist for MTV's *Beavis and Butt-head* comic book from Marvel. Parker's comic strip *The Bossmen* and weekly cartoon *The Bullpen Bullseye* were also published by Marvel. *(Page 156)*

JOE PHILLIPS
In nine years I've done over fifty issues and close to 120 covers and cards. Titles include: *Ex-Mutants, Speed Racer, Justice League, Fantastic Four,* and *Spider-Man*. Upcoming project: *The Heretic* from Dark Horse. *(Page 158)*

WOODROW PHOENIX
Phoenix has dated several weirdos in his time, ranging from somewhat odd to certifiably lunatic. Credits: *The Sumo Family* (Manga Mania) and the forthcoming *Orson Welles: Secret Agent*. *(Page 108)*

FRANK QUITELY
Born in Glasgow, Scotland 1968. Unsuccessful spell in Glasgow School of Art. Dabbled in small press while freelancing for several years. Became full-time comic artist in early 1993. *(Page 138)*

RICHARD PIERS RAYNER
Russ Manning Award-winner for Most Promising Newcomer in 1989, Richard has illustrated *Dr. Fate, L.E.G.I.O.N. '90, Swamp Thing* and *Hellblazer*. He is also drawing *Road to Perdition,* a graphic novel in the Paradox Mystery line, written by Max Allan Collins. *(Page 11)*

JAMES ROMBERGER
James has been attacked by fascists in America and Europe. His drawings are in many private and museum collections. He lives in New York's Lower East Side. *(Page 25)*

GREG RUTH
At 6:45 A.M. I got a "bowl cut" and went to elementary school. At 10:53 A.M. I got the family station wagon and went to high school. Graduated Pratt at 12:37. Had a turkey sandwich around 1:12 P.M. *(Page 36)*

ZINA SAUNDERS
Zina Saunders's illustrations have been used in advertising, books, videocassette covers, and in the *Star Wars, Mars Attacks,* and *Superman: Man of Steel* trading cards. *(Page 135)*

WILL SIMPSON
While painting in a potato field Will drew *Big Ben: The Man With No Time For Crime* for Warrior. Other work: *Judge Dredd* for *2000 AD,* and *Hellblazer* and *Vamps* for DC/Vertigo. *(Page 78)*

ROBIN SMITH
Robin was the art director for *2000 AD,* an artist on *Judge Dredd,* and the illustrator of *Bogie Man*. He once had the opportunity to vote for Screaming Lord Sutch in an election. Robin is drawing *Green Candles,* a graphic novel in the Paradox Mystery line. *(Pages 63 and 207)*

JOE STATON
Joe has worked for Marvel on *The Incredible Hulk,* and for DC illustrating *Superman, Batman, Plastic Man, Green Lantern,* and many others. Joe is the artist on *Family Man,* a graphic novel written by Jerome Charyn for the Paradox Mystery line. *(Page 60)*

ALEC STEVENS
Alec Stevens *almost* enjoys music more than art. He cites Bela Bartok, Stravinsky, Miles Davis, Coltrane, early Zappa/*Mothers,* Nick Drake, *Focus, Glassharp,* and Jukka Tolonen as favorites. *(Page 170)*

TOM SUTTON
TFS, a.k.a. Tom Sutton, really loved drawing this story. He hopes the publisher will assign him another one real soon. The rent is due. *(Page 188)*

GREG THEAKSTON
Greg has been working in comics since 1970. He's also known for his work bleaching classic comics, his work at *Mad Magazine,* and as editor/publisher of *Tease!* *(Page 120)*

JAMIE TOLAGSON
Mr. Tolagson (a lean, strapping 7' 2", 215 lbs.) believes that his large form distracts people from his true artistic nature. Jamie now lives in Phuket, Thailand, with his four lovable dobermen. *(Page 178)*

MITCH WAXMAN
A sturdy fellow who lives in New York City with his carnivorous turtle. Writer/artist of *Plasma Baby* and *Vengeance of the Aztecs*. *(Page 203)*

ART WETHERELL
I worked mainly in magazine illustration, with odd stints in comics (*Tarzan, 2000 AD,* Marvel U.K.). But comics stop me feeling bad, and I intend to stick around for a while. *(Page 126)*

MARK WHEATLEY
Mark holds the Inkpot and Speakeasy Awards for his creations, including *Mars* and *Breathtaker*. Current projects: *Radical Dreamer* for Blackball Comics and *Batman: Legends of the Dark Knight* and *Argus* for DC. *(Page 193)*

MICHAEL ZECK
Mike attended Ringling School of Art in Sarasota, Florida. For the past twenty years he's worked on many comics, including *Captain America, Punisher, Spider-Man,* and *Batman: Legends of the Dark Knight*. *(Page 44)*

BIBLIO-GRAPHY

IDI AMIN
Martin, David, *General Amin*, Faber, London 1974
Kyemba, Henry, *A State of Blood: The Inside Story*, Ace Books, New York 1977

DR. JAMES BARRY
Rose, June, *The Perfect Gentleman*, Hutchinson, London 1977
"Lady's Man," *Hoaxes and Deceptions*, Time-Life Library of Curious and Unusual Facts, Alexandria, Virginia 1992

JEREMY BENTHAM
Ogden, C.K., *Jeremy Bentham, 1832-2032*, Kegan Paul, Trent, Timbunen, London 1932
"Stuffed Shrimp," *Odd & Eccentric People*, Time-Life Library of Curious and Unusual Facts, Alexandria, Virginia 1992

SARAH BERNHARDT
Skinner, Cornelia Otis, *Madame Sarah*, Houghton Mifflin, Boston 1967
Row, A.W., *Sarah The Divine: The Biography of Sarah Bernhardt*, Comet Press Books, New York 1957
"Dramatic Flair," *Odd & Eccentric People*, Time-Life Library of Curious and Unusual Facts, Alexandria, Virginia 1992

AMBROSE BIERCE
Bartlett's Familiar Quotations, Little Brown, Boston, 1992
Hayman, LeRoy, *Thirteen Who Vanished: True Stories of Mysterious Disappearances*, New York, Julian Messner 1979
Wiggins, Robert A., *Ambrose Bierce*, University of Minnesota Press, Minneapolis 1964
"Old Gringo," *Vanishings*, Time-Life Library of Curious and Unusual Facts, Alexandria, Virginia 1992

CLARA BOW
Anger, Kenneth, *Hollywood Babylon*, Straight Arrow Books, San Francisco 1975
Stenn, David, *Clara Bow: Runnin' Wild*, Doubleday, New York 1988
"Losing It," *All the Rage*, Time-Life Library of Curious and Unusual Facts, Alexandria, Virginia 1992

WILLIAM S. BURROUGHS
Morgan, Ted, *Literary Outlaw: The Life and Times of William S. Burroughs*, Henry Holt, New York 1988
Burroughs, William S., *Junkie: Confessions of an Unredeemed Drug Addict*, Viking Penguin, New York 1977
"Dead Shot," *Shadows of Death*, Time-Life Library of Curious and Unusual Facts, Alexandria, Virginia 1992

CALIGULA
Barnett, Anthony A., *Caligula: The Corruption of Power*, Yale University Press, New Haven 1989
"Little Boots," *Manias and Delusions*, Time-Life Library of Curious and Unusual Facts, Alexandria, Virginia 1992

THE COLLYER BROTHERS
"Strange Case of the Collyer Brothers," *Life*, April 7, 1947
"Collyer Mansion Yields Junk, Cats," *The New York Times*, March 26, 1947
"Body of Collyer is Found Near Where Brother Died," *Ibid*, April 9, 1947
"Homer Collyer, Harlem Recluse, Found Dead at 70," *Ibid*, March 22, 1947
"Langley Collyer Dead Near a Month," *Ibid*, April 10, 1947
Kernan, Michael, "The Collyer Saga and How It Grew," *The Washington Post*, February 8, 1983
"Slaughter on Fifth Avenue," *Odd & Eccentric People*, Time-Life Library of Curious and Unusual Facts, Alexandria, Virginia 1992

MARCELLO CRETI
"Of Cabbages and Things," *Manias and Delusions*, Time-Life Library of Curious and Unusual Facts, Alexandria, Virginia 1992
del Re, Emmanuela C., *Il Figlio di Ergos. Marcello Creti: Scienziato, Santo e Mago*, Pontecorbolli, Florence 1992

ALEISTER CROWLEY
The Mind and Beyond; Magical Arts; Mysterious Creatures; The Mystical Year; Secrets of the Alchemists; Visions and Prophecies; Witches and Witchcraft; Mystic Places, Time-Life Mysteries of the Unknown, Alexandria, Virginia 1988-1991
Encyclopedia Britannica macropedia 15th Edition, Chicago, 1985

SALVADOR DALI
Decker, Andrew, "Unlimited Editions," *Art News*, Summer 1988
Richard, Paul, "Dali and the World of Dreams," *The Washington Post*, January 24, 1989
Sargent, Winthrop, "An Excitable Spanish Artist, Now Scorned by His Fellow Surrealists, Has Succeeded in Making Deliberate Lunacy a Paying Proposition," *Life*, September 24, 1945
Violet, Ultra, "Goodbye Dali — It's Been Surreal," *The New York Times*, January 30, 1989

FERDINAND WALDO DEMARA JR. ("THE GREAT IMPOSTOR")
Crichton, Robert, *The Great Imposter*, Random House, New York 1959
Garvey, Jack, "Ferdinand Demara Jr.," *American History*, October, 1985
"Occupation: Imposter," *Hoaxes and Deceptions*, Time-Life Library of Curious and Unusual Facts, Alexandria, Virginia 1992

FYODOR DOSTOYEVSKY
Dostoyevsky, Fyodor, *Great Short Works of Dostoyevsky*, Harper and Row, New York 1968
Grossman, Leonid P., *Dostoyevsky*, translated by Mary Mackler, Bobbs-Merill Co., Indianapolis 1975
Hingley, Ronald, *Dostoyevsky, His Life and Work*, Scribner's, New York 1978
Encyclopedia Britannica, Vol. 7, Chicago 1955

ISADORA DUNCAN
Desti, Mary, *The Untold Story: The Life of Isadora Duncan, 1921-1927*, DaCapo Press, New York 1981
"Fatal Flourish," *Shadows of Death*, Time-Life Library of Curious and Unusual Facts, Alexandria, Virginia 1992
Encyclopedia Britannica micropedia, 15th Edition, Chicago 1985

THOMAS EDISON
Gillespie, C.C., ed., *Dictionary of Scientific Biography*, Scribner's, New York, 1980
James, Clive, *Fame in the 20th Century*, BBC Books, London 1993
Jehl, F., *Menlo Park Reminiscences*, Dearborn, Michigan 1938
Josephson, Matthew, *Edison*, McGraw-Hill, New York 1959
"The Wiz," *Inventive Genius*, Time-Life Library of Curious and Unusual Facts, Alexandria, Virginia 1990

ELAGABALUS
Encyclopedia Britannica, 15th Edition, Chicago, 1985

KING FAROUK
McBride, Barrie St. Clair, *Farouk of Egypt*, A.S. Bauer, South Brunswick, 1968
McLeave, Hugh, *The Last Pharaoh*, McCall, New York 1970
Stern, Michael, *Farouk*, Bantam, New York 1965
"Klepto King," *Odd & Eccentric People*, Time-Life Library of Curious and Unusual Facts, Alexandria, Virginia 1992

HENRY FORD
Cohn, Norman, *Warrant for Genocide,* Harper & Row, New York 1967
James, Clive, *Fame in the 20th Century,* BBC Books, London 1993
Encyclopedia Britannica macropedia, 15th Edition, Chicago, 1985

WALTER FREEMAN
Shutts, David, *Lobotomy: Resort to the Knife,* Van Nostrand Reinhold,
    New York 1982
Restak, Richard, "The Promise and Peril of Psychosurgery," *Saturday Review
    World,* September 25, 1973

JUNE AND JENNIFER GIBBONS
Wallace Marjorie, *The Silent Twins,* Prentice-Hall, New York 1986
"Britain's Silent Twins," *Mysteries of the Human Body,* Time-Life Library of
    Curious and Unusual Facts, Alexandria, Virginia 1990

HETTY GREEN
Sparkes, Boyden, and Samuel Taylor Moore, *The Witch of Wall Street: Hetty Green,*
    Doubleday Doran, New York, 1933
"The Color of Money," *Odd & Eccentric People,* Time-Life Library of Curious and
    Unusual Facts, Alexandria, Virginia 1992

GREY OWL
Brower, Kenneth, "Grey Owl," *Atlantic Monthly,* January 1990
Dickson, Lovat, *Wilderness Man: The Strange Story of Grey Owl,* Atheneum,
    New York 1975
"Fly By Night," *Hoaxes and Deceptions,* Time-Life Library of Curious and Unusual
    Facts, Alexandria, Virginia 1992

GEORGES GURDJIEFF
The Mind and Beyond, Mysteries of the Unknown, Time-Life Books, Alexandria,
    Virginia 1990
Kherdian, David, *On a Spaceship with Beelzebub by the Grandson of Gurdjieff,*
    Globe, New York 1991
Moore, James and Paul Kegan, *Gurdjieff and Mansefield,* Routeledge,
    London 1980

WILLIAM RANDOLPH HEARST
"A Unique Tour of San Simeon," *Life,* August 26, 1957
Tebled, John, *The Life and Good Times of William Randolph Hearst,* Dutton,
    New York 1932
Swanby, W.A., *Citizen Hearst,* Charles Scribner's Sons, New York 1961
Loe, Nancy E., *William Randolph Hearst,* ARA Service, Philadelphia, 1988
Aidala, Thomas, R., *Hearst Castle, San Simeon,* Harrison House 1981
Murray, Ken, *The Golden Days of San Simeon,* Doubleday, Garden City, 1971
"Pleasure Dome," *Odd & Eccentric People,* Time-Life Library of Curious and
    Unusual Facts, Alexandria, Virginia 1992

ADOLF HITLER
Fest, Joachim C., *Hitler,* translated by Clara and Richard Winston, Harcourt Brace
    Jovanovich, New York 1974
Langer, Walter C., *The Mind of Adolf Hitler,* New American Library,
    New York 1973
Morton, Frederic, *Thunder at Twilight,* Scribner's, New York 1989
Picker, Henry, *The Hitler Phenomenon,* Translated by Nicholas Fry, David &
    Charles, London 1974
Picker, Henry and Heinrich Hoffman, *Hitler Close-Up,* Translated by Nicholas Fry,
    Macmillan, New York 1973
Center of the Web, *The Third Reich,* Time-Life Books, Alexandria, Virginia, 1991
"Der Fuehrer," *Manias and Delusions,* Time-Life Library of Curious and Unusual
    Facts, Alexandria, Virginia 1992

J. EDGAR HOOVER
Lambert, Pam, "Hoover Unveiled," *People,* March 22, 1993
Summers, Anthony, *Official and Confidential: The Secret Life of J. Edgar Hoover,*
    G.P. Putnam & Sons, New York 1993
Urquhart, Sidney, "Partners for Life," *Time,* Februaury 22, 1993
Encyclopedia Britannica micropedia, 15th Edition, Chicago, 1985

HARRY HOUDINI
James, Clive, *Fame in the 20th Century,* BBC Books, London 1993
The Mystical Year; Mind Over Matter; Psychic Powers; Spiritual Summonings,
    Time-Life Mysteries of the Unknown, Alexandria, Virginia 1988-1991
"The Missing Elephant," *Vanishings,* Time-Life Library of Curious and Unusual
    Facts, Alexandria, Virginia 1991
Dawes, Edwin A., *The Great Illusionists,* Chartwell Books, Secaucus,
    New Jersey 1979
Desfor, Irving, *Great Magicians in Great Moments,* Lee Jacobs Productions,
    Pomeroy, Ohio 1983
Henning, Doug, and Charles Reynolds, *Houdini: His Legend and His Magic,*
    Times Books, New York 1977

HOWARD HUGHES
Fay, Steven, Lewis Chester, Magnus Linklater, *Hoax: The Inside Story of the
    Howard Hughes-Clifford Irving Affair,* Viking, New York 1972
Encyclopedia Britannica micropedia, 15th Edition, Chicago 1985

IVAN THE TERRIBLE
The Cambridge Encyclopedia of Russia and the Soviet Union, Cambridge University
    Press, Cambridge 1982
Hook, Donald D., *Madmen of History,* Jonathan David, Middle Village,
    New York 1976
Payne, Robert and Nikita Romanoff, *Ivan the Terrible,* Thomas Y. Crowell,
    New York 1970
"Czar Tissue," *Manias and Delusions,* Time-Life Library of Curious and Unusual
    Facts, Alexandria, Virginia 1992

ALFRED HENRI JARRY
La Belle, Maurice Marc, *Alfred Jarry and the Theatre of the Absurd,* New York
    University Press, New York 1980
Stillman, Linda Klieger, *Alfred Jarry,* Twayne Publishers, Boston 1983
Beaumont, Keith, *Alfred Jarry: A Critical and Biographical Study,* St. Martin's
    Press, New York 1981

FRANZ KAFKA
"Close Czech," *The Mystifying Mind,* Time-Life Library of Curious and Unusual
    Facts, Alexandria, Virginia 1991
Encyclopedia Britannica, 15th Edition, Chicago 1985
Benet, William Rose, *The Reader's Encyclopedia,* Cromwell, New York 1969

SHIPWRECK KELLY
"Old Glory," *Above and Beyond,* Time-Life Library of Curious and Unusual Facts,
    Alexandria, Virginia 1993
Obituary, *Time,* October 20, 1952
Obituary, *The New York Times,* October 20, 1952

WILLIAM LYON MACKENZIE KING
Robertson, Heather, "Kingsmere: Retreat for an Eccentric," *Reader's Digest*
    (Canada) 1987
Stacey, C.P., *A Very Double Life: The Private World of William Mackenzie King,*
    Macmillan, Toronto 1976
Fraser, Blair, "The Secret Life of Mackenzie King, Spiritualist," *MacLean's,*
    December 15, 1951
"King's Secret," *Time,* December 24, 1951
"Spirited Performance," *Odd & Eccentric People,* Time-Life Library of Curious and
    Unusual Facts, Alexandria, Virginia 1992

T.E. LAWRENCE
James, Clive, *Fame in the 20th Century,* BBC Books, London 1993
Knightley, Phillip and Colin Simpson, *The Secret Lives of Lawrence of Arabia,*
    McGraw-Hill, New York 1970
Lawrence, T.E., *Revolt in the Desert,* Folio Society, London 1986
Thomas, Lowell, *With Lawrence in Arabia,* Doubleday, Garden City,
    New York 1967

EDWARD LEEDSKALNIN
"Coral Castle: An Engineering Feat Almost Impossible to Believe!"
    Coral Castle brochure, Homestead, Florida 1988
"Coral Castle English Tour Guide," Coral Castle brochure, undated
"Coral Camelot," *Odd and Eccentric People,* Time-Life Library of Curious and
    Unusual Facts, Alexandria, Virginia 1991

LUDWIG II, KING OF BAVARIA
Blunt, Wilfrid, *The Dream King, Ludwig of Bavaria,* Hamish Hamilton,
    London 1970

BERNARR MACFADDEN
Oursler, Fulton, *The True Story of Bernarr MacFadden,* Lewis Copeland,
    New York 1929
Wood, Clement, *Bernarr MacFadden: A Study in Success,* Lewis Copeland,
    New York 1929
Yagota, Ben, "The True Story of Bernarr M. MacFadden: Life and Loves of the
    Father of the Confession Magazine," *American Heritage,* 1981
"Fast to Last," *Odd & Eccentric People,* Time-Life Library of Curious and Unusual
    Facts, Alexandria, Virginia 1992

STEWART AND CYRIL MARCUS
Cassill, Kay, *Twins: Nature's Amazing Mystery,* Atheneum, New York 1982
Rosenbaum, Ron and Susan Edmiston, "Dead Ringers," *Esquire,* March, 1976
"Twinned to Die," *Mysteries of the Human Body,* Time-Life Library of Curious and
    Unusual Facts, Alexandria, Virginia 1991

GUY DE MAUPASSANT
Lerner, Michael G., *Maupassant,* George Braziller, New York 1975
"Vice Guys Finish Last," *Manias and Delusions,* Time-Life Library of Curious and
    Unusual Facts, Alexandria, Virginia 1992
Encyclopedia Britannica micropedia, 15th Edition, Chicago 1985
Benet, William Rose, *The Reader's Encyclopedia,* Crowell, New York 1965

AIMEE SEMPLE MCPHERSON
Austin, Alvyn, *Aimee Semple McPherson,* Fitzhenry and Whiteside, Don Mills,
    Ontario 1980
"Vaudeville at Angelus Temple," Selton Bissell, *Outlook,* May 23, 1928
"Aimee Semple McPherson," Julia N. Budlong, *Nation,* June 19, 1929
"Aimee Semple McPherson, Prima Donna of Revivalism," Sarah Comstock,
    Harper's, December 1927
"Once in Love With Aimee," *Manias and Delusions,* Time-Life Library of Curious
    and Unusual Facts, Alexandria, Virginia 1992

FRANZ ANTON MESMER

Darnton, Robert, *Mesmerism and the End of the Enlightenment in France,* Harvard University Press, Cambridge 1968

Bramwell, J. Milne, *Hypnotism,* Julian Press, New York: Institute for Research in Hypnosis 1956

Rosen, George, "From Mesmerism to Hypnotism," *Ciba Symposia,* March-April, 1948

LORD MONBODDO

Cloyd, E.L., *James Burnett: Lord Monboddo,* Clarendon Press, Oxford 1972

"Head For Tails," *Science Astray,* Time-Life Library of Curious and Unusual Facts, Alexandria, Virginia 1992

MOONDOG

"Moondog Returns from Hippie Years," Allan Kozin, *The New York Times,* November 16, 1989

"Street Beat," *Odd and Eccentric People,* Time-Life Library of Curious and Unusual Facts, Alexandria, Virginia 1991

MAD JACK MYTTON

Bridgeman, Harriet and Elizabeth Drury, *The British Eccentric,* Clarkson N. Potter, New York 1975

Lamont-Brown, Raymond, *A Book of British Eccentrics,* David & Charles, London 1984

Timbs, John, *English Eccentrics and Eccentricities,* Singing Tree Press 1969

"High Spirits," *Odd and Eccentric People,* Time-Life Library of Curious and Unusual Facts, Alexandria, Virginia 1991

VASLAV NIJINSKY

Ostwald, Peter, *Vaslav Nijinsky: A Leap into Madness,* Lyle Stuart, Secaucus, New Jersey 1991

Le Sacre du Printemps, Editions Minkoff, Geneva 1980

Hodson, Millicent, "Nijinsky's Choreographic Method: Visual Sources from Roerich for Le Sacre du Printemps," *Dance Research Journal,* Winter 1986-87

"Leap Into Darkness" and "The Rite Stuff," *Manias and Delusions,* Time-Life Library of Curious and Unusual Facts, Alexandria, Virginia 1992

JOSHUA ABRAHAM ("EMPEROR") NORTON

Canfield, Catherine, *The Emperor of the United States of America, and Other Magnificent Eccentrics,* St. Martin's Press, New York 1981

Parker, Joan, "Emperor Norton I," *American Heritage,* December 1976

"Heart in San Francisco," *Odd & Eccentric People,* Time-Life Library of Curious and Unusual Facts, Alexandria, Virginia 1992

LIEUTENANT HIROO ONODA

Onoda, Hiroo, *No Surrender: My Thirty-Year War,* translated by Charles S. Terry, Kodansha International, Tokyo 1974

"The 'Last' Japanese Soldier Fights for Nature," *Asahi Evening News,* December 27, 1985

"Diehard," *Above and Beyond,* Time-Life Library of Curious and Unusual Facts, Alexandria, Virginia 1992

EDGAR ALLAN POE

Campell, Killis, *The Mind of Poe and Other Studies,* Russell & Russell, New York 1969

Prescott, F.C. (ed.), *Selections from the Critical Writings of Edgar Allan Poe,* Gordian Press, New York 1981

Quinn, Arthur H., *Edgar Allan Poe: A Critical Biography,* Appleton-Century-Crofts, New York, 1963

RASPUTIN

Cowles, Virginia, *The Romanovs,* Harper & Row, New York 1971

Garber, Janet Serlin, *Rasputin: The Mysterious Monk,* Contemporary Perspectives, New York 1979

Encyclopedia Britannica micropedia, 15th Edition, Chicago, 1985

WILHELM REICH

Gardner, Martin, *Fads and Fallacies: In the Name of Science,* Dover, New York 1957

"Energy Glut," *Science Astray,* Time-Life Library of Curious and Unusual Facts, Alexandria, Virginia 1992

WILLIAM ELLSWORTH ROBINSON (CHUNG LING SOO)

Andrews, Virginia, *A Gift from the Gods: The Story of Chung Ling Soo, Marvelous Chinese Conjurer,* Goodliffe, Warwickshire 1981

"The Vanish of a Lifetime," *Vanishings,* Time-Life Library of Curious and Unusual Facts, Alexandria, Virginia 1991

Stashower, Danile, *Elephants in the Distance,* Morrow, New York 1990

MARQUIS DE SADE

Hunt, Lynn, "The Prisoner of Pleasure," *The New York Times Book Review,* August 15, 1993

Lever, Maurice, *Sade,* translated by Arthur Goldhammer, Farrar, Straus, & Giroux, New York 1993

Encyclopedia Britannica micropedia, 15th Edition, Chicago, 1985

WILLIAM JAMES SIDIS

"Bent Twig," *The Mystifying Mind,* Time-Life Library of Curious and Unusual Facts, Alexandria, Virginia 1992

Radford, John, *Child Prodigies and Exceptional Early Achievers,* Macmillan, New York 1990

EDWARD ASKEW SOTHERN

Pemberton, T. Edgar, *Lord Dundreary: A Memoir of Edward Askew Sothern,* Knickerbocker Press, New York 1908

Smith, H. Allen, *The Compleat Practical Joker,* William Morrow, New York 1980

"Sothern Exposure," *Hoaxes and Deceptions,* Time-Life Library of Curious and Unusual Facts, Alexandria, Virginia 1991

LORD SUTCH

Harris, Martyn, "Lord of Misrule: Sutch a Level Headed Loony," *Sunday Telegraph,* November 11, 1990

Purcell, Steve, "Sutch a Loony After All," *Daily Star,* May 28, 1991

"Peer Group," *Odd & Eccentric People,* Time-Life Library of Curious and Unusual Facts, Alexandria, Virginia 1992

CYRUS R. TEED

Landing, James E., "Cyrus R. Teed, Koreshanity and Cellular Cosmogony," *Communal Societies,* Autumn, 1981

Herbert, Glendomin M., and I.S.K. Reeves, *Koreshan Unity Settlement 1894-1977,* Division of Recreation and Parks, State of Florida 1977

Fine, Howard D., "The Koreshan Unity: The Chicago Years of a Utopian Community," *Journal of the Illinois State Historical Society,* June 1975

STEPHEN TENNANT

Hoare, Phillip, *Serious Pleasures: The Life of Stephen Tennant,* Penguin Books, New York 1992

NIKOLA TESLA

Cheney, Margaret, *Tesla: Man Out of Time,* Dell, New York 1981

Johnston, Ben, *My Inventions: The Autobiography of Nikola Tesla,* Hart Brothers, Willston, Vermont 1982

"Eccentric Emigre," *Inventive Genius,* Time-Life Library of Curious and Unusual Facts, Alexandria, Virginia 1991

VINCENT VAN GOGH

"At Last, Medicine Really Listens to Van Gogh," *The New York Times,* July 25, 1990

"Ear Trouble," *The Mystifying Mind,* Time-Life Library of Curious and Unusual Facts, Alexandria, Virginia 1991

Leymarie, Jean, *Van Gogh,* Tudor Pub. Co., New York 1956

Encyclopedia Britannica micropedia, 15th Edition, Chicago, 1985

ERICH VON STROHEIM

Anger, Kenneth, *Hollywood Babylon,* Straight Arrow Books, San Francisco 1975

Encyclopedia Britannica micropedia, 15th Edition, Chicago, 1985

ANDY WARHOL

James, Clive, *Fame in the 20th Century,* BBC Books, London 1993

Finkelstein, Nat, *Andy Warhol, The Factory Years,* St. Lawrence Press, New York 1989

Warhol, A., *Philosophy of Andy Warhol: From A to B and Back Again,* Harcourt Brace Jovanovich, New York 1989

Warhol, A., and Pat Hackett, *POPism: The Warhol 60s,* Harcourt Brace Jovanovich, New York 1980

SARAH WINCHESTER

Burgess, Michele, "This is the House That Sarah Built," *Travel-Holiday,* March, 1986

Flanagan, Mike, "Sarah Winchester's Mystery House," *Empire,* October 27, 1985

"Hauntings," *Mysteries of the Unknown,* Time-Life Books, Alexandria, Virginia, 1989

"Winchester Cathedral," *Odd & Eccentric People,* Time-Life Library of Curious and Unusual Facts, Alexandria, Virginia 1992

ED WOOD JR.

Grey, Rudolph, *Nightmare of Ecstasy,* Feral House Press, Los Angeles 1992

Rose, Lloyd, "The World's Worst Filmmaker — And Why We Love Him," *The Washington Post,* August 15, 1993

COPYRIGHT INFORMATION

INDEX